C 978 006 027 134 24 08 97

C000063313

WITHDRAWN
FOR
RE-SALE

SOLD

Two generations of Ogilvies have served — and in their time commanded — the 114th Highlanders, the Queen's Own Royal Strathspeys. James Ogilvie is the third generation. Pitchforked with mixed feelings first into Sandhurst, then into the family regiment, he finds himself in 1894 a subaltern en route for India. He is given no time to discover how well he is really suited to the military life, the command of men and to meeting the expectations of an irascible father who will be his Divisional Commander on the North-West Frontier. The passage out teaches James many things about the army the hard way. Viceregal India has lessons of a different sort for a young second lieutenant, but action brings new emotions and a new testing, as the Royal Strathspeys are sent through the Khyber Pass to contain the rebel Ahmed Khan outside Jalalabad. To the British public at home the impudent manœuvres of an obscure rebel in a too long protracted campaign on a remote frontier of the Empire are of little consequence. But the engagement is James's military baptism of fire and leads to an exciting climax. It also leads to the discovery that to emerge with credit is not to emerge without doubts.

Recent Titles by Philip McCutchan from Severn House

CAMERON'S CONVOY
CAMERON IN THE GAP

THE
FIRST COMMAND

Philip McCutchan

NOTTINGHAMSHIRE LEISURE
SERVICES

Morley Books	23.9.97
	£16.99

This title first published in Great Britain 1997 by
SEVERN HOUSE PUBLISHERS LTD of
9–15 High Street, Sutton, Surrey SM1 1DF.
Previously published 1972 in Great Britain and the USA
as *Drums Along the Khyber* under the pseudonym *Duncan MacNeil*.
This title first published in the U.S.A. by
SEVERN HOUSE PUBLISHERS INC of
595 Madison Avenue, New York, N.Y. 10022.

Copyright © 1972 by Philip McCutchan

All rights reserved.
The moral right of the author has been asserted.

British Library Cataloguing in Publication Data

A record for this title is held at the British Library.

ISBN 0-7278-5290-6

All situations in this publication are fictitious and
any resemblance to living persons is purely coincidental.

Typeset by Palimpsest Book Production Limited,
Polmont, Stirlingshire, Scotland.
Printed and bound in Great Britain by
Hartnolls Ltd, Bodmin, Cornwall.

One

"MR. OGILVIE!" It was Black's voice, sharply critical, coming up in his rear. "Can you, or can you not, read a heliograph?"

James Ogilvie turned with a start, cursing under his breath as his right hand rose towards his Wolseley helmet. He had failed to see the winking field heliograph, its mirrors reflecting the sun, for the simple reason that it was coming from behind him. No doubt, however, subalterns were expected to have eyes in the backs of their heads; and it would not have occurred to him to pass the blame to his men for being no more vigilant than he. His face scarlet, he read off the message. It was from the Colonel, who was currently resting the main body of the regiment back along the cruel pass that ran through out of India. Ogilvie had been sent ahead with a corporal and three recruits to scout. This would, Black had suggested to Ogilvie's company commander and the Colonel, be excellent experience for a young officer and green soldiers.

The message told James Ogilvie that Ahmed Khan had scouts out too, that the party had been spotted and was about to be ambushed if they went ahead. They were therefore to remain in cover while the regiment advanced and overtook them, after which the expeditionary force would press forward under covering fire from the sharpshooters on the flanks.

Black, the adjutant, snorted. "Damn you, Mr. Ogilvie, we've been trying to raise you for the last fifteen minutes. Kindly remember in future not to neglect your rear. The Colonel's not at all pleased about this—and as for me, I'm damned if *I'm* pleased at having the regiment saddled in action with boys fresh from Sandhurst!"

"I'm sorry," Ogilvie said awkwardly, but Black had already turned away and was making his retreat towards the main body, his horse slipping and sliding on the atrocious surface of the track, disapproval in every line of his ramrod-straight back. There had been something in the adjutant's sallow, discontented

5

face, however, that had said he wasn't especially sorry to be able to speak adversely to Lord Dornoch about Ogilvie, and Ogilvie was uncomfortably aware that he, as the scout, should have seen the enemy before the Colonel. But there wasn't time to worry about that for now. Already there was the distant sound of rifle fire and bullets snicked off the mountainside ahead of Ogilvie's party. At the moment, they couldn't be reached; they were in some sort of cover, more by good luck than good judgment, but there wouldn't be much more of that as they advanced. As Ogilvie waited for the regiment to come up he heard across the unfriendly, watchful spaces of the rough terrain of the Sufaid Koh the curious noise that accompanied the first few puffs of wind into the bagpipes; and a moment later they burst out in the full throat of their savage but exultant notes, playing Pipe-Major Ross's own fairly recent composition —A Farewell to Invermore. A phrase from the past slipped suddenly into James Ogilvie's mind, even though he himself had never failed to respond to the sound of the pipes: '*C'est magnifique, mais ce n'est pas la guerre.*' Still, they'd been seen already, as the helio had said, so they might as well advance with spirit and with dash . . .

To the skirl and beat of the pipes and drums, the 114th Highlanders, The Queen's Own Royal Strathspeys, came on in column of route, kilts a-swing below the khaki-drill tunics, to face the sporadic rifle-fire from the crests, to assure the enemies of the Queen-Empress that the British Raj responded with fire and sword to every tweak of the lion's tail. And to ensure that it was known far and wide that wherever the flag waved rebellious natives would, in the greater interest of the majority, be put down with that same fire and sword so that the Pax Britannica would not long be broken.

This was to be James Ogilvie's first experience of fire and he felt a disturbing looseness in his stomach as he waited to take his party into the column of advance, wondering how he would be likely to conduct himself when they came within range of the rifles—and more, how he would conduct himself when they reached Jalalabad, if ever they did without being cut to pieces on the way, and came under the guns of the fortress. He thought, too, about the past; thought about his year at Sandhurst, which he had to admit had been no shining example of a

6

successful start to a military career. It wasn't that he had done anything wrong, but certainly he had never been singled out for honours. His instructors—his officers, his Company Serjeant-Major, his platoon Colour-Serjeant—had regarded him as a burden to be borne, stoically if not cheerfully, and, to some limited extent, as a butt for their not-unkindly-meant wit. After many years spent, on his mother's insistence, at a private tutorial establishment instead of a public school, he had had difficulty in adapting himself, in spite of the military traditions of his family, to the rush and bustle of a Gentleman Cadet's life. He had been bewildered by the constant parades and the constant shortage of time which, among other things, had entailed being dismissed daily from the last parade at 7.25 p.m. and being expected to be in the Mess, washed and in full mess order, at 7.30 precisely. Other aspects of life had not appealed, either—among them the ceremonious but vicious unofficial treatment accorded to the new entrants, when for instance they were forced in a body at bayonet-point, by senior cadets, to descend a steep iron staircase cluttered with tables and chairs, at the rush. This had before now resulted in broken arms and legs. The ducking in the lake on the first occasion on which a cadet wore his mess uniform could prove costly, too. Of course there had been the lighter moments in this, the unofficial side of Sandhurst life—such as the senior term's passing-out ball soon after he had joined, when at dusk the great lake had been covered with hundreds of chamber-pots from the Gentlemen Cadets' bedrooms, each of them carrying a single lighted candle to entrance the military ladies of Camberley and Aldershot . . . but such moments had been few and didn't really appeal in any case to Ogilvie, whose Scottish ancestry had tended to make him more serious-minded and sensitive than many of his fellow cadets. Now, through the blare of the pipes moving closer along the remote frontier pass, voices came back to James Ogilvie, the voices of men whose drill movements were as precision-perfect as machines and who couldn't comprehend what motivated a young Gentleman Cadet who, after a full year on the square, was still virtually unable at times to force a decent military control upon his limbs. Or even to keep his ears open . . .

"Mr. Ogilvie, I really do believe you have got cloth ears. Sir! Will you kindly pay attention to the orders! They are given in a

7

well-thought-out sequence as laid down by minds greater than your own." The Company Serjeant-Major of A Company, purple in his sweating face, bristled a ginger moustache close to James Ogilvie's nose. "Did you 'ear what I said, Mr. Ogilvie, you terrible Gentleman Cadet, you?"

"I'm sorry, Staff." Ogilvie looked, in accordance with Queen's Regulations for the Army, straight ahead—neither up nor down, right or left. He was aware of very blue eyes bulging beneath the gold-rimmed peak of C.S.M. Apps's cap. Apps, on long-suffering detachment from the Grenadiers for service as an instructor at the Royal Military College, was as tall as himself.

Apps's pace-stick trembled beneath a hammy arm. He stepped backward and to his left, away from Ogilvie. His voice rose to a hoot, a scream that tore across the parade ground and echoed off the walls behind. "I said—*right marker*! Sir!"

Ogilvie, already at attention, moved into action as commanded. He took six short, sharp paces forward and halted, drawing his extended right foot down with a guardsman's crash. He then waited for Apps's order that would form the remainder of A Company up on his left. The order didn't come. Instead, he was left standing like a flushing statue while the C.S.M. addressed the young gentlemen in thunderstruck tones. "Gentlemen! Did you see the way Mr. Ogilvie halted! No—do *not* answer me back! I realize you saw! But perhaps you do not know *what* you saw. I shall tell you. Gentlemen, you have seen the way *not to bloody-well halt*!" He marched quivering up to Ogilvie. "Tomorrow you will pass out, Mr. Ogilvie, and I shall become a sane man again with God's help. Tomorrow, at the passing-out parade, you will march past the Duke of Cambridge. His Royal Highness is an old gentleman, Mr. Ogilvie. You are very likely going to give him an apoplectic *fit*."

Ogilvie swallowed. "Yes, Staff."

"It will be a case of murder. You must buck your ideas up, Mr. Ogilvie. His Royal Highness is a stickler for smartness. His Royal Highness is a first cousin of Her Majesty the Queen, Mr. Ogilvie. His Royal Highness led a division of Guards and Highlanders at the battle of the Alma, Mr. Ogilvie. His Royal Highness had his horse shot from under him at Inkerman. His Royal Highness has faced shot and shell and has *survived*, Mr. Ogilvie. But as God's me judge, 'e hain't going to survive *you*!

8

I am astonished that you 'ave been accepted for the 114th. The 114th is a crack regiment with a reputation for spit and polish. As you should know. Sir!"

"Yes, Staff."

"Besides the which, *long* gentlemen look funny in a kilt. Now let us try again, Mr. Ogilvie, for the sake of the 114th. About ... *turn*! Quick ... march. Left-right-left ... '*alt*. About ... *turn*. Right marker."

James Ogilvie knew very well that it was inexcusable that he should put up such a showing the day before the passing-out parade. There had been so many times when he had felt the army was not, after all, for him. He was perhaps too dreamy ever to become a man of action, to lead men confidently in battle. At his prep school he had never liked games for one thing — to his father's dismay — and in today's army there was beginning to be quite an insistence on games. The army was changing rapidly and the old type of blood and guts officer — like Ogilvie's own father and grandfather, like His Royal Highness and his horse at Inkerman — was on the way out, though they still lingered in high places. Ogilvie wished he could sort out his own mind. His ideal concept of a military officer was frankly someone with a dash of that blood and guts outlook, though he was pretty sure he personally could never have stomached all that had gone with it — the floggings, the squalors of barrack-room life, the injustices of arrogance. His concept, however, was decidedly not that of a cricketing, footballing officer. But there had been that emphasis on games at Sandhurst and he had been the odd man out once again, the loner among the muddied oafs. And drill movements failed to fascinate him as much as C.S.M. Apps and the Colour-Serjeants expected them to. Yet all the same he had the army in his blood — to some extent he was a romantic on this point — and there were the aspects of it that appealed to him very strongly indeed. Among these were its traditions, the stories of the regiments and corps that made up the most far-flung and victorious army of modern times. It was an army now comfortably astride a magnificent Empire, ruling the heathen in the name of the Queen-Empress — that little old lady in black, with the bun and the arrogant bearing who, when his father had been commanding the depot in Invermore, had once bidden him to

tea in the castle at Balmoral. James had been scared stiff and
hadn't been able to open his mouth when Her Majesty had
barked a condescending word at him, and his father and mother
had been scarlet with embarrassment, though normally it took
a good deal to embarrass his irascible father. James Ogilvie
loved martial music—even enjoyed marching when behind the
crash and thunder of the brass. There was something that
stirred his very soul as he thought of the days that had gone, of
the men who had marched away into history behind the
regimental colours, carrying the flag of England to a glory that,
unlike them, was immortal. He thrilled to the valour and
sacrifice that had built the Empire, forged it by fire into what it
was today—solid, prosperous, utterly and finally unassailable.
The pride of it, the pride of being one of a gallant company of
men, weighed very heavily in the balance and he knew inside
himself that, despite his doubts, he could never have been
anything other in life than an officer of the 114th Highlanders,
lately commanded by both his father and his grandfather before
him.

Next day, as the passing-out company led the parade past the
elderly charger-mounted figure of the Duke of Cambridge—
the old man who was soon to hand over as Commander-in-
Chief to Lord Wolseley—James Ogilvie's heart beat fast with
an increased sense of that inherited pride of soldiery. It seemed
to him, as the band crashed out The British Grenadiers so that
the music beat through a heat haze and echoed off the yellow-
white walls of the college, that here on the parade at Sandhurst
the heart of the Empire beat, that here were gathered, somewhere
in the mists, the ghosts of men from a splendid past to en-
courage those who, once gazetted to their regiments, would
carry the honour and the glory on into the future, those who
held in fresh hands the sacred traditions so dearly bought,
those who would widen the scope of British might till all the
map were red. Stiffly Ogilvie marched past the old Commander-
in-Chief, eyes front behind the Senior Under-Officer of A
Company, a young man bound for the Coldstream Guards and
a life of ceremonial and palace duties, debutantes and London
seasons, hunting, grouse-shooting, tea-parties in duchesses'
town houses. Such a life made no appeal to James Ogilvie; he
knew that much at least, though he had not yet arrived at the
happy state of knowing just what it was he did want of his

chosen career. But there would be no London seasons for James Ogilvie for many a year, for the 114th were presently under orders for India. Among other things this would mean he would see his parents again for the first time in three years. His father, now a major-general, was on the staff of Southern Army H.Q. at Ootacamund. The prospect of seeing his mother was delightful, of seeing his father both welcome and unwelcome. Ogilvie's father set high standards and expected his son to contribute more honour to the family's name. And he was much inclined to outspokenness, especially when in a tantrum. This tended to make James even more unsure of himself, of his ability to make a success of his profession of arms.

But meanwhile he could savour the moment, the present. There was the band and the pageantry and the dream. And that afternoon, when the passing-out ceremony was over for another year, Company Serjeant-Major Apps addressed him.

"He's still alive an' breathing, Mr. Ogilvie! Couldn't never 'ave clapped eyes on you, he couldn't! I thank you from the bottom of me 'eart for not letting me down, Mr. Ogilvie. Maybe you'll make an officer yet. And here's me very best wishes that you do. Sir!" His right arm cut a swathe through the air in front of Ogilvie's nose and the hand quivered in front of his forehead. "You've got the makings in you, spite of all I've ever said. You're not such a block'ead as some."

Two days later Ogilvie had been in London, staying with a friend, a Guards subaltern who maintained rooms in Half Moon Street off Piccadilly. Ogilvie had fourteen days' leave before he was due to report to the 114th's depot at Invermore, and he filled those fourteen days with late risings, with rowing on the river at Henley, with expensive dinners, and a round of the shows and the music halls. He enjoyed the music halls especially, liked the full-throated, uninhibited roaring out of such songs as Soldiers of the Queen, or The Girl I Left Behind Me. In a curious way it made him feel he was embarking for active service, that the singing was, as it were, for him personally — even though he was naturally wearing mufti his profession would be fairly obvious. He found this a satisfactory feeling, but it worried him nevertheless, for he was seeing himself already for what he had not yet in fact become, and that was altogether too easy a way to be a soldier, too vicarious. It was like a non-combatant, a regimental paymaster say, revelling in old ladies' admiration at a tea-party. He felt the need to be blooded, to test himself. There were other things he had to be blooded in as well, and one of them was liquor. One night during that leave he had far too much champagne, followed by far too much brandy at the Cafe Royal, and Jackie Harrington, his friend, took him home senseless in a hansom. In the morning he felt like death and vowed never to repeat that particular experience. And another night Mr. Harrington took him rather furtively behind the scenes at the Gaiety Theatre and introduced him to a girl named Freddie something-or-other, and they all went on to a curious sort of club in Soho, and then Freddie came back to Harrington's rooms and was still there in the morning . . . all night James Ogilvie had known she was there and he'd had almost no sleep as a result, letting his imagination—and at that stage of his life it was only imagination—run riot. He felt intense desire, and a blind envy of Harrington, and when the girl had gone he couldn't stop himself asking a few immature questions.

"You—er—you're not thinking of marrying Freddie, are you, Harrington?" he asked.

Harrington burst out in a roar of highly astonished laughter. "A girl of that class, a show girl? Good God, Ogilvie, do have a little sense!"

"But you . . . she was here all night."

"So she was indeed, you ass! Damn good at it too." Harrington twiddled at his moustache. He was a good-looking man, with a firm thrustful chin and a high forehead, and had a very well cultivated guards officer laugh. "Isn't it time you grew up, old man?"

"What d'you mean?"

Harrington looked at him with a twinkle in his eye. "I mean," he said deliberately, putting a match to his pipe, "a man doesn't need to marry every girl he sleeps with. One couldn't anyway, in this ridiculous country. Women of that class are *different*. One doesn't compromise a girl of family, naturally—it's just not done, I'd agree—same as you wouldn't put one of your own household's maids on her back, though it's quite all right to bed someone else's. You know that. Girls like Freddie are, well, fair game. They're already compromised!"

"Who by, in the first place?"

"Someone like me." Harrington laughed; there was no malice in it at all. "They know what's what and Freddie'd never expect marriage."

"Doesn't seem right." Moodily, Ogilvie thrust his hands into his trouser pockets and wandered across to the window. He could hear the horses' hooves in Piccadilly, passing along the side of the park. "They all have feelings."

"I suppose they have," Harrington said carelessly, "and perhaps it's wrong, but it's very highly natural all the same. Didn't your father ever tell you?"

Ogilvie turned from the window, frowning. "No," he said seriously. "As a matter of fact he didn't. I've not seen an awful lot of him—you know that. He's had more than his share of foreign service—"

"*I* learned quite a lot at school, Ogilvie. Tell you what: let me pass on my experience, old man! I'm the one to teach you, right enough! But don't expect too much, will you? I mean . . . well, look here, Ogilvie, you'll get a girl of your own before long, and I know damn well that's what you want. Do you good, too. Women grow a man up. You'll be all right—you're not exactly repulsive to look at with that fine, tall body and intelligent patrician look! Women go for your sort of eyes, too. But you won't find them as easy as I do, let me warn you. You've got a kind of pure look, you're not an old reprobate like me, and girls who do what Freddie does, don't go for innocence, believe me. It can lead to complications. I've already said they don't necessarily want marriage or even to lose their freedom in over-involvement—and you're the sort that goes for love and marriage, I'll be bound. It'll be an overwhelming passion when it comes! And as like as not, it'll be the fair damsel from the manse or whatever it is you have in your native glens. A parson's daughter, anyway, or something equally pure and modest."

Ogilvie laughed. "I don't know that I'd want a parson's daughter."

"Well, anyway," Harrington said, "your time'll come. Your lot's under orders for India, and the wives don't mind changing beds out there, so I'm told. Then there's the chi-chis. I wouldn't mind an exchange into the Bengal Lancers, myself. It's a rotter's paradise, dammit! Hot weather makes hot women and the moment they get east of Suez they throw the bedclothes right off. Just one word of warning: never, never sleep with your

13

company commander's wife unless he's away on detached service. They'll drum you out for less! You'll find yourself in the Supply and Transport, or whatever fancy name they've given 'em these days." He pulled his watch from his waistcoat pocket and flipped the gold case open. "Come on, Ogilvie; let's walk along to the Berkeley grill. And don't worry too much. As I said — your time will come, you mark my words!"

Marking Harrington's words failed to help during the rest of his leave, failed to quieten the emotions that tumulted through his mind and body. Ogilvie had not been unaware of women in more recent years, but never before had he been so close to a largely forbidden world, and the night Freddie had spent with Harrington had made an inordinately large impression on him. Just before his leave was up Harrington suggested he might have a word with Freddie and see if she could produce another girl, and he laughed when Ogilvie refused. "Why not?" he asked. "Afraid you mightn't be able to perform?"

Ogilvie flushed deeply. "Heavens, no," he said quickly. "It's . . . oh, really, I don't know . . . it's just that it makes it all sound so — cold-blooded, so mechanical."

Harrington just shrugged; he very clearly didn't understand in the least. In due course James Ogilvie, still a virgin, but feeling he had learned a little about himself, caught the night express from King's Cross to Edinburgh, arriving at Waverley at 7 a.m. From Edinburgh he entrained for Grantown-on-Spey, where he was met by regimental transport in the form of a brake that took him and his gear to Meerut Barracks in Invermore and his first induction as a member in his own right of the 114th Highlanders, The Queen's Own Royal Strathspeys.

Two

As the regiment advanced in column along the Khyber Pass Ogilvie watched the austere figure of the Colonel as stiff and straight in the saddle as if he had beeen riding between the ranks on inspection back in Invermore. Lord Dornoch's sharp gaze swept him but nothing was said; the reprimand would come later, and in private. The Colonel was a remote man in some ways, but a just one and friendly enough in the Mess. As a rattle of rifle fire came down from the hills, the sharpshooters returned it. Smoke drifted; some way ahead a robed figure toppled from a crest, and fell, his rifle falling with him. As if from nowhere, vultures appeared, big black scraggy brutes that hung and circled and waited. The pipes and drums moved on, now beating out a savage tune as wild as the land that had given it birth, as wild as the land through which the Royal Strathspeys were now advancing with the native support train, the *bhistis,* and the stretcher-bearers who were going to be much in demand before long.

The day James Ogilvie had joined his regiment some months before he had, after reporting to the adjutant, been welcomed by Lord Donoch over a glass of sherry in the Mess. Dornoch's eyes, cold blue and very steady, had summed him up shrewdly and had looked pleased. "There is little I can tell you about us that you don't know already for yourself, Ogilvie," he'd said in a clear, incisive voice. "In a sense, you've been one of us from birth, haven't you? I've watched you grow up, you know. I always knew you'd be joining us one day."

"Yes, Colonel."

"Well, I'm glad the day has come while I'm still with the regiment. I'm glad to have you—and proud to serve with another Ogilvie. I hope you'll follow your family tradition, young man, and command the battalion in due course." The Colonel's eyes twinkled at Ogilvie. "That's what your father hopes too, isn't it?"

Ogilvie smiled, and flushed a little. "Yes, Colonel."

"Well, I'm sure you won't disappoint him," Lord Dornoch said with hearty friendliness. He laid a hand on his arm. "You'll already have met my adjutant, of course — Captain Black." Ogilvie had; and had been aware at once that the stiff-faced adjutant was no lover of his fellow-men. "Let me introduce you to some of the others."

He did so. Ogilvie was introduced to the second-in-command, a tall, stooping man with a long face slashed by heavy eyebrows and a light brown moustache — Major Hay. He seemed, Ogilvie thought, a very pleasant officer, with a friendly if reserved smile; not a demonstrative man, but a genuine one. There were three captains present in the Mess that evening — Willington, Graham and MacKinlay, also the quartermaster, an old soldier named McCrum wearing the two stars of a lieutenant on his mess uniform. There was a surgeon major of the Army Medical Staff, and four combatant subalterns. These were to be Ogilvie's close associates for perhaps many years, the men with whom he would receive his first taste of foreign service, possibly his first experience of action. They would all, in varying degrees, affect his life and help to mould his character. That first night in the mess James Ogilvie held his tongue, spoke only when spoken to. This was due partly to a natural and inherent shyness and to good manners, but also partly to prudence. Time alone would reveal to him what these men's interests were, how he should respond to each, how far he should go with each in revealing his own self. Friendships were not to be rushed into, they were the better for being slowly developed and thereafter prized and respected. This he had discovered for himself at the tutoring establishment and again later at Sandhurst; at neither place had he had many friends, but those he had were sincere, genuine, and the relationships had been deep and would last. That night he was too full of new impressions, too excited, to sleep much. After breakfast next morning, a silent meal at which, again, instinct told him not to open his mouth except quietly to give his order to the mess servants — it was a meal at which officers only grunted out good mornings — he reported again to the adjutant for instructions.

Black sat coldly sallow-faced behind a bare table in his office. "You'll be aware you have a lot to learn, Ogilvie," he said. "You haven't started yet. Sandhurst's just the kindergarten.

16

Here is where you begin to learn how to be a soldier. Are you willing to learn?"

"Yes, of course, sir."

"Then you shall start now. You should know that in the 114th all officers other than the Colonel are addressed by their christian names except when on parade. Mine is Andrew. You will use it. The regiment is a family and we are brothers."

Ogilvie merely nodded; he was well aware of the convention but had yet to forget Sandhurst, where Gentlemen Cadets did not use christian names to the instructors; besides, Captain Black, with that hard face beneath hair as black as his name, looked altogether too cold, too haughty, for anything but a very formal 'sir'.

Black went on, "You'll be aware of the duties of a subaltern. In the field you will command a half-company. Your company will be B Company, under Captain MacKinlay. In quarters you also have the command of the half-company. Further, subalterns are detailed as signalling officers, transport officers and so on, and also to command the two machine-guns allocated to a battalion. Tell me now . . . James: what do we have in the way of transport and animals?"

Ogilvie said at once, "Seventy-one horses, sixteen vehicles when mobilized—which is the strength we should be at now, since we're under orders for service in India."

"Oh, very good, very good indeed," Black said with a touch of sarcasm. "Now, a little more precisely, if you please."

Ogilvie said, "The vehicles include six small-arms ammunition carts, and wagons for tools and equipment and stores. There are eight pack animals for ammunition—one to each company—and another eight for stores."

Black nodded; there was a curious look in the man's eyes. He said abruptly, "Don't imagine you know it all, James. Now—for today you will be attached to me and will accompany me on my own duties—this may last for several days depending upon how you shape. In due course you'll understudy the senior subalterns in their various responsibilities, until I decide what your particular function will be. Understood?"

"Yes . . . Andrew."

Over the next few weeks James Ogilvie realized just how little he knew of soldiering, of the actual day-to-day routine and responsibilities of a junior officer of infantry. The days were

17

long and active, there seemed always to be something to superintend, some exercise to take part in, and there were social duties too, obligatory attendances at dinners and balls in the Mess and in some of the great houses of the district—houses where the name of Ogilvie was already well known. He found this pleasant enough in a way, but was irked on occasions by the aspect of so much of it being 'duty' rather than pleasurable. It was scarcely soldiering and one could weary of dancing in a stately manner with the Speyside matrons. There would be plenty of that in India, too, of course, but he felt it would be different out there, and he looked forward to going. In point of fact he was to get his wish earlier than expected. One morning, after James Ogilvie had been six weeks in barracks at Invermore, a frock-coated major-general stood in the War Office, with an aide, in front of a large wall map of the Indian North-West Frontier district. The major-general was studying in particular the border with Afghanistan, and was drawing heavily on a cigar.

He said throatily, "Damn natives. Far too uppish these days. Nothing's been the same anywhere in the Empire since the confounded mutiny, of course—goes without saying. Well, we simply have to cope with the situation as it is—what?"

"Exactly, sir. But frankly, I'm far from certain what the situation *is*, if—"

"Well, then, listen," the major-general said irritably, pulling at a white walrus moustache. "We all thought the whole frontier was settled by the Durand Mission, didn't we—when they agreed to the Durand Line last year. Seems it isn't! The Afghans still have their internal problems. There's been a cable . . . from the Commander-in-Chief India. You'll recall that one of the Pathan princelings rebelled and seized the town and fortress of Jalalabad a few weeks ago—"

"Ahmed Khan, sir?"

"Yes, that's right. The Amir asked officially for British assistance in driving him out. Well, it appears things are going pretty badly—pretty badly!" The major-general gnawed anxiously at the trailing, yellowed ends of the moustache. "It'll be in all the blasted papers by this evening, I shouldn't wonder! We'll have everyone screaming out for action. And Ahmed Khan won't be easy to eject, I can tell you, from what I hear. Jalalabad's not an easy town to defend, agreed, but the rebel has the superiority in manpower." He blew exasperatedly

18

and the moustache rose like leaves in a breeze. "Now, the problem seems to be this: the Peshawar garrison, as well as the Division before Jalalabad, is very badly depleted by sickness — indeed that applies to the whole of the Northern Army command. They're depleted by the leave situation too. Murree's over-extended already."

"Can't leave be cancelled?" the aide suggested.

The major-general was doubtful. "Not very well. Dammit, it's the leave season! You know how it is out there. So many social engagements in the calendar ... Viceregal Lodge wouldn't like it at all. Damn shame anyway ... wives and that. Polo. One doesn't like to interfere with a feller's polo unnecessarily, I always say. Know how I'd feel about it myself." He reddened as he saw the pointed way his aide was looking at his stomach. "Oh, I'm past active riding myself, but that doesn't alter the fact I can *feel* for those fellers out there." He glared at the map for a while longer, then turned away towards the window. Then he said over his shoulder, as he stared out at the horse-drawn omnibuses and clasped fat hands over that vast midriff, "Of course the internal disposition of troops is *entirely* up to the Commander-in-Chief India and I've not a doubt he'll move some men up from the Southern Command. But it still means they want us to speed up our drafts from home — and as it happens the blasted Amir especially wants as many *British* troops as possible rather than Indian units. It's the old story, of course, at any rate on the Indian side of the border — we don't conflict with their caste system. All castes and creeds'll take from us what any one of them wouldn't from another. Dammit, I suppose you *can't* expect a prince to like being chased by an Untouchable or — or a Parsi! Ever served in India?" His eyes bulged at the aide.

"No, sir —"

"Don't, then, if you can avoid it. Think yourself lucky! Smelly lot of buggers, all of them, even the maharajahs, and no morals at all. Still, they're ours and they look to us and we have to take the rough with the smooth. Who's next on the list for India, Soames?"

Soames hastened the seal of James Ogilvie's fate for years ahead. "The Royal Strathspeys, in depot at Invermore —"

"Dammit, quote me *numbers*!" The major-general hadn't quite taken in the reorganization.

19

"The 114th, sir. Also, the 88th—"

"Who're they?" the general demanded contrarily.

"The Connaught Rangers, sir. They're at the Curragh."

"H'm. When are they due to go?"

"Three weeks' time, sir, to join Southern Army command."

"Hrrrmph." The major-general swung round abruptly and released his waist-line. "They'll do for a start. Damn fine regiments, both of them, *excellent* records. Fighters. I wonder . . . I think I'll recommend they don't join the Southern Army at all. I'm quite sure Sir George White'll find them most useful to back up the Peshawar garrison direct—quite sure! Draft a telegram, Soames, to each of the colonels. Tell 'em to inform War Office soonest possible, how early their regiments can be fit to embark. Tell 'em it's urgent. And in the meantime you can arrange for the *Malabar* to be brought forward to troop 'em to Bombay. She'll be jam-packed but it can't be helped."

Next morning at Invermore, Daily Orders announced that the battalion was to be made ready to embark at Portsmouth Hard on the following Monday, and that they might be moving into action on the North-West Frontier a good deal sooner than normal after arrival at Bombay. From that time onward the tempo of life in barracks changed. James Ogilvie was projected into the colossal task of seeing to it that upwards of a thousand men and seventy horses and pack animals, with all their equipment, were made ready within a matter of days for a long spell of Indian service. Foreign service kit, already prepared in the quartermaster's store, had to be issued and checked by sections, and the barracks themselves left in an orderly condition. Full medical inspections had to be carried out on both men and animals, all stores mustered and shortages made good, weapons inspected, domestic details settled, family problems that always arose when a regiment was ordered on foreign service unexpectedly or as in this case earlier than expected. There were the scrimshankers who pleaded special cases—very few of these—there were illegitimate babies, sick wives, expectant wives, the girls who wanted to become wives 'on the strength' so they could go out with their newly-acquired husbands. In the midst of all this activity, the normal training programme for recruits was proceeded with so far as possible.

Ogilvie, so lacking in drill co-ordination at Sandhurst, had already found himself in the position of having to take charge on the parade-ground, and now, as a very junior subaltern, he was given the task of personally drilling the recruits' squad so that the sergeants could be released for the more immediately important business of moving the regiment out. To his surprise, he found this a not too formidable task. Oddly enough, when watching other young men struggling with the very movements that he himself had found so hard to master, he suddenly realized how very simple it all was. Looking as it were from Olympian heights, the whole thing seemed to lose its mystery. He wondered why, and towards the end of that frantic week he believed he had arrived at the answer: at Sandhurst he had had no responsibility towards anyone but himself; and the enormity of his offences on the parade-ground, so often remarked upon by C.S.M. Apps, had filled his mind. Now, the single star he wore on each shoulder — and which he tried not to appear pridefully conscious of — made him responsible under Captain MacKinlay for almost every facet of the lives of his half-company, which was a responsibility he would not be taking lightly; and such things as drill movements had slotted into the correct order of priorities in his mind; and with the relaxation of concentration had come understanding. The fears had flown away. And now he managed very competently with the occasional discreetly whispered comment from his Colour-Sergeant, an N.C.O. named MacNaught. MacNaught encouraged James Ogilvie a great deal but failed, it seemed, to prevent him incurring the displeasure of the adjutant.

"A word in your ear, James," Captain Black said on the Saturday morning before the departure from Invermore. He had come out on to the square while Ogilvie had been drilling his squad, and having spoken had turned away from the men, waiting for Ogilvie to fall in beside him. Thereafter they marched in step, kilts swinging, up and down the square, and it seemed to Ogilvie that the adjutant might well have kept his voice down a little. "Rumour has it," Black said, "that you didn't exactly impress your betters at Sandhurst. And in any case Sandhurst's one thing, my lad. The 114th's another. I'm not taking the regiment to India to be made a laughing-stock of. It's very important the drill standard is high. The natives expect that. Do I make myself clear?"

"Clear enough," Ogilvie answered shortly, "except for one thing."

"Well?"

"What have I done wrong?"

"In precise terms, you have done nothing *wrong*. Only, what you have done right has not been done right enough, James. You're not making the men move smartly enough, with enough spirit and alertness. Do you understand?"

Ogilvie nodded. "Yes."

"Good! Then you and I will get along together well enough," Black said with a tight smile, looking Ogilvie up and down as they marched. "Now go back to your squad, James, and put them through it. Never be afraid to use your voice, James. These men are not Gentlemen Cadets, they are raw soldiers—peasants, farmers' sons, tinkers, loafers. Some of them are the same sort of scum the army put up with at the Crimea. They enlisted for the glamour of the uniform and the pipes and to cut a dash with their women in the kilt of the Royal Strathspeys. They have to be made to realize they have to work as well, that they must become a credit to the regiment so that others may enlist after them because of the pride that is felt in the Royal Strathspeys in our recruiting area. Any slackness will lead to a dilution of that pride, James. So they must be driven, here on the square, as later they must be driven into action when we reach India. You are one of the drivers, James, so start driving right away. Please carry on."

He stopped suddenly, stock still. Ogilvie moved away, his face burning. The adjutant's voice almost screamed at him. "Mr. Ogilvie—if you please!"

Ogilvie halted, turned. He looked at the adjutant; the man's normally rather cadaver-like face was working with fury. "Yes?"

"I have given you an order, Mr. Ogilvie, and we are on the barrack square." Captain Black's eyes were hard and bright, as hard and bright as the great silver badge on his glengarry. A light wind gently swirled the kilt around spindly, hairy legs. "Have you learned nothing at Sandhurst?"

"I'm sorry, sir." Ogilvie slammed to attention, his right hand flew to the salute. "Permission to carry on, sir?"

Black smiled, thinly; it was more a grin, a sadistic one. "I have already granted that, Mr. Ogilvie. What I am still awaiting is the proper acknowledgement in accordance with the Queen's Regulations."

Once again Ogilvie saluted. Black returned the salute and Ogilvie about-turned smartly and marched back to his squad, his face flaming now, conscious that he had undoubtedly and appallingly slipped up in terms of military etiquette. Shame and anger at what the men had overheard about his time at Sandhurst sharpened his voice and after that he put the recruits through the hoop and left them breathless. By the time the drill was over there was anger in their faces too, and he was conscious of the dark backward looks at him across the square after they had been dismissed. He was sorry; and he felt the whole thing had been unfair. He had been made to appear in their eyes what he was not. Disliking being driven himself, he disliked driving others. Perhaps, after all, he would never make an officer of the standard required of the Royal Strathspeys. If the adjutant was right, he was expected to treat the men more or less as superior animals, pawns to be used to enhance regimental pride; that had undoubtedly been Black's personal attitude. Regimental pride, to Ogilvie, was something real, something to be safeguarded certainly, but it was not an end in itself and human considerations, he felt, could be disregarded only, in the last resort, at the peril of that very pride they all sought to instil. But later that day he was able to see matters in perspective and to realize he had perhaps over-dramatized himself.

At 5.30 on the Monday morning the barracks came alive under the notes of the bugle sounding reveille. There was the almost immediate noise of orders, the rattle of equipment and neighing of horses; and then at 7.30 the battalion formed up on the square and, after the muster by roll-call, was reported correct to Lord Dornoch. The order was given to move to the right in fours and advance in column of route. With the Colonel riding ahead, the pipes and drums under Pipe-Major Ross, the depot brass in support, led the column out. It seemed as though the whole of Invermore had come to cheer and wave goodbye to their own regiment as it started out on its seven and a half thousand mile sea and land journey to the remoteness of the North-West Frontier. Ogilvie, ahead of his half-company, his broadsword bumping his thigh, felt a lump come into his throat as the savagery of the pipes echoed out along the grey streets of the little Scots town and out into the wild Monadliath Mountains behind. Women were crying as the men marched by to the tunes of Highland Laddie and Will Ye No Come Back Again. As the head of the column reached the station yard where the wives and families were waiting to entrain, the pipes and drums broke off and marched to form up on one side with the depot band; and as the regiment marched past towards the platform the brass burst with an intensity of sheer emotion into Auld Lang Syne. Last of all to entrain before the Colonel were the pipers, led by Pipe-Major Ross in his own tune, Farewell to Invermore. Two minutes after this the train was chuffing out leaving behind it a feeling of emptiness, a vacuum that would not wholly be filled until the Royal Strathspeys came home again to Invermore. Ogilvie had read in the faces of the women left behind, that they would live now in dread that their own men would not be coming home with the regiment; and their faces were much on his mind as the train drew those men away from the heart of Scotland, towards a Sassenach land where the inhabitants were wont to liken the sound of their beloved pipes to the squeals of dying pigs . . .

At Portsmouth the following evening, just as the sun went down, the regiment, along with the Connaught Rangers from the Curragh, was marched up the gangways of H.M. Troopship *Malabar* lying at the South Railway jetty, which had been cleared for her by the departure of the flagship of the Channel Fleet. Once again the pipes and drums beat out, playing them aboard section by section, company by company. It was the same as yesterday but different; here in Portsmouth town there was no feeling of home, the regiment was not native here — except that Southerners were apt to regard all kilted Scots as 'natives' in a different sense — but the moment of leaving was one of even greater poignancy, for now the last land links were being cut with friends and families and soon they would be away, out at sea, remote, untouchable, on their own until the first coaling port, Gibraltar, was reached. That would not be for four, maybe five, days. Just before a harbour tug edged alongside with its paddles churning up the water, and as the last lines fell slack and were hauled aboard by the seamen, Ogilvie witnessed a scene that shocked and upset him. A young woman ran to the quayside, pursued by three of the Metropolitan policemen responsible for dockyard security. She was calling out, "Jamie, oh Jamie, come back to me! Jamie, I'll not let them have you, I'll die if you'll no' come back to me, Jamie!"

As the constables reached her and seized her, a kilted soldier leapt up on to the guardrail, shouting down to her. He jumped from the rail, landed badly on the stone jetty, cried out that his leg was broken. Men rushed to him and Black's voice rang out from the troopship's boat deck: "Down there — down there, I say! Have that man sent aboard on the end of a rope and look sharp about it."

So the young woman — God alone knew how she'd come from Invermore, she must presumably have stowed away aboard the train with the authorized wives — wasn't allowed to keep her Jamie, who in pain and anger was secured with a heavy rope cast down from the deck and hauled, shouting obscenities, up the side of the departing troopship.

They left to the sound of the Pipe-Major's music and steamed out from the harbour mouth, past Point Battery and Fort Blockhouse, on between the channel buoys and past the old sea-forts built by Lord Palmerston as a precaution against invasion by the French, forts manned by the Royal Garrison Artillery. As the *Malabar* steamed past, beneath a great cloud of smoke discharging from her funnel, men waved from the forts and then the ship was heading out to turn south around the Isle of Wight and start her long haul through the English Channel and past Ushant into the Bay of Biscay for Cape St Vincent and the Gibraltar Strait.

Two days out from Portsmouth Ogilvie happened to be walking past the cabin that had been allocated as a regimental office to the Royal Strathspeys when he heard Black call his name. He turned and went into the office. "You called?" he asked.

"Yes, James." Black was seated behind a littered table, rolling a heavy walking-stick between his hands. "I believe I gave you the job of assistant troopdeck officer under Captain Graham — am I not right?"

Ogilvie nodded warily. "Quite right," he said.

"I've just had word this moment that Captain Graham's reported sick with a fever, and there's some sort of trouble down on C Company's section of the deck," the adjutant said carefully. "Get down there at once, James, find out what's happening, put a stop to it, and report to me."

"Do you know what sort of trouble?"

Black stared at him coldly. "The devil I do! I've told you to ind that out, have I not?"

"Yes, but—"

"But what?" Black's pale, corpse-like face seemed to bulge, to grow larger, to move closer, to deepen in pallor. "Are you trying to tell me you're afraid you'll not be able to deal with it?"

"No—not that—"

"I'm very relieved to hear it, James. Very relieved indeed. Now go about your duties, if you please."

Ogilvie turned away and went along an alleyway towards the companion leading down to the troopdecks. He wasn't entirely sure Black had been entitled to give him the order. Whatever was going on along the troopdeck, it was surely a company matter and should have been referred to C Company commander. The adjutant's job was generally to assist the Commanding Officer in his administrative duties, and certainly it was his job to issue all regimental orders and keep the roster for duties, as well as to superintend the drilling and musketry instruction of young officers and recruits, and to keep an eye on the way all military duties were performed. But captains of companies were wholly responsible for the discipline and administration of their own commands, and the adjutant's duties in that respect were merely to ensure uniformity along the lines laid down by the Colonel. However, in the circumstances an order was an order and had better be obeyed.

It was sheer good fortune that, on his way down to the troopdeck, Ogilvie happened to meet the Regimental Sergeant-Major, Mr. Cunningham, a real old soldier, a warrant officer with a bulbous nose, a waxed grey moustache, and a magnificently out-thrust chest that had earned him the nickname of Bosom. Bosom slammed to the salute. "Sir! Is there anything I can do for you, Mr. Ogilvie?"

"I understand there's some trouble—"

"Aye, sir. I'm on my way down now to sort it out. You'll not need to worry."

Ogilvie said hesitantly, "I'll come with you, Sarn't-Major."

The R.S.M. stood in front of him like a rock, a rock that rolled a little with the ship's motion. "You'll pardon me saying so, sir, but there are occasions when Her Majesty's Commission is better out o' the way. If you take my meaning. When there's trouble, an officer can be struck. That aggravates the charge against the man concerned. Striking an officer is a court martial offence. Sir."

"I've been ordered to go down, Sarn't-Major, by the adjutant."

Bosom's lips framed a silent whistle. "I see, sir. So that's the way of it, is it? I think, in that case, the thing's maybe different." He hesitated a moment, then said, "You'll allow me to lead the way, Mr. Ogilvie," and turned about smartly, marched along the alleyways and down another companion, his boots banging on the steel. He was thinking: *why yon ghoulish-looking bastard's always got it in for the young officers I'll never know, but sure as fate he has ... Young gentleman's no more notion in his skull of how to handle a troopdeck brawl than I would have of how to talk to a duchess at a tea-party.* As they neared the troopdeck Ogilvie caught the animal smell of it, the sweaty smell of hundreds of men living in close proximity, of damp serge, of sea-sickness, of overcrowded ablutions and urinals. There was a sudden scamper, a wild rush of feet as the R.S.M.'s approach was seen, and then his voice bellowed out: *"Silence along the troopdeck! Silence there, all! Shut your bloody din. Stand still!"*

Men obeyed on the instant, stood rigid at attention as R.S.M. and subaltern moved along the narrow space between the mess tables. Right down here the smell was almost overpowering and Ogilvie wondered, as he had wondered on previous visits of inspection, how the men could put up with it without vomiting. It would, he knew, increase a hundredfold once the *Malabar* moved through the Suez Canal into the Red Sea, down towards the Strait of Bab el Mandeb—the Gates of Hell as seamen called it. This sort of atmosphere, this sort of living, must lead inevitably to tensions, and ahead of him, as he went along behind Cunningham's thick back, he witnessed the first of them. There was a free fight going on. Authority's approach had not yet been marked here. Belts were swinging viciously, their solid brass buckles biting hard into flesh and bone, and the air was blue with profane and filthy language.

Two men lay on the deck, which was slippery with blood. Cunningham stopped some feet clear of the *mêlée* and drew a

27

deep breath. Already men on the fringes were coming to attention, dissociating themselves from what was happening. "You, you and you," Cunningham rapped out. "Go in and put a stop to that." The men he had addressed were all privates; no N.C.O.'s. The men moved to obey, shouting out that the R.S.M. was present with an officer. The air became, for a space, bluer; but the fighting stopped. One big private, a trouble-maker whom Ogilvie recognized as a man named McFee, who came from a family of tinkers, looked at him with red-eyed hatred and made a move in his direction till he was stopped by two of the men the R.S.M. had sent in. Cunningham had stepped back, almost on Ogilvie's foot. To strike the R.S.M. would be serious too. Ogilvie recognized that McFee would undoubtedly have struck *him* if he'd come down on his own.

"Get yourselves to the ablutions," the R.S.M. said stonily, "and get cleaned up. Where's the corporal in charge of this section?"

"Sar-Major!" A man in shirt sleeves came forward.

"A nice mess, Corporal Morrison, that'll maybe lose you your stripes. See that these men clean themselves and the troopdeck. I want all blood shifted, and quickly. When that's done, Corporal Morrison, you'll pass the word that I want to see all the N.C.O.'s of this troopdeck in my cabin in half an hour. If there's any repetition of this there'll be some of you broken and I'll have every man on double drill and fatigues right the way through the voyage to Bombay and after."

He turned about, caught Ogilvie's eye and gave a fractional jerk of his head. "All's well, sir," he said, and marched stolidly away behind Ogilvie. When they were out of sight and hearing of the troops the R.S.M. stopped and said, "You did fine, sir. All that was required of an officer at that stage. Next time, you'll know more what to do yourself. Now I'm coming with you to report to the adjutant."

In Black's office the R.S.M. said briskly, "I had reached the scene before Mr. Ogilvie, sir, and the matter was settled. I shall deal with the N.C.O.'s myself, sir. With your permission."

"Oh, that's granted all right, Sarn't-Major," Black said, his eyes glinting. "What about the men involved?"

"I'd not press it, sir. Conditions are far from ideal along the troopdeck." There was gravity, and a warning, in the R.S.M.'s voice. "We have the hot weather to come, sir."

"I'm aware of that, Mr. Cunningham, thank you."

"Sir! My view is, a little blood-letting doesn't do any real harm. A slow build-up, now, would be far worse. Punishments now would do more harm than good in my opinion, sir. You have my word I'll shake up the N.C.O.'s and leave them in no doubt as to what their duties are in anticipating trouble. Sir!"

Black drummed his fingers on the table. "Very well, Sarn't-Major," he said abruptly. He nodded, "That's all."

"Sir!" Cunningham gave a swinging salute, turned about and left the office.

Black stared at Ogilvie and gave a thin, acid smile. "So the R.S.M. beat you to it," he said softly. "Yes—or no, James?"

Ogilvie hesitated for a second then said, "Yes." In a sense it was true enough; Cunningham had been first into the troop-deck.

Black smiled again. "You're a bloody liar, Mr. Ogilvie," he said, "and so is the R.S.M. And you and I—and the R.S.M.— know that, do we not? I'll say no more about this for now. But you'll remember in future that I expect my orders to be obeyed to the letter. Now get out of my sight."

Two more days and the *Malabar*, past St. Vincent and Trafalgar now, sliding through a glassy sea, steamed slowly round Tarifa and Carnero Point and entered Gibraltar Bay. Soon after this she was brought alongside the coaling wharf and the all-pervading filth of coaling ship began and went on throughout the rest of that day and some of the night—hours of slogging in which the soldiers took part as well as the ship's company and in which the 114th Queen's Own Royal Strathspeys, and the Connaught Rangers, lost their shine and turned temporarily into blackened chimney-sweeps. The officers were given leave and Ogilvie went ashore with MacKinlay, his company commander. The afternoon had turned hot and sticky with a Levanter—the wind that came out of the east to bring high humidity to hang like a misty pall over the garrison. MacKinlay and Ogilvie hired a gharry at the Land Port and were driven past Casemates into Waterport Street. There were soldiers everywhere, and sailors from the British Mediterranean Fleet whose ships lay at anchor in the bay or secured alongside the jetties in the inner harbour. The Rock was Britain's key to all the East, the guardian of the Mediterranean sea routes, and was garrisoned accordingly. The visitors made a point of seeing all they could; it would be years before they passed this way again. Many decades earlier, during the great siege, the 114th had served on the Rock. This place was part of the regiment's history, a living, tangible link with its past. Ogilvie revelled in the very names, names that also were a part of history, commemorative of men and regiments that had served the British fortress-outpost: Cornwall's Parade, Chatham Counterguard, Forbes's Battery, Hesse's Demi-Bastion, Green's Lodge — Red Sands, where the military columns had formed up for a great attack on the Spanish lines during the siege to write a page into British military history. The 114th had taken a leading part in that attack. Ogilvie and MacKinlay climbed the rock itself as high as they could go, looked out over the deep blue waters of the bay towards the barren, light-brown Andalusian hills, across the Strait to the hills of Africa. Ships passed below them as they looked down from Europa Point at the southern tip of the Rock, naval vessels, merchantmen bound to or coming from the great waterway of the canal at Suez. They made their way north again, through the town, past some of the barrack buildings, back again to Casemates and the Land Port, the old gateway into the neutral ground and to the Spanish frontier at La Linea. They walked back to the Water Port and found a boat going out to the coaling jetty. Aboard ship the air was filled with coal dust and there was a continual clatter and roar as the slings were tipped down the chutes to slide into the *Malabar*'s bunkers. The ship was battened right down as if for heavy weather; it was close and airless below decks. Even the officers' cabin alleyways began to smell like the troopdecks. It was a relief when the ship got under way in the early hours of next morning, and, passing out into the open sea to turn eastward around Europa, was able to open up ports and weather doors and let good clean air blow through. The moment they had come off the jetty the washing-down operation had begun and by the time Ogilvie went on deck before breakfast, the *Malabar*'s topsides were as clean as a new pin. As he looked out over the guardrail beneath a clear blue sky he saw dark shapes approaching from the eastward, dark shapes with heavy white bow waves pushing ahead of them, and soon a squadron of heavy ironclads, cruisers he believed they were, swept in line ahead down the troopship's port side. It was a splendid sight as the ships moved past: the guns trained strictly to the fore-and-aft line in their turrets, White Ensigns streaming out along the breeze from the main peaks as the squadron steamed for Gibraltar. Ogilvie heard later that this was the Fourteenth Cruiser Squadron, hurrying home to Portsmouth after three years' service on the China station and the Hong Kong base.

Some days later, the *Malabar* entered Port Said roads to await the pilot and entry to the canal. Here no shore leave was given and very soon the troopship moved out of the roads into the narrow confines of the waterway, passing between the great banks of sand with the occasional green cultivated patches standing out like oases. By now the heat had intensified and to make matters worse a light wind meant that the great bell-mouthed ventilators began to suck down sand, so that they had to be turned away from what air there was. The men stayed mostly on deck, watching the banks of Egypt slide past. Every now and again the *Malabar* tied up to bollards on those banks to allow north-bound shipping to pass. It was a slow passage but at last they passed into the Bitter Lakes and down to Port Tewfik, and eighteen hours after entry they moved past the pilot station and out of the canal into Suez roads to begin the searingly hot passage of the Gulf of Suez and the Red Sea. A fierce sun beat down on the ship and the warm sea heated her from below like a kettle on a stove. Later they endured the worst of all Red Sea conditions—a following wind, which negated the effect of the head-wind made by the ship's own speed, so that the air remained as it were stationary, so that they were in a virtual suspension of heated air, and no draughts blew through to cool down the cabins and public rooms, alleyways and troopdecks overcrowded with two battalions embarked.

Tempers became frayed, men grew lethargic. Many reported sick; there were several cases of fainting along the troop-decks, and the ship's own boiler-room staff was much reduced from the same cause. It was no joke, to be tending furnaces right down below decks in such conditions. Major Corton, the 114th's Medical Officer, and his Rangers counterpart, had their hands full now. Black found plenty of things to keep the 114th busy, to occupy hands and minds, but largely this acted as an irritant since he overdid it; and then frayed tempers grew violent. There were more outbreaks of fighting on the troop-decks and at the next Defaulters before Aden, a corporal was reduced to the ranks and six men were placed in the ship's cells.

This was a sharp example and it had its due effect. Tempers, still potentially violent, were held in check, the N.C.O.'s became even more vigilant than before under another tongue-lashing from Cunningham and, this time, from Lord Dornoch as well. In this state of suppressed violence the ship at long last secured to buoys in Aden for another long coaling operation—a longer one this time, for the bunkers were a good deal emptier after the long haul from Gibraltar than they had been when only a few days out from England. By this time the sickness had increased to high proportions—there had been a severe out-break of stomach trouble in the Red Sea—and the subalterns were detailed to assist the coaling operation in place of such of the senior N.C.O.'s as were sick. So Ogilvie had no opportunity of going ashore; instead he worked almost around the clock supervising the loading of the coal from barges that came along-side in an apparently endless stream. The *Malabar's* winches lifted each basket as it was filled by the men sweating it out on the mounds of coal, and the baskets were tipped out on the canvas-lined decks and shovelled down to the bunkers by more sweating, cursing, semi-naked maniacs who had once been the dashing Royal Strathspeys. Now and again Captain Black would appear, cool and comparatively clean, to stand and stare at the demoniac scene, shouting out a criticism, loudly drawing Ogilvie's attention to the fact, or rather the non-fact as it happened, that they were slacking. After this had happened three or four times Ogilvie made a mild and polite protest on behalf of his men.

He said, "They're doing the best they can. It's heavy work."

"Really? What do you know about heavy work, Mr. Ogilvie?"

Ogilvie, his patience at breaking point, grinned through a mask of coal dust. "As much as you, I dare say. Sir."

Black stiffened. His face quivered. "Are you answering me back, sir?"

"No, sir." Already Ogilvie was regretting his sudden forth-rightness, but he stuck to his point all the same. "I'm only pointing out the facts. If I press them any harder, we'll get more sickness. They've had just about enough."

"Malingerers, scrimshankers, mother's boys! As for you, sir, you're nothing but an insolent young puppy that needs to be whipped. You'll have to toughen up, Mr. Ogilvie—yourself as well as your men. This isn't a kindergarten and the *Malabar* isn't the first ship that's coaled in Aden after a bad passage of the Red Sea. It won't be the last, but this may well be the last time *you* come this particular way if you don't tighten up your ideas! Watch your step, Mr. Ogilvie, watch your step."

The adjutant swung away sharply, his usually pale face red as a beetroot and his lips pressed tightly together. When he had moved out of hearing Ogilvie felt a nudge in his back and turned round to see a grimy figure grinning at him. This was an elderly private of his own company, a long service man with no ambition for promotion, named Jock Burns. "Weel done, Jimmy lad," Burns surprisingly said. "The boys'll like fine to know ye stood up to that perishin', fornicatin' bastard and his great big yap. Je-sus! But I'd like fine to see the bugger humpin' some of these baskets and gettin' a wee bit dirt under his lady-like finger-nails . . ."

There was loud laughter from other men nearby and under the covering of coal dust Ogilvie's face flushed a deep red. Thoroughly embarrassed, he had no idea how to react. He turned the matter off with a rather strangled grunt and began doing some shouting of his own. He'd been oddly pleased, in a sense, by what the man had said, but knew he was now on highly dangerous ground. If Black should ever catch a whisper that he'd been spoken about in such terms, and that an officer had failed to deal with the situation, he was finished. Besides, it could be tricky from another angle. If the men should be allowed to feel he might be on their side against the adjutant, it could lead to all sorts of difficulties—possibly even in action. It didn't do an officer any good to become known, for instance, as a Popularity Jack.

The path of the subaltern was devious and was beset with difficulties, with difficult personal decisions and assessments. Sometimes, but not always, it was better to let things ride. But this time Ogilvie felt he had missed an opportunity of letting the men know he was not only willing to speak up for them on occasions, but that he was also firm and, above all, loyal.

"As indeed you did, my lad," MacKinlay said later when all was cleaned up and they were pushing down the Gulf of Aden, eastwards for the Arabian Sea. Ogilvie's company commander had happened to overhear Private Burns's remarks since he'd been standing directly overhead behind a lifeboat. "That was bloody foolish, James. We all know Black's a bastard, but we

33

don't let the men say so! Black won't get to know — you needn't lose a wink of sleep over that. But you really must remember the kind of material you're dealing with. Oh, the men are all *right* — they're decent enough at heart, and they'll fight well when they have to. But they must always, always be in your control. You can never let up on that. If you do, you'll lose their respect and it'll show. After that — well, you'll not be much more use than my Aunt Fanny's left tit, to put it concisely. Let 'em get away with remarks like that, talk about any officer to another officer as Burns did, and there'll be no end to it, and no end to the embarrassments they'll cause you. Then you'll be well on the way to a most singular lack of promotion prospects."

"I'm sorry," Ogilvie said dejectedly. "What can I do about it now?"

"For God's sake," MacKinlay answered, "nothing! What's done is done. Just remember it, that's all, and never, ever, let it happen again. But don't," he added with a disarming grin, "go and worry about it all the way to Bombay! You'll learn ... dammit, man, you've got plenty of time! You're young yet."

Very, very young, MacKinlay thought as Ogilvie went off to watch the stars hanging thick and low over Arabia. Very young — and that was just his trouble. Been kept too young too long, somewhere along the line ... in spite of Sandhurst. Perhaps the tutor business had had a lot to do with that. He had to grow up. He hadn't yet the capacity for weighing things up fast and coming to a firm conclusion. An officer simply had to have that, above all other things. The British private soldier — not to mention the British adjutant — was a very wily bird indeed and it never had taken him an instant of time to sum up his officers ...

That night the 114th's company commanders were summoned to speak with Lord Dornoch in a cleared corner of the boat deck and next morning the whole regiment was assembled to be addressed personally by its Colonel. He said in his clear, carrying voice, "Men, I have news for you, news that reached me in a despatch from India while we were in Aden. I'm sorry to have to tell you that events are not proceeding too happily in Jalalabad. Although the town is under siege by our forces, the rebel, Ahmed Khan, has consolidated his position and has in fact managed to keep a supply line open to the west. His Highness the Amir is worried and so is our Commander-in-

Chief. Serious casualties have been suffered by our besieging Division. A cavalry brigade has been cut to pieces, so has the 23rd Madras Light Infantry. They have lost most of their British officers." He paused. "I am informed that we shall be moving into action through the Khyber Pass very soon after we enter cantonments at Peshawar . . ."

Lord Dornoch's voice was lost in the wild, tumultuous cheering that went up from the massed men, a cheer that echoed exultantly across the Arabian Sea. Coaling, sickness, troopdeck fighting were all forgotten now. The Colonel raised a hand for silence, smiled as the cheering went on and on, then Captain Black shouted for them to stop and the Colonel proceeded, "It's going to be up to the Royal Strathspeys to teach the rebel a lesson he'll never forget, and to avenge the deaths of our brothers in arms. I need hardly say, we shall give a showing in accordance with our traditions . . ."

This time nothing could stop the demonstration. The R.S.M. didn't even try; with his pace-stick wedged beneath his arm, he was grinning all over his face. Cheer after cheer went up. It was the same from the ranks of the Connaught Rangers, who were being addressed by their own colonel in the after part of the ship, and this time Pipe-Major Ross was beaten to it by the Irish regiment. The skirl of the bagpipes was heard from aft, playing some wild air from out of the mists of Ireland's past, and then this was drowned by a deep-throated roar as, it seemed, every man aboard the trooper burst spontaneously into song that must surely have carried across the water to Arabia itself:

> "For we're Soldiers of the Queen, my lads,
> We've been, my lads,
> We've seen, my lads,
> We're part of England's glory, lads,
> For we're Soldiers of the Queen!"

Three

THERE was still a keeness to be in action but much of the spontaneity and high spirits had worn away by the time the *Malabar* had picked up the Bombay pilot and had steamed past Colaba Point into the Gateway of India to berth at Prince's Dock. The heat and the smells of the East reached out to meet and surround the troops as they lined the decks, the majority of them indulging their first sight of the mysterious, teeming sub-continent. There was an intense curiosity, a real desire to get to know the country in which they would spend perhaps the next five years or maybe longer. There was also an awareness even in the greenest recruit that none of them would pick up the homeward pilot untouched by India, an awareness that here they would leave their youth, that they would return to Scotland purged by fire and sword and an unusual experience of life; and an awareness, too, that in fact not all of them were destined to go back. India took her toll by way of terrible sickness as well as by battle flame. Cholera, dysentery, bubonic plague were the enemies to be faced as much as were the warring tribes waiting for the 114th beyond Peshawar.

Men gazed down as the troopship neared the berth, saw some of the results of the presidency's humid, enervating climate: the low-caste dock workers lying inert in the shade of the great sheds and warehouses that accommodated one quarter of all the seaborne commerce of the sub-continent. The smells increased as the vessel secured alongside beneath a metallic sky; suddenly-fastidious noses wrinkled and there was some raucous comment and a ripple of laughter that was at once silenced by the N.C.O.'s as the gangways were sent aboard from the dockside. No time was being lost; already the trains were waiting in the station near the dock, waiting to draw the fresh troops along the track north for Peshawar and the reinforcement of the Division outside Jalalabad. And as soon as those gangways had been secured and the arrival formalities completed by the self-important clerks who swarmed aboard like flies, the disembarkation started by sections.

While this was going on a despatch was delivered to Lord Dornoch in his stateroom, together with a private letter from a friend at Army headquarters in Murree. After reading these he sent for Black and his second-in-command, Major Hay. Then he lit a cigar and stared thoughtfully out through the port at the dusty dock and at the regiment beginning to form up alongside the warehouse, the clean khaki-drill tunics already showing sweat-stains. When the two officers arrived he swung round and said abruptly, "I've just had word, gentlemen, as to our high command." He hesitated, and when he went on he seemed to be studying Black's reaction in particular. "Sir Iain Ogilvie is being posted from Ootacamund to Murree on promotion to Lieutenant-General. He's to have the Division which we'll be joining."

"What's happened to Sir Henry Fane, Colonel?" Hay asked.

"It seems he's gone sick. You'll remember sickness was one of the difficulties of the campaign . . . and generals aren't exempt."

Black, Dornoch had noticed, was looking put out. The adjutant asked, "This is young Ogilvie's father, Colonel?"

Dornoch compressed his lips a little, and nodded.

"I see." Black cleared his throat. "Was this appointment made — d'you happen to know, Colonel — at his own request?"

Dornoch moved across the stateroom to catch some of the movement of air from a punkah. He said flatly, "Unofficially, I'm told it was. Why d'you ask, Andrew?"

Black shrugged with an elaborate and unconvincing lack of concern. "Oh, nothing, Colonel — nothing at all." He hesitated. "Only I was wondering why he should make this request . . . at this particular moment, I mean. That is all."

Dornoch said, "Sir Iain's a very experienced frontier fighter. What's more, he's said to like action. He'd have been appointed even if he hadn't asked. All the same — and this is why I wanted to speak to you, Andrew — I'd agree with your unspoken thoughts, I think."

"The son?" Hay put in.

There was a curious sound, and a smirk, from the adjutant. "Exactly!" he murmured.

Dornoch raised his eyebrows. "Andrew, don't let there be

37

the smallest misunderstanding. I am simply suggesting that Sir Iain might very well want to see how his son acquits himself in action. That would be a perfectly natural thing, and many fathers would feel the same."

"I doubt that, Colonel," Black said, frowning. "I think most fathers would see to it they commanded a Division as far away as possible from the son. With the best will in the world, the presence of a high-ranking father can be . . . *confining*, shall I say, to the Colonel who commands the said son."

"And to the adjutant?"

Black flushed. "And to the adjutant, since you make the point yourself, Colonel — yes."

Dornoch seemed about to snap, but changed his mind. "It's not the happiest of situations," he admitted, speaking slowly, "but I'm in no position to give orders to the Staff, so we'll have to make the best of it. Sir Iain will not be expecting, or condoning, any favours to his son. And that's all, gentlemen — I simply wanted you both to know the position. This is not to make any differences." Then he looked directly at Black, and added, "In any direction. Clear, Andrew?"

Black nodded, but his face had gone tight. There had been the clearest message in Dornoch's voice, the clearest possible warning, and Black didn't like it. Dornoch said nothing further, but Black noted an air of faint unease. The Colonel wasn't the man to be scared of generals in the very least, but he was extremely proud of his regiment and highly jealous of its reputation and he would be most strongly averse to any outside influences affecting it.

When the 114th and the 88th had been formed up on the jetty and reported to their respective Colonels, the word was given for them to march off and once again Pipe-Major Ross was given his head. With the Royal Strathspeys in the lead, the British reinforcements marched along through the dust behind the pipes and drums, the wild war-notes echoing off the port buildings to announce to all concerned the arrival of more soldiers of the Empress of India. They marched the short distance into the bare, lofty station, were halted alongside the trains and then dismissed by sections to pile aboard. Within an hour all men, animals and equipment of both regiments had been entrained, and the long journey north began. They would

38

go by way of Baroda, Jaipur, Delhi, Lahore and Rawalpindi—a journey of some 1500 miles through an intensification of the heat, and sometimes of the smells, to which Bombay had introduced them. And as the miles wore away behind them, they made frequent stops for men and horses and mules to be watered at small wayside halts, where the *bhisties* brought their full skins that were quickly and thirstily emptied. Occasionally along the route, as the trains chuffed slowly through the parched country, they saw the gaping remains of animals with the carrion birds hovering, circling overhead as the steaming monsters on the track disturbed their meals. From the carriages behind James Ogilvie there came the voices of the men, roaring out the music-hall songs, army version, accompanied now and again by mouth-organs. The volume of sound diminished as the heat and discomfort of that tedious journey sapped men's energy and when at the halts Ogilvie made his rounds he found the troops mostly trying to find sleep, stretched out in all manner of curious positions on the seats and even on the floors of the carriages. As they came farther north into the foothills of the Himalayas they rolled over high, rickety bridges spanning immense drops into gorges that were currently empty of all but a trickle of water, but which in their season would be rushing torrents. Here in the north the air grew cooler; flagging spirits revived, and at night the men felt a chill in their khaki tunics.

At last, three days out from Bombay, the troop-trains pulled in to Peshawar to be greeted in person by their newly appointed Divisional Commander wearing full-dress uniform. James Ogilvie, marching ahead of his half-company out of the station, watched the portly but straight-backed figure of his father, who was chatting to Lord Dornoch. Ogilvie had not welcomed the news of the appointment; and now, with misgiving, he saw his father's gaze sweep over and past him with no hint of recognition.

Behind the pipes and drums the 114th Highlanders marched to quarters in cantonments, kilts a-swing above knees still white from lack of foreign service. The depleted garrison and its ladies, wives and women—for officers, N.C.O.'s and men—turned out to watch them march in and give them a cheer. They were formed up in a hollow square on the parade-ground to be addressed by Lieutenant-General Sir Iain Ogilvie—short, plump, red in the face, the redness accentuated by the contrast of the dazzling white plumes that cascaded down his cocked hat. He addressed them from horseback in a stentorian voice that carried over every inch of the parade and seemed to his son to blast in every window in the barrack buildings behind.

"I'm damn glad to have you in my command," Sir Iain said. "Damn glad! My own regiment especially, I confess. You're needed, let me tell you—and you've not arrived a moment too soon. In fact I may as well start by telling you this: you move out in two days' time—two days—that's to say, the 114th does. I intend holding back the 88th as a fresh relief column until they're needed indispensably—here on the North-West Frontier one doesn't throw in all the reserves straight away. It always pays—always pays—not to let the niggers know your whole strength." He paused. This time there was no wild cheering, no jingoistic singing. The men were tired, overawed by their first acquaintance with India—and overawed by the first sight of their Divisional Commander, who looked as if he would burst a blood-vessel if any man should so much as cough on parade. So they kept their feelings to themselves and stared woodenly at the officer on horseback. Sir Iain went on, "I gather you know the general situation, men. It has not changed a jot—except that as time passes it becomes more difficult to eject the rebel from Jalalabad, in spite of the fact the area outside the walls is badly encumbered—which makes defence a problem. He continues to reduce our strength—that's the point! At this moment, we have troops almost ringing the town, but the rebel still has that vital route open to the west, a route through which he's being supplied and reinforced. It is this route that the 114th, as fresh replacements and fit men, which most of the Division are *not*, will be under orders to close by taking one of the hills that command its entry. This will be difficult, but it will be done, and when it *is* done, the whole force will be moved along a contracting circle. I intend to grip the town and fortress—*like that*!" Sir Iain Ogilvie had lifted his right hand high in the air, fingers fanned. Now he closed his fist with a snap that seemed very nearly audible to his audience. "Imagine a man's neck caught like that," he observed. "*That* is how I want Ahmed Khan. And you are here to see to it." He added, "I myself will be riding with you through the Khyber to join my Staff and the Division outside Jalalabad. Do not underestimate the Khyber Pass, those of you who have not served here before. The Khyber is hell upon earth. Although strictly the area is within our sphere of influence it has been considered feasible to march a regiment through at this particular time only because the forts of Ali Masjid and Landi Khotal are in friendly hands — hands friendly, that is, to the legitimate ruler, the Amir in Kabul, not necessarily to the British as such, though certainly I would not expect the forts to act against us on this occasion since we march as the Amir's allies. Bear in mind, all of you, that you'll come under potentially strong fire positions along every foot of the way outside the range of those forts — fire positions that may well have been infiltrated by Ahmed Khan's rebel levies. Every man will need to be constantly alert to spot snipers before they can fire on the column — damned alert! The most rigorous punishment will be awarded any man who fails to show alertness, damned if it won't!"

There was a good deal more of this; and the men, James Ogilvie thought as the parade was at last marched off and dismissed, seemed suitably impressed with his father, which was as it should be, though before he was out of earshot he had overheard a certain amount of gloomy tooth-sucking about a hidebound old bastard. He was settling into his quarters in the cantonments later, after having supervised the taking over of barrack-room accommodation by his own men, when he was interrupted by a messenger knocking at his door.

"Come in," he called.

The man entered and stood at attention. "Sir! The Colonel's compliments and he'd like to see you in his office at once." He added on a solemn, warning note. "The General's no' away yet, sir, and I think he's with the Colonel."

"Thank you," Ogilvie said. From the man's tone and bearing he deduced that the barrack-room had not yet learned of the relationship. If this was so, then the bush-telegraph must have slipped up somewhere, though generals were so remote normally from the rank and file that many private soldiers never did come to know the names of their most senior commanders. As he automatically straightened his uniform, James Ogilvie felt the old familiar sensation of an imminent carpeting. He was about to be lectured by his father; almost all his memories were of lectures, and criticisms, of standing to attention like a soldier on a charge. What was to come would scarcely be anything in the nature of a family reunion—indeed, he wouldn't have expected it to be in the circumstances, but still . . . There would be much gruffness and throat-clearing, a touch of awkwardness possibly, steely looks from steady blue eyes. His father was in basis a *good* man, he knew, and he had often been aware of the affection that lay concealed behind the façade; he was, after all, the only son. Two sisters, married to soldiers though they were, didn't quite count. But perhaps there was in fact more hope than affection, and it was the knowledge of that burning hope that lay in his father that gave the son many of his self-doubts. He walked along smartly behind the messenger to the Colonel's newly-taken-over office, hesitated outside the door, pulled his tunic straight again, checked with his hand the angle of his pith helmet, and knocked.

He went in and halted. He saluted, eyes looking rigidly towards Lord Dornoch. "You sent for me, Colonel?"

"Yes, James." Dornoch, seated behind a desk, spoke abruptly. "Your father—"

"All right, Dornoch, thank you," Sir Iain said. He had been standing by a window, looking out across the parade-ground towards the flagstaff and the distant bluish hills. Now he swung round. He cleared his throat; the steely gaze flashed across the room towards his son. There was absolutely no awkwardness; seeing his son for the first time in the uniform of the regiment failed, at any rate visibly, to affect him. He said, "I'm glad to see you, boy. You look fit. The army's done you good—damn sight more good than that damn tutor your mother found— hey?"

"Yes, father—"

"No, boy, no." The voice, cutting in at once, was curt, hard, dominating—an order had been given. "Your Colonel has already referred to me as such. I don't deny my damn paternity, but once is enough! We're here on active service, and this is the army—the regiment. I am your Divisional Commander. There is no other relationship, Ogilvie." The use of the surname was a shock and was meant to be. "That is why I asked your Colonel to send for you—to make this crystal clear beyond a doubt, you understand me, Ogilvie?"

"Yes, sir," James Ogilvie answered.

Sir Iain seemed to relax a little. He nodded, blew through his moustache, and said, "Good, that's better. Now a few words of

42

advice—same as I'd give any young officer in my command. Do your duty, obey your orders, respect your betters, show no fear in action even when you feel it. We all feel it. You will feel fear when you march into the Khyber Pass in two days' time. You'll feel scared to blasted death! Respect the feeling, allow it to instil a sensible caution in you, but never give in to it. And don't be squeamish about killing the enemy. Remember they're only niggers, and you're British, a soldier of the Queen-Empress. You're the cream of the world's armies, the very best." He paused, his gaze not wavering for a moment. "You're young. You've not seen blood spilt yet. You will. You won't like your first sight of death. You'll grow accustomed to it. You'll miss a friend or a man of your own company when he's killed, but after a time you'll find that the fact of death *per se*, the sight of it, will mean nothing whatsoever to you. The first time I saw death was in battle, too. China—the taking of Peking under General Gordon. It was horrible and I was sick on the spot. That didn't stop me killing others. The first time I killed a man, I twisted my sword about in a Chinees's guts. I used my handkerchief to wipe the blade and kept it for weeks afterwards as a trophy." His son stared at him; he had never been told so much about his father before. "I repeat, I wasn't so damn sick I couldn't kill others. Remember that. You are here to do well for your country and your regiment, Ogilvie. Remember that too." Sir Iain, coming to the end of his somewhat disjointed morale-lifter, shifted his gaze to the Colonel. "If you don't want this young man any more, Dornoch, I'm finished with him."

Dornoch said, "Yes, sir," and nodded at Ogilvie, smiling kindly. "Very well, James, that's all."

"Yes, Colonel. Thank you." Ogilvie slammed his hand to the salute. "If I may ask one question, sir?"

He had addressed, not the Colonel, but his father. Sir Iain said abruptly, "Well?"

"May I ask, sir . . . how is my mother?"

There was, for a moment, a softer look in the hard blue eyes, as though the question was pleasing. The Divisional Commander vanished for that moment and the father took his place. "Your mother's well, boy. She's presently in Simla." He added, "She sends her love."

That was all. Ogilvie saluted again, said, "Thank you, sir," and turned about with precision and a heel-slam. He wondered

43

if his mother's simple message would ever have reached him if he hadn't made an enquiry.

When he had gone Sir Iain cleared his throat again and took a pinch of snuff from a small gold box, transferring the dust to the back of his hand, whence he drew it into flaring nostrils with a tremendous inrush of air. Dornoch almost laughed; the sight reminded him of a horse snorting in reverse. He asked, "Is this a new habit, sir?"

"Damn it, no, been taking snuff for some years now. You should keep up to date, Dornoch."

"We've not met for some years," Dornoch reminded him.

Sir Iain made an irritable movement, as though he felt his quirks should be heralded ahead of him. "Don't like some of our traditions," he stated. "Never did—not that one."

"The snuff? That's not a—"

"No, no, damn the snuff! I didn't mean that at all." The general sneezed. "This Christian name business. I was always against it, but even when I commanded the battalion, the damn tradition was too strong and too old to be changed by a bird of passage. Always thought it gave a young feller the wrong ideas, to be calling older men, senior men, Charlie or Harry or Eustace. Not right at all, but there you are. Now I'm going to bring my arse to an anchor, as my naval brother says." He sat down, heavily. "Very formal way of addressing one's seniors in *his* service, y'know, it's all aye, aye, sir and fiddlemetits. Good thing, I say. Now about my son. You may be right—what you said earlier. He seems to be shaping reasonably. Too damn young for his years still, though. Colours up like a virgin."

"He's young, I agree, but we'll overcome that."

"His mother's fault, of course. Mothers aren't the best things for young men." He added, "He'll not be too brash in action, I hope. Men's lives are at stake—men in his company."

"We'll be finding that out, but I've every confidence in him, sir. And the men like him—that's half the battle."

"Is it? Popularity's never a good end in itself, Dornoch."

"I didn't mean to suggest it was." The Colonel spoke patiently. "But he's the kind of young officer they'll trust and follow, when he's had the right experience."

"Why d'you say that—hey?" The blue eyes fixed their gaze on Lord Dornoch.

"It's a little hard to be precise, it's a feeling I have. You'll

44

agree that any man who commands a battalion acquires an ability to sum men up. If I may say so without offence, sir, it may be that I can see him from a greater distance than you, as his father, can ever see him."

"Well? Go on!"

Dornoch said, "He has integrity, sir. That comes through, to the men as well as myself. Integrity and a clear honest decency go farther than anything else—once the experience is there also."

"H'm..." The General pulled briefly at his moustache, and a frown creased the flesh between his eyes into a deep groove. "Well—no favours, mind. No holding back because he's my son—no soft jobs. But I know I don't need to tell you that, Dornoch," he added as he saw the way the Colonel was lifting his eyebrows. "That adjutant of yours—what's his name again?"

"Black—Andrew Black."

"Black, Black. Can be a good name, but on the other hand ... Any family to speak of?"

Dornoch knew well what was meant by that. "They're not landed, sir."

"Not in Burke's?"

"No."

"Good God. Trade?"

"I believe there's trade in the background."

The General rustled irritably. "Damn it, man, what *sort* of trade?"

"I understand the grandfather, the paternal grandfather, was a steelmaster, Sir Iain."

"Good *God*!" Sir Iain was startled, and showed it. Brewing, say, would have been *moderately* respectable if not exactly desirable. Steel was neither. But it meant money. Money, however, was not important; of itself, it had never made a Royal Strathspey. Birth had, and very efficiently. After all, the men respected a gentleman; they didn't like serving under an officer who was basically of their own sort and if a man came from the common people then he remained common however much money he had. The general made a sour noise in his throat. "A feller of that background could be impressed ... see a way into society, don't you know. Could be a snob—try to curry favour. That sort of thing."

45

With a touch of impatience Dornoch said, "I doubt if that would apply in the case of Captain Black, sir."

"Hope you're right." After that the two men began discussing some of the details of the military campaign that lay ahead of them and in the course of the discussion it became clear that Sir Iain Ogilvie was still a good and wise soldier despite his having the fixed social prejudices of his years.

If the adjutant had known of the conversation between his Colonel and the Divisional Commander, he would have agreed wholeheartedly with Dornoch's final remark. Many years before, Black's father, like Ogilvie's, had sent him into the army. The reasons had been utterly different from Sir Iain's but had been nonetheless heartfelt, nonetheless urgent. In the Black family there was absolutely no military tradition at all; Andrew Black was there to establish it and thus to become a gentleman. His father, who had any amount of money, aspired to rise socially, and considered the best way to do this was to have a son in the army, and not only in the army, but in one of the very best regiments. It would be an open sesame. So Andrew Black had gone to Sandhurst and had duly passed out very creditably. In the meantime all kinds of strings had been pulled and various financial pressures applied with the utmost discretion, for Black senior was a brilliant man of business and had good friends who were important bankers holding the accounts of landed families and military families and even families in Government itself . . . and young Andrew Black had been gazetted to the Royal Strathspeys, which was a regiment of panache as well as of distinction — more so, in the father's view, than the Guards. For this gift of a military career Andrew Black had never forgiven his father, even though he had made himself become a good soldier and enjoyed many aspects of army life, most especially the power it gave him over many men's lives. The truth was that he had never felt easy in the company of his brother officers. He saw slights in everything, in every conversational gambit which he didn't quite understand, in every amusedly raised eyebrow when he himself had made some small gaffe, in every smile, in every reprimand that had come his way as a subaltern. He had grown to dislike the officer caste to the point of hatred, though mostly he had managed to keep this dislike to himself. He had never become

46

a Royal Strathspey in his heart. He had quickly become moody, self-reliant, a man who walked alone, and frequently these days drank alone as well. He was drinking now, not in the Mess, but alone in his quarters — sinking a bottle of whisky rather too fast for tomorrow's health and fitness. He was thinking about the people who called themselves the landed gentry, a class that practically everyone but he in the Mess belonged to. James Ogilvie did, *par excellence*! Dornoch was a lord — a *bloody* lord Black told himself vindictively. Not that Dornoch was ever in the least ostentatious about it, but it came through naturally in all he did and said, and in all he *didn't* say or do as well. It rankled; Black couldn't hope to compete and he knew it, though he'd managed to master the secret language of the upper classes well enough, the particular inflexions and accents and pronunciations and grammatical constructions that indelibly marked a man apart from the others; he had even largely learned which *incorrect* speech had to be used to the same end, for sometimes correctness could stamp one with the stamp of bounderism. And Ogilvie again ... as conceited a young puppy as ever he'd met. Dumbly insolent to him ever since he'd joined from Sandhurst, and couldn't take a reprimand without looking soulful and hurt — damn his eyes!

Savagely, Black gulped at the whisky. Ogilvie was as aristocratic a name as you could find anywhere — hence the fellow's appointment to the 114th, no doubt. And then the father! His appointment to the high command smelt, by God, it stank to heaven of nepotism, even if on this occasion it was nepotism in reverse, if there was such a thing. Where the son is, so also is the father — to protect him, cosset him, ladle him with the syrup of high rank, and eventually promote him over Captain Andrew Black's head ...

Finishing the bottle, Black lurched to his feet, his eyes red and angry, went over to a cupboard and brought out another. Half an hour later his head sunk over the table, going down into the crook of his elbow, and he slept. To him soon after this came Major Hay, dropping in, on his way to Lord Dornoch's quarters, to tell him the Colonel wished to discuss certain details of the forthcoming movement of the battalion through the Khyber Pass. Major Hay — aristocrat like the others, fussy as an old hen, shook his greying head sadly at what he saw. He clicked his tongue in distress; for he understood a lot about

47

Andrew Black. He removed the bottle and the glass out of sight, lifted the adjutant's head—lifted the adjutant, dragged him with some difficulty across to his bed, sat him on it, lifted his legs up and rolled him on to his side towards the wall. Then he went, not to the Colonel, but to the Medical Officer, Surgeon Major Corton, who was sitting reading in the Mess.

"I'm sorry to bother you, Doctor," he said.

"That's all right." Corton looked up. "Sit down. Have a brandy?"

"Thank you, but I won't. Andrew's sick. I was wondering if you'd look in?"

Corton stretched and grinned, ran his fingers through thick sand-coloured hair. "I was hoping for a quiet evening, John. Been at it ever since we marched in, checking medical stores—trying to get us a decent kit, though you'd think I was asking for all the treasure of the Orient. How d'you beat cholera—if it comes our way—or stop bleeding, with half a ton of Gregory Powder?" He sighed. "So Andrew's sick—what of, John?"

"A fever of some kind, I think."

Corton grinned again. "That man's riding for a fall," he observed. "All right, John, if it'll make you feel any easier, I'll go along and give him a powder."

Hay said gratefully, "Thank you, thank you indeed," and went off to report to the Colonel that the conference was off so far as the adjutant was concerned since Black was currently in the doctor's care. It was true in a sense, but it was also a damnable lie really, and no one realized better than John Hay himself that he would never have done the same for a private soldier or a junior N.C.O., which was a circumstance Hay saw as a simple and inevitable fact of regimental life. And, of course, what he had done was a kindly enough act; but next morning Black, staggering under the weight of his hangover and shaking in every limb, gave no credit for that. The bloody gentry had once again got him at a disadvantage.

That same morning Lord Dornoch held Defaulters and, by the sheerest coincidence, had to deal with a corporal who, the night before, had been found unfit for guard duty because he had been drunk on a bottle of gin slipped to him by a member of the crew aboard the troopship. Dornoch, as he was bound to do, gave the man a severe tongue-lashing and spoke at some length about the perniciousness of such behaviour so hard on the heels of their arrival in India and especially when the battalion was about to go into action. Major Hay was present when the Colonel sentenced the corporal to reduction to the ranks and in addition, since the battalion could already, by stretching a point, be considered to be on active service, to one day's Field Punishment Number One. It was a harsh sentence, intended as an example, and Hay saw little inconsistency in his tacit approval of the sentence and his own action the night before in regard to Captain Andrew Black. An officer was an officer, the men were something very different, and you really couldn't give them much leeway. When later he saw the ex-corporal lashed securely and with devilish discomfort to the wheel of a gun-carriage, out on the parade for all to see in the searing sun, without water, Hay was visited by a touch of irritation. Really, it was too bad of Black to behave like a ranker.

That night the barrack-room saw the difference between the gentlemen and the rank and file in a rather more lurid and vivid light.

The man James Ogilvie had failed to reprimand during coaling-ship at Aden was the spokesman. "It's all very fine for the bleedin' gentry," he said in a loud, hectoring voice. "Why, what are they after all, but wee tin gods, up yonder in their muckin' palatial splendour, wi' sairvants to wait on them an' all, even to spread the bleedin' toothpaste on the bloody brushes for them like as not? Can ye tell me that?" No one bothered to answer; Private Jock Burns, self-appointed barrack-room lawyer, had all the answers already. "I'll tell you," he said. "They're mortal, same as us, though ye'd never so much as dream it the way they behave. If one o' them doesna get a good Scots bullet up the bum when we enter the Khyber, I'm not Jock Burns! Look now—His bloody Lordship almost quoted the Bible when he stripped yon Robbie Main o' his stripes today . . . battalion's virtually in bloody action now, he says!" Burns's seamed face lowered and his jaw came out like an underhung bulldog. "Well, then, aren't the bloody officers in action wi' us? So why are they goin' to a bloody ball the night, dancin' and drinkin' and messin' around wi' the women— *ladies*, I beg their bloody pardons—and gettin' themselves as unfit as Robbie Main for marchin' off tomorrow? Can ye tell me *that*?"

In point of fact, Private Burns was not the only one who thought it inappropriate that the officers should attend a ball the night before marching into action. James Ogilvie would have agreed with him, even though the great Iron Duke himself had set the precedent before Waterloo. This was not 1815 and the British Army had changed its character more than a little since those far-off days. But India was India and the social obligations, though perhaps they did not occur, at least along the frontier, so frequently as at Invermore depot, were rigidly observed whenever possible. Tonight, Lord Dornoch had decreed as possible. More than that—imperative. For in a palace outside Peshawar lived a princeling from Afghanistan named Feroz Khan, cousin of the Amir on whose behalf the British regiments were to fight. Feroz Khan had extended his invitation to the newly arrived officers of the garrison and it would be most impolite—even impolitic, which was more important—to refuse. Action or no action, every available officer would be expected to attend, wearing full Mess dress with decorations.

James Ogilvie was one of those instructed to attend, and as it happened that night was to be an important one for him. It was also to be an impressive one, one in which he received his first taste of the extravagant glory that was high-caste native India. But first he was given a taste of something else. As the officers were driven out from the cantonments at dusk they swayed on their carriage springs past the dereliction of the other half of India, the Untouchables lying crowded and stinking in dark doorways, in filthy side alleys, in the streets as the gentry passed through the town. A sickening stench rose to Ogilvie's nostrils, almost making him retch, recalling the smell along the troopdecks of the *Malabar* but a thousand times more concentrated. No wonder the Peshawar garrison had been so badly hit by sickness. Hands reached out, unintelligible voices addressed the splendid British officers beseechingly.

"What do they want?" Ogilvie asked.

MacKinlay, his company commander, was with him in the carriage and he laughed at the question. "My dear James, are you really so ignorant of the world? They want alms. It's all they have to live on."

"Do we give them alms, then?"

Again MacKinlay laughed. "If you want every beggar-man

in Peshawar to drag you out of the carriage, then by all means chuck 'em an anna or two! But I'd advise against it, James. Leave 'em well alone—they're happy enough as they are."

"Happy!" Ogilvie gave him an indignant look. "How can you say that?"

"They've never known any better life," MacKinlay answered with complete indifference. "Believe me, I know India. You have to close your eyes to a hell of a lot—if you don't, you'll start to think too much and then you'll go off your head."

"You don't believe these things ought to be thought about?"

Carefully, MacKinlay snipped the end from a cigar with a small gold cutter. "It's better not, old boy, it's far better not. You're a British officer, one of God's chosen people . . . your job's to safeguard the Empire, and help to rule it, not to sow the seeds of its dismantlement by talking or acting like a blasted radical, James! God knows, there's quite enough of *them* around these days." He reached out and tapped Ogilvie's arm. "There's one thing above all you'll learn in India, and that is, the natives have to be kept down hard. Let 'em once get above themselves, old boy, and the Empire's done for, you mark my words!"

Ogilvie didn't respond; he sat in silence, and in the expensive fragrance of MacKinlay's cigar, as the carriage rolled on through the town and out the other side. He had been surprised by MacKinlay's viewpoint, by the vehement way in which it had been expressed. MacKinlay had always seemed a tolerant man, with the standard paternalism towards the men but with more sincerely-meant kindliness than many other officers. All at once he was different; Ogilvie didn't entirely realize it, but he had come up against the built-in shift in values that affected so many of the officer class when they were one of a comparatively small garrison in a native and largely hostile land. It was a defence mechanism at work, a defence against the cringing, wily hostility which they felt in their bones lay so close beneath the servile veneer of the masses. Men inspired less fear when they had become, by process of rigidly instilled thought-patterns, objects to be despised.

They left the city behind them and with it the smells and the whining, deformed beggars and holy men. They came out into moon-filled countryside, bare open land stretching to the

51

distant hills lying below the farther snow-covered Himalayan peaks. Out here the air seemed cooler and fresher, with a hint of those distant snows borne along a light evening breeze. Soon across the plain they saw the lights of the palatial residence for which they were bound and MacKinlay said with a sigh of relief, "That's the India you want to cultivate, dear boy. Mind you, the princes are probably even bigger rogues than the Untouchables — must be, in fact — but they do know which side their bread's buttered these days!"

Ogilvie wondered just what MacKinlay meant by his use of the word 'rogue' in connection with the seedy beggars of the town, who had looked to him merely poor outcasts without the opportunity of aspiring even to roguery; but he sensed that MacKinlay would be unable to explain other than by some airy comment to the effect that so far as he was concerned all natives were rogues, varying only in degree. If this was so, it struck Ogilvie as an arid attitude to take towards a country in which, for better or worse, they were to spend so many years of their lives. Soon the officers in their carriages passed under a battle-mented gatehouse set across the roadway, past a splendid quarter-guard of dismounted private cavalry, huge, black-bearded men dressed in dazzling white satin with gold scarves and jewelled turbans, and high, shining boots that caught the flicker of the great guard-lanterns that shone on either side. The carriages went on across a wide courtyard with a fountain playing in its centre, a courtyard brightly lit by more lanterns and by hundreds of coloured fairy-lights hanging from trees and poles like a Chinese garden. Brittle Indian music was coming from somewhere inside the palace. At the head of a flight of marble steps, His Highness Feroz Khan was greeting his guests as they filed past. The officers of the 114th joined the queue, with Ogilvie at the tail. His Highness was an old man, bent and wizened like a monkey, grinning from beneath an ornate sky-blue turban whose peacock-feather rose from an immense ruby set in gold — a head-dress that almost extin-guished him. He bowed to each guest, then took his hand with a dry, claw-like touch. He grinned and bobbed away, showing blackened teeth, but said nothing. They filed past into an enormous space — Ogilvie felt that 'hall' was not quite the word for it — and on behind the extravagantly-dressed queue into a long apartment with an ornate ceiling patterned in gold and blue tiles. In here half the British and Indian Armies appeared to have gathered, together with most of the Indian civil and political services in their dress uniforms. It was a breathtaking sight—the variegated uniforms of Scots and Irish, cavalry and infantry, gunners, sappers, rifle regiments, scarlet and blue and gold and green, and the extravaganzas of the Indian regiments—Guides, Mahrattas, lancers—it was brilliantly colourful. Ogilvie found himself wondering how it was that Whitehall had ever decided the Royal Strathspeys were needed at all to support so vast a garrison—unless the sickness and the casualties that had afflicted the men had passed the officers by (which was not too unlikely a thought, perhaps). The ladies, though providing yet more colour, were overshadowed by their gorgeously-clad menfolk. Servants circulated, bringing endless trays laden with liquor. After a while Ogilvie's head began to swim with the heat from the close-packed bodies, from the chandeliers, from the amount of drink he had felt obliged to take. Slowly, separated now from the rest of the battalion, he made his way through the ante-room towards the ballroom, where the music was coming from. This had changed now to an English waltz, extremely badly played, and the floor was a most glittering sight. Hairy-faced officers, streaming with sweat, moved past Ogilvie as he stood staring, their elegantly gloved hands holding the bare, powdered backs of their ladies—or someone else's. It was probably no more than coincidence that Ogilvie's thoughts went back to London and the remarks of his friend Jackie Harrington at precisely the moment when his Colonel, coming up behind him, laid a hand on his shoulder. Dornoch asked, "Enjoying yourself, my boy?"

"Yes, thank you, Colonel."

"You look a trifle lost. Not surprising really—your first taste of princely Indian life! I remember when I was your age . . . I felt a genuine sense of awe that one man should have such immense riches. That was Haidarabad. I was staying with the Nizam for a tiger shoot. We never did kill a tiger that time—but there were enough dusky maidens to satisfy any young man's wildest dreams!" Dornoch laughed, and the laugh faded to a small, rather whimsical smile that played around the corners of his mouth; he seemed cool enough, and unimpressed with his present surroundings. He went on, "I'd like you to meet a lady whose husband is currently in action outside

53

Jalalabad — and whose escort for this evening has had to leave to attend to a small matter in the native cantonment." He turned aside and put a hand on the arm of a young woman with mischievous eyes and a cloud of dark hair around a pale, oval face. "My dear, may I introduce Mr. Ogilvie of my regiment? James, this is Mrs. Archdale, whose husband is distinguishing himself with a Mahratta brigade. I'm sure she'd like to dance." His eyes twinkled at the girl — she was little more really — with a kind of fatherly wickedness. "You'll excuse me, my dear? I'm afraid it's my job to circulate at these affairs, just as it is in my own Mess."

She gave a small, formal bob of her head. "Oh, but of course, Lord Dornoch, you really mustn't mind about me —"

"But I do," he cut in gallantly. "I leave you with regret — but in good hands, I'm glad to say." Then he was gone. Again Ogilvie had had a surprise. This was no longer the correct Colonel of the 114th Highlanders; there had been a light in his eye that was never there in the Mess or the battalion office or when Lady Dornoch, that rather formidable and important woman in subalterns' lives, was with him — which currently she was not, having been confined to quarters with a touch of lumbago. Ogilvie swallowed, found his hands sweating lightly in the palms, and asked nervously, "Will you dance, Mrs. Archdale?"

Her eyes seemed to mock him. "Colonel's orders, Mr. Ogilvie? I heard what Lord Dornoch said, you know! Or do you really want to?"

As a matter of fact he didn't; he felt an obscure sense of danger because this girl was highly attractive and already he was feeling a response to her in his body. That would never do. He took a grip on himself, realizing he was being callow and foolish. What was a dance, after all? Very likely he would have the one dance and she would be off, looking for a more proficient partner. He said with a stiff reserve, "Yes, I really want to. May I have the honour?"

Gaily she said, "Yes, Mr. Ogilvie, you may indeed," and in fact it was she who took him and swept him into the whirl. Once there he took over, his masculinity vaguely affronted. He liked the touch of her bare flesh through his thin glove, wondered what it would be like without that absurd formal covering on his fingers. He found nothing to talk about, was as

54

hopelessly tongue-tied as on that far-off day with his father at Balmoral, and the old Queen's frosty stares. But this girl was vital and alive and not at all regal, not at all frosty, and she held her body close to his own; more closely, a quick glance around told him, than most of the others were doing. She seemed to know a great many people, which was rather off-putting, because she kept meeting eyes over his shoulder, and smiling, and now and again lifting her hand in a somehow appealing gesture. He felt her basic disinterest in himself despite their physical closeness, and this further inhibited his ability to muster any small talk, but after a while a thaw set in and he found himself answering her questions, which were mainly concerned with army matters, until the music stopped and the dancers moved off the floor to be replaced by others. Ogilvie guided Mrs. Archdale towards a door leading on to a dimly-lit terrace that ran right along one side of the ballroom and where there were tables and chairs. He said diffidently, "It should be cooler out there, don't you think?"

She giggled. "That's what they all say!"

"Oh—do they?" He flushed uncomfortably, as though he had made an advance and had been rebuffed.

"Yes," she said, "but never mind, I'd quite like to sit for a while."

On the terrace they went first to a marble balustrade and looked down a long drop to bare earth below where there was a moon-splashed cluster of mean-looking huts. Ogilvie remarked, "I wonder who lives down there."

"The sweepers, and creatures like that," she said with the same lack of interest and feeling as MacKinlay had displayed when talking about the beggars. She changed the subject. "I think I'd like a drink."

"Of course." Ogilvie turned away and signalled to a servant, who came up with a tray. Mrs. Archdale swept the native with a glance, turned her back and made for a table. The man followed. She sat, then disdainfully took a glass from the proffered tray—a glass of brandy. Ogilvie, scarcely aware of what he was choosing, took a glass that turned out to contain an excellent, full-bodied French wine. He raised the glass. "Your good health," he murmured.

"I have a feeling," she said, smiling, "you should be saying 'Her Majesty the Queen-Empress.' Shouldn't you?"

He felt she was laughing at him. "I doubt if that would be appropriate," he said, realizing how stiff he sounded.

She was still smiling. "You're awfully regimental," she said surprisingly. "If you're not careful you'll end up like Tom."

"Tom?"

"My husband. Major Archdale to you." She did something to her hair, and the movement of her arm did something to the arrangement of her dress. Ogilvie found himself staring down into the valley between her breasts; he looked away. "The army can get too deeply into a man's life," she said with a hint of pensiveness. "It can be lonely for a woman. I gather you're not married, Mr. Ogilvie."

He laughed. "Married subalterns are a rarity, Mrs. Archdale!"

"I know that, but you won't always be a subaltern, one hopes. Something tells me, in fact, you're going to get on well. Is there a lucky girl, waiting somewhere in those remote Scottish hillsides?"

All at once he felt a wave of nostalgia, a homesickness for Scotland, for its clean honesty and its glens and lochs and the crispness of a Highland morning. He said seriously, answering her question, "No one in particular at all events. Why do you ask, Mrs. Archdale?"

She shrugged and said, "Oh, just put it down to the curiosity of army wives on remote stations. Your father's the Divisional Commander, isn't he?" she asked suddenly.

"Yes," he said in surprise at the sudden shift—it was his night for surprises—and again asked, "Why?"

"Because he's just come on to the terrace with His ghastly little Highness our host."

"The devil he has!"

"My dear Mr. Ogilvie, he's not going to eat you, surely?"

He had got quickly to his feet, almost knocking over the table and glasses. His father, attended by an *aide-de-camp,* was coming along towards him, an important-looking figure in the Mess uniform of the General Staff, all scarlet and gold and garnished with tassels and medals and orders. Half a pace behind him, His Highness Feroz Khan grinned and shuffled and darted sharp glances to left and right. The native prince was accompanied now by three young eunuchs, his hand running up and down the satin-skinned arm of one of them.

56

Ogilvie stood at attention as the procession moved past. His Highness gave him a sly sideways look and a slack-mouthed, suggestively approving grin. His father nodded distantly. "Evening, Ogilvie," he said.

"Good evening, sir." The men moved on past; his father kept edging distastefully away from the eunuchs. As Ogilvie sat down once again Mrs. Archdale said, "Well, well! A regimental father, too. Very!"

"Yes."

"Has he always been like that?"

"Yes." Ogilvie was about to say something more, to excuse his father, when he saw the A.D.C. coming back towards him, a man of captain's rank whom he didn't know.

The A.D.C. bowed to Mrs. Archdale then turned to Ogilvie. He said, "Mr. Ogilvie, the General suggests you make a point of attending His Highness's special entertainment. It's being held in the Throne Room, which leads off the terrace at the end." He bowed again to Mrs. Archdale, then hurried away in Sir Iain's wake.

"Off you go as bidden," Mrs. Archdale said brightly.

"Won't you come?"

She gave a peal of laughter and tapped him with her fan. "My dear Mr. Ogilvie, no, I will not! I wouldn't be admitted in any case—and when you get in there you'll see for yourself why."

"Oh—I think I see. Well, I certainly don't want to go."

"Oh, yes, you do," she said good-humouredly, "and anyhow, you've been *ordered* to. And it may be good for your education—which is no doubt what was in your father's mind. It'll teach you a little more about India, and you're going to be here a long time, so you mustn't let any chivalrous thoughts of me detain you."

"Shall I see you again . . . after the entertainment?"

"I doubt it," she said. "Ladies usually stay well away from unattached males after the kind of show Feroz Khan's going to put on!"

But he did in fact see her again after the special entertainment, and in the meantime he had certainly had his eyes opened. Fairly inexperienced with women even in a purely social sense, James Ogilvie was still totally inexperienced when it came to the bedroom, was still as virginal as he'd been when staying with Jackie Harrington. What he saw that night stirred up the latent urges that had been stimulated back in Half Moon Street when the girl Freddie something-or-other had spent the night there. But this time nothing at all had been left to the imagination. It was an orgy, nothing less. The women—he was not sure if they were His Highness's wives—disported themselves fantastically and entirely naked except for large jewels whose facets glittered from navels and nipples and elsewhere. They threw themselves frenziedly into the most extreme, and occasionally absurd, postures. The music was erotic, the action, in part of which the eunuchs were engaged, was more so. During the entertainment, more drink was served. Ogilvie sweated, became the victim of an urge so strong that he felt his body must explode. Now and again he stole a glance at his father; that irascible gentleman was staring as if transfixed, his eyes bulging, his mouth slightly open. Ogilvie—again—was intensely surprised; for perhaps the first time in his life he saw his father as a human being with all a man's emotions. Never had he seen him like this; neither, he was willing to bet from the basis of a sudden flash of insight, had his mother, in front of whom his father behaved publicly as did Lord Dornoch in the company, or rather the presence, of Lady Dornoch. He looked at the other officers, singling out the Royal Strathspeys. Black had an intent, hungry look. He was at one and the same time eager and disapproving. Major Hay was looking appalled, though presumably, having served in India before, he was no stranger to this kind of entertainment. The Colonel was smiling slightly, had adopted a bored, patrician look of tolerance. MacKinlay and the other company commanders and Ogilvie's brother subalterns seemed to be enjoying it well enough and were in no way embarrassed as Ogilvie himself was. Ogilvie's attention went back to the performing women. He was surprised at the lack of beauty in them; always he had imagined that Eastern women, the women in the harems, were good-looking and seductive. These were not, in the main. One or two were reasonably so, but the majority were skinny, haggard even, with dirty, tousled hair and sagging breasts and lined faces, and there was a smell of uncleanness as though the palace was short on soap and water, which it probably was. But that didn't matter to Ogilvie; he found, to his shame, that he was seeing Mrs. Archdale in those unlovely bodies, that he was mentally projecting her in their places, that he was seeing her as he was seeing them, her nudity displayed with eager abandon before him; and this was the more shame-making because—regimental thought!—he didn't even know her Christian name . . .

Soon after the officers had rejoined the ladies, Ogilvie, sweating still from drink and excitement and with his pulse racing, saw Mrs. Archdale in the centre of a group of young officers, none of them as it happened from the 114th. Laughing, she excused herself and left the group to join Ogilvie. "Well?" she asked challengingly.

He stared at her, blood pounding through his head, visualizing again all that he couldn't see. Licking his lips he said, "I do understand . . . why you couldn't come."

She nodded, then said with sudden compassion and understanding, laying her fan against his chest, "Don't let it all disturb your dreams too much. There are plenty of unattached girls in India. You'll see. When you have leave to visit Simla, or Poona . . . they'll come running. I promise you that, James."

"James?" he repeated.

She said, "It's your name, isn't it? I made enquiries. You don't mind, do you?"

"Of course not."

"Mine's Mary. Why don't you come and sit down for a minute, you look unwell."

"Yes," he said stupidly, and almost staggered across the floor towards the terrace, pushing into people and getting a number of eyebrows raised at him. He was really more than a little drunk. As they sat down at one of the tables in a dark corner he said in a thickish voice, "I've had a damn sight too much to drink."

"You've had a damn sight too much of other things too," she said crisply. "They ought to give people a course on Indian social life before sending them out here!"

"Yes," he said again; then, speaking as thickly as before, he said, "Mary, d'you know something?"

She looked at him curiously. "Well, go on."

He said, "I've never even kissed a girl."

She laughed. "Oh dear, don't let your friends hear you confess *that*!" Then she saw his terrible seriousness and her voice softened and she said, "Well, then, you may as well begin now as later," and very gently she moved into his arms and she lifted her face towards him and their lips met. He kissed her clumsily but hungrily and with a strange, consuming passion, and he was reluctant for it to end. It was she who drew away, as gently as she had begun. She said in a matter-of-fact voice, "Well, James, that's that. I don't know what's been started but it mustn't go on . . . and I know I'm to blame."

He said, "Tell me about yourself."

She hesitated, then said, "Oh, all right, I will. Better if *I* do, rather than have someone tell you what isn't true, which is sure to happen sooner or later in a place like Peshawar. I'm told I look like twenty, but in fact I'm twenty-seven, which is far too old for you even if I wasn't married to Tom. So don't get ideas of – of falling in love with me, which I see is at least half on the cards – and don't tell me I'm too frank, I know I am. Just remember you're a little drunk and you've had an emotional evening, and this is India. It can be terribly, dangerously romantic – all those hills, and the silence of the plains, and the glamour, which is horribly false really, of serving the Queen and being treated as God because of it. And the fighting, and the coming back as heroes because you've killed some poor starving tribesmen who didn't want to change their way of life and who were defending their own just as much as the English tried to do way back in 1066 – and the Scots at Flodden Field and Culloden. Which are sentiments dear Tom would simply hate to hear expressed," she added in a voice that had gone very hard. "Which leads me to the next thing I have to tell you before someone else does. I do not love Tom, I loathe him. He's an old man, James – fifty-three. He's the *stupidest* man I've ever, ever met and he's the Brigade Major of the Mahratta Brigade, and I don't know if there's any connection or not. And he's a killer. He adores India because it lets him be a high-level killer and gives him medals for being one. It's his outlet. He has no time for sex, he hasn't even the ability, poor Tom!" He felt a sense of shock at such forthrightness from an officer's wife. "But I'll tell you something you're going to be sorry to hear in your present state of mind and it's this: I've never been in any man's bed but Tom's and though I may fall one of these days, it's not going to be tonight or with a boy of your age. So go back to cantonments with your Colonel and the regiment, James dear, and tomorrow go off to fight. And if you happen to run into Tom when you're through the Khyber, and

I pray God you do get through safely, you'll feel much better because you'll be able to look him in the eye. All right?"

He nodded, his head reeling, his body still on fire. "All right," he said in a low voice and, looking up, saw Captain Black coming towards them.

Black had merely come to round up the officers for a return to cantonments, Dornoch having sought His Highness's leave to extract his battalion early so that they could the better march next morning. Normally, these affairs went on into the small hours or even right through the night, it seemed. Black said nothing at the time about Mary Archdale but Ogilvie guessed from the disapproving look in his eye that he was only storing it up. He was right. Next morning at dawn the skirl of the pipes aroused the battalion and, soon after, the bugles sent the men running on to the parade where, with their baggage train, native bearers and mountain artillery, they formed up before Lord Dornoch. As the sun went up the sky in many-coloured splendour, striking fire off the hills, the 114th Highlanders marched away from the cantonments in column of route, behind the pipes and drums and the Colonel on his charger, with Sir Iain Ogilvie on his right, marched away on action bent, all of them with high spirits but all of them wondering who would be the ones who would not return. And later as James Ogilvie marched ahead of his half-company, the adjutant, mounted and wearing trews, wheeled his horse out of the line and waited beside the dusty track until Ogilvie drew level with him.

"A word in your ear, James," he said. "You'll kindly fall out."

Ogilvie did so. "Yes?" he asked.

"You were in a compromising situation last night. I refer, of course, to Mrs. Archdale, as I understand the woman's name to be."

"There was nothing compromising about that," Ogilvie snapped back, his colour—and his temper—rising. "We were simply talking, that's all."

"Aye—alone, on a darkened terrace!" the adjutant said furiously.

"What's wrong with that?"

"What's *wrong* with it—what's *right* with it you mean, my lad! Do you think such conduct would go unremarked in Scotland?"

"Yes—by all but a handful of miserable, hypocritical kirk props."

Black's face grew mottled and he sucked in breath harshly. "You'll not take that line with me, young Ogilvie, no, not even though your father's the Divisional General. You damned aristocrats . . ." His voice trailed away into a muffled curse as he realized that for the first time in his career he had given the game away, let the veneer slip. God, how Ogilvie would laugh now behind his back! He almost screamed as he went on, "I'll not permit that kind of misbehaviour so long as I'm adjutant of the 114th. I'll not see the regiment dragged through the filthy mire of—of *fornication*! May I be forever *damned* if I do! You'll not see that woman again. Man, man, I'm told she's a married woman!"

"You've been busy, haven't you," Ogilvie said, "finding things out. I know quite well she's married. And I have every intention of seeing her again if she wishes it."

He'd said it, because he was furiously angry at Black's ridiculous and hysterical exaggeration; but from then on fear of Andrew Black was to march with him all the way to Jalalabad. Later he felt that if he could have withdrawn it, he would have done so. He never knew how Black kept control of himself. There was a terrible pause then Black said in a deadly quiet voice, "What I have just said cannot be given as a military order, I realize that. Nevertheless, there are ways and means, Mr. Ogilvie. So just keep it in mind that if you disobey me and see that woman again, I shall make the necessary representations to have you removed from India, from the regiment, and from the Army, on the grounds that you have failed to conduct yourself as an officer and a gentleman." Then he banged his spurs in hard and shot away up the line of advance.

They marched, a proud and still fresh, unwearied column of kilted soldiers with their attached mountain battery of six ten-pounder breech-loading guns, officered by the Royal Artillery with the mules driven by natives, past the old Sikh fort of Jamrud eight miles west from Peshawar. Beyond this they rested briefly, falling out by the wayside, then pressed on the four miles that took them to the eastern entry to the Khyber Pass. From Jamrud to Torkham at the western end was a full fifty miles, which meant long days of forced marching, much of it

62

in single file along narrow ledges that would prove especially hard on the animals, whose hooves would slither dangerously towards deep drops. Entering the pass, they pressed on through the stalking terror where every high crag, every peak along the way could hide a skilled Afridi or Shinwari marksman. On the way they made contact with isolated men of a field telegraph company guarding the miles of wire, unreeled from drums, that kept the division outside Jalalabad in touch with base. It was two days later, when they were well inside the pass and beyond the fort of Ali Masjid on its rocky perch, that Black suggested to the Colonel that Mr. Ogilvie might gain valuable experience by taking over the advanced scouting party as the column began to approach Landi Khotal.

Four

THEY were all tired now, weary from the slog along the Khyber, weary of the dust and sun and from the constant watch that had to be kept on the peaks and crags that towered above them for most of the way. Their feet were blistered, their uniforms dirty with sweat and with dust that the sweat had turned to a thin layer of near-mud on their bodies. Their kilts were bedraggled from the immersion from time to time in the river that ran along the gorge and in places crossed the track so that they had to ford it with their rifles held high above their heads. The pitiless sun of high summer seemed to burn right through the pith helmets; but a winter passage would probably have been worse, even if it were possible at all. In earlier days whole companies of British soldiers had perished in the Khyber snows, frozen into the very ground where they had sunk to exhausted rest.

So far there had been no action of any sort but there was a strong feeling that it could not go on like this for long, a feeling that the rebel was drawing them on, allowing them to come thus far unhindered, lulled into a false sense of security, until they were past the point of no return. The column had straggled under the guns of the fortress of Ali Masjid; they had seen the native garrison, the friendly garrison, watching them from above, lean stringy men with hawk-like faces and tattered clothing, remotely watching from behind old-fashioned long-barrelled rifles; there had been no word from them even though the Divisional Commander had set the heliograph into the sun to wink out a message of goodwill and felicity. He might have saved the signallers' time. The lack of response was discouraging and seemed to indicate that even though the fort was currently friendly enough not to fire on the passing regiment, such friendliness might be wearing a trifle thin under some pressure from the rebel in Jalalabad. This was another good reason for scouting well ahead towards Landi Khotal.

Allegiances sometimes changed swiftly on the Frontier, and most of all, perhaps, here inside the Khyber . . .

When James Ogilvie and his scouts had been joined by the main column the pipes continued their weird skirl along the pass towards the now uncovered ambush ahead, the wild thin notes beating off the mountains, rising up to reach the hovering, expectant vultures, those inevitable accompaniments to the exchange of rifle fire among opposing human disturbers of the peace. And now there was such an exchange in progress. Soon after the sharpshooters on the flanks of the column had scored a bull's-eye on one of the advanced snipers, those vultures dived down for their meal, but rose again with the next crackle of rifle fire. A moment later the Colonel's hand went up and the column halted. The pipes died. Men eased their packs, wiped the streaming sweat from their eyes. Talking rose, dwindled back again as the adjutant cantered down the line. Black called, "Break ranks, move off the track, take what cover you can find. Look sharp now." He moved on. The company commanders repeated the order and the platoon sergeants scattered the men to left and right under the ferocious sun. For the moment there was no more firing from the peaks. Ogilvie found himself behind a large boulder with his Colour-Sergeant, MacNaught. He said, "I wonder what's in the wind?"

"If you're asking me, sir, I'd say the Colonel's decided to pick off all the snipers and reduce the ambush before continuing the march."

"Nothing more than that?" Ogilvie stared around, met the bleak eye of a descending carrion bird, and shuddered.

"Nothing more than that, Mr. Ogilvie?" MacNaught gave a short, entirely humourless laugh. "We'll be bound to lose some men, sir, and to them it'll be just the same as if the whole bloody Afghan army had been set on to them."

Ogilvie coloured. "Of course." He looked around again, at the men steady behind the rifles, their eyes scanning the pass and the high, rocky sides that hemmed them in. There was a tense and utter silence, the kind of silence that comes only in high places, and a dead stillness in the air. The only things that moved, it seemed, in all the landscape were the slow-motion wings of the hovering carrion birds and above them a few strands of high cloud. Time hung in the air, a suspended

65

sword. Ogilvie felt, not exactly fear as yet, but a kind of horrible anticipation and a strong desire for something to start happening, anything to break the mounting tension. He was conscious of a corporal's rather wheezy breathing over his shoulder, and this began to irritate him beyond all reason, as though something might in fact happen and, because of the corporal's heavy breath, drawn through a drooping moustache, he would be unable to hear it. But when it did come, which was within the next thirty seconds, there was no doubt about whether he could hear it or not. It was a tearing screen of fire, of bullets that whistled down from the seemingly uninhabited peaks to smash into rocks and hard earth and human bodies. There were yells and cries and shouted orders and the 114th answered with every rifle and with the battalion's two machine-guns, the Maxims. As more fire came down upon them they began to isolate the smoke bursts and find their targets. Bodies crashed down to the pass, falling with outflung arms and legs to bounce bloodily off the rocky crags. Behind Ogilvie, the heavy breathing had stopped, and it had stopped because the corporal was dead. A wetness that Ogilvie felt on the back of his neck was the corporal's blood that had welled and spurted from a hole in his neck and another in his forehead. As his father had warned, Ogilvie felt sick. The scene spun around him, oddly woven in drifting acrid gunsmoke. Near him, two more men lay dead, another worked the bolt of his rifle with blood streaming down his right arm. Then, as suddenly as it had started, the shooting stopped.

Ogilvie lifted his head, looked out over the top of the boulder. Distantly, Lord Dornoch was standing with his father and Major Hay, out in the open, looking through field glasses, scanning the peaks. From behind, hooves rang on the hard track, Black's horse came back up the line at a fast canter, slipping on loose stones. Black's uniform was awry, his helmet had gone, his trews were dark with blood, he was leaning down to one side and his right hand was gripping the wrist of a tribesman whose body bumped cruelly along the rough, lacerating ground. Black, it seemed, was taking his prisoner to the Colonel. Or attempting to. He had gone past Ogilvie when his grip slipped and the man fell and lay still. Four soldiers jumped him, started kicking him. He made no sound. No officer interfered, no order was given to stop the kicking. Again Ogilvie

66

felt sick. Sandhurst had failed to prepare him for this. Sandhurst produced gentlemen, not mindless brutes. You played up and you played the game. Surely this was not the way British soldiers behaved? At Sandhurst, as well as in the story books, the British soldier had been represented as a chivalrous hero who treated his enemy with courtesy once vanquished. When the Colonel reached the spot he said briefly, "All right, men, that'll do. Stand him on his feet." The tribesman was dragged brutally upright, bayonets pressed into his back, another booted foot took him hard in the groin. He had a proud face, hawk-like as the men who had stared down from Ali Masjid, with an out-thrust bearded chin. He stared boldly up at the Colonel on horseback. Lord Dornoch spoke to him in some hill dialect that Ogilvie couldn't follow. There was no answer, but after a while the man's head jerked forward like a snake's and a stream of stained spit landed fair and square on Dornoch's shabraque.

Dornoch's head went back and his lip curled. He glanced at Black. "Have you been following what I was saying?" he asked.

"I'm afraid not, Colonel. I'm not familiar with—"

"Well, I'm asking him for information as to the strength and disposition of any more tribal forces along the pass. I've told him that if he doesn't give me a satisfactory answer he's going to die."

Hay, who had ridden up by this time, said, "I doubt if he'll talk, Colonel. These men don't mind death."

Dornoch gave a bleak smile. "They don't fear death by shooting, John, but they do fear a dishonourable death, and he knows quite well what he's going to get. I'm pretty sure he understands me, but I'll try another dialect to make quite certain."

He did so; he tried patiently, several times more. At last he said, "He understands. I can see it in his eyes. But you're right, Major. He's not going to talk." He spoke once again to the captive tribesman. There was no reaction beyond a shrug. Dornoch studied him hard for a few more moments, then said indifferently to the adjutant, "Very well, Andrew. Set up a sheer-legs, if you please."

Black saluted and wheeled his horse. He shouted orders. Men ran to bring out three lengths of heavy timber from the baggage-train. These were lashed together at one end with rope belonging to the gunners; another rope was rove over the join, and then the three lengths were drawn inwards at the foot and the top thus raised until it was some twelve feet above the ground. Black personally tested it for firmness by swinging on the rope, then a dozen men tailed on to the trailing part of the rope while the farrier-sergeant made a hangman's knot at the end falling between the sheer-legs. The tribesman was lifted on to a horse with his hands tied behind his back and the horse was led to its position below the dangling knot, which was looped over the man's head and pulled taut around his neck. With the soldiers standing by, ready to take the strain, just a little slack was allowed and then the horse was given a sharp welt on its flank with a whip. The animal shot forward and Ogilvie believed he heard the sharp click from the man's neck as his weight came with a jerk on to the rope. The body was left to dangle while the British dead were decently covered with cairns of stones. Lord Dornoch read a simple service over them, the dead man was then cut down and his body left in the sun, the sheer-legs were dismantled and the timbers stowed away again, and then the battalion formed up in column and continued along the pass towards Jalalabad. It had been a small and un-noteworthy engagement. And had left its mark only in a handful of wounded and in the dead they had abandoned to the company of the many others that signposted earlier engagements of British regiments that had brought the Raj to the sub-continent.

As night fell, the 114th were once again halted, this time to fall out and make camp and then find much-needed sleep. Ogilvie was trying to make himself a comfortable bivouac in the entry to a fissure in the rock when MacKinlay came to him.

"Brooding, James?" MacKinlay asked.

Ogilvie straightened. "A little, perhaps."

"Well, you've had a minor blooding today and you came through it well. You'll feel just as scared next time, though. And the time after that." He looked quizzically at Ogilvie. "I take it you *were* scared? No disgrace, old boy, you know."

"I wasn't as scared as I'd thought I might be. The whole thing seemed rather . . . well, impersonal. As though it wasn't happening to me."

"It doesn't happen to you till it's you that stops a bullet. I know just what you mean, James." MacKinlay squatted and lit

68

up his pipe. Fragrance wafted over Ogilvie, pleasant in the cool evening air. "We'll be getting more of today's little effort. We're in the danger zone now and the Pathans won't have used up all their tricks by any means."

"I didn't think they would've," Ogilvie said shortly. "It's not that that bothers me."

MacKinlay looked at him over the bowl of his pipe. "What, then?"

Ogilvie said, "The way our fellows kicked that poor devil half to death—"

"Oh, come! That's an exaggeration, James!"

"Well, anyway, they did kick him. And no one stopped them. And the hanging—just to make it more beastly. The Colonel could have had him shot, couldn't he?"

MacKinlay nodded sombrely. "He could, but thank God he didn't. The Colonel was right, James, even if your kicking beauties were not. But even their conduct is perfectly understandable. They're as green as grass, just as green as they can be in terms of Indian service, and they're scared, and they'd lost some friends. To them, that one man was the whole enemy and they took it out on him. If it had gone on too long, it'd have been stopped, but a good officer lets his men have their head for a space when necessary. You'd do well to bear that in mind, James." He grinned. "It purges the system!"

"It's still not British."

"No, it's not, I agree—not what we've all been taught at home and at school is British, at all events. Cricket—not hitting a man when he's down—walloping some bounder who's annoyed one's sister—the hunting field . . . though I doubt if we're awfully British towards the fox when all's said and done!" He frowned. "What *is* British, James? Do *you* know?"

"Fair play," Ogilvie answered. "A touch of chivalry towards a beaten enemy."

"Again I agree," MacKinlay said. "Or rather, I would agree west of Suez, say. But out here we're dealing with natives. They're different. The whole way they look at things is different. I remember my grandmother saying once that the villagers at my mother's family home in Sussex didn't feel things the way people of our sort did. You know what I mean—they were closer to the earth, to life and death—if they lost a child, say, they simply got down to it and had another, it didn't affect them as it did us. The inference, of course, was that they were a kind of unfeeling species, almost sub-human. I don't say I agree with that view at all. But it does illustrate what the Pathan, and the Indian too, really is. They have totally different values out here, my lad! They wouldn't know the difference between fair play and a fried egg. They wouldn't show you or me any fair play, and chivalry is just weakness to them—to the low-caste ones anyway." He shook his head, blew a great cloud of tobacco smoke around. "There's lots of things that aren't British by Sandhurst standards—you'll find out! No, take it from me, the Colonel was dead right today. That hanged body's going to be a warning to the tribes, all of them, as to what'll happen to them when we've settled the Jalalabad rebel's hash. It may make them more amenable to surrender as soon as they can do so without losing too much face. I repeat once again, the Colonel was right, James. Right from another point of view as well: us! Or most of us, that is. As I said, the men are green, and they're going into action far too soon after arrival out here, really. Dornoch knows that. So does the Staff—so does your old man, of course. And what we're badly in need of is a crash course in the ways of the North-West Frontier. That's what the Colonel started to give us today, old son, and you'll find you won't feel so badly about it next time."

"I suppose anyone can get coarsened if they try."

MacKinlay said quietly, "That's not the way to look at it. You want to survive, don't you? You've got to get used to the idea that this isn't Buck House guard duty. Well—'nough said, old boy. I'll take myself off to bed. 'Night, James."

"Good night . . ."

MacKinlay got heavily to his feet, seemed about to say something further but evidently thought better of it. He turned away. For a while Ogilvie watched him making for his own bivouac and after he had vanished he heard the crunch of his footsteps. And after that, silence, and the night, and the moon over the cruel peaks, and a scud of dark cloud, and time to think. And, one way and another, plenty to think about.

A strong guard had been mounted to keep watch throughout the night all around the perimeter of the bivouacs. The men forming the guard—twenty rank and file, two corporals, a sergeant and a subaltern—were relieved at two-hourly intervals

70

and at five minutes to two a.m. James Ogilvie was roused out by the sergeant of the off-going guard.

"Time for your watch, sir."

Ogilvie struggled through clouds of weariness. In due course he would learn to wake at the slightest touch, the slightest sound—but not now. Patiently the sergeant waited till he was fully awake, then said, "Mr. Syme is away at the western end, sir. He says to tell you he's bloody tired and cold and ready to drop down where he stands, sir."

Ogilvie yawned, tried to smile. "Is everything quiet, Sergeant?"

"Everything's quiet, sir." The sergeant hesitated. "Begging your pardon, sir. The R.S.M. told me to say when I woke you, he'd be much obliged if you'd call him if you're at all worried about anything."

"That's very kind of Mr. Cunningham," Ogilvie said cautiously, "and I'll keep it in mind."

The sergeant straightened, took a pace backward, and came briefly to attention. Then he turned about and marched off with his rifle at the short trail. Ogilvie got to his feet. He felt a twinge of annoyance with the R.S.M. Bosom Cunningham was treating him like a child, didn't want to risk having the whole battalion roused out by any alarm to arms as a result of a green subaltern misinterpreting the sound of a night bird's cry. Nevertheless the R.S.M. meant well and was a sure shield against a young officer making too great a laughing-stock of himself when there was an element of doubt in a situation. Ogilvie went off in a westerly direction to take over from Second-Lieutenant Syme, picking his way with a certain amount of difficulty between the strewn boulders casting their shadows grotesquely beneath a high, bright moon. The air now was crisp, really cold, and Ogilvie needed the blue patrol jacket his servant had got out for him from his baggage. When handing over the guard, Syme repeated the sergeant's earlier summary: "Nothing doing, old boy. It's everywhere as quiet as a church."

"And damn cold." Ogilvie shivered.

"You should be wearing trews." Syme himself was. "When the wind blows up your kilt, you'll get a touch of the brass monkeys. Want to go and change? I'll wait."

"No, it's all right, thank you, I'll manage." Ogilvie hesitated. "By the way, where's Bosom sleeping?"

Syme laughed. "See that boulder over there—the big one between the two little 'uns? Cunningham's in its shadow. You can't see him, but now and again you'll hear a snore if you listen for it." Syme pulled off his glengarry and ran a hand through thick fair hair that gleamed in the moonlight like gold. "Did you have a message from him, too?"

"Did you, then?" Ogilvie asked in surprise. He'd always regarded Syme as one of the more knowledgeable subalterns.

"I did indeed—don't worry, you're not the only one! Bosom loves us like a father, and trusts us just about as far too! And if I were you, James, I'd take his advice—that is, if you're not at the other end of the perimeter when things start going bump in the night."

As it happened Ogilvie was in the precise spot at which he had taken over from Syme when he heard the eerie whistling note but it was so similar to the cry of that hypothetical night bird he'd had in mind that he didn't react until it was almost too late. It was a mysterious and frightening sound in the night, a high warbling note three times repeated. It came from rising ground away to the right and some distance ahead of them where the rocky sides of the pass tended to fall away. Ogilvie stood listening, waiting for a repetition. The sergeant, standing by his side with a bugler, was as puzzled as he.

"I don't know what to make of it, sir," he said. "It sounded like a bird of some sort . . . and yet at the same time it didn't, sir."

There was no other sound. Ogilvie said uncertainly, "It may have been *meant* to sound like a bird. I'm going to rouse out the R.S.M. and—"

"Already roused. Sir!"

Ogilvie and the sergeant swung round, startled. The R.S.M., approaching fast from the rear, hadn't made any sound. He said, "I heard a noise I did not like at all, Mr. Ogilvie. If I was you, sir, I'd sound the alert and quickly."

"But—"

"Quickly, Mr. Ogilvie. Look ahead there. Man, the pass is alive and is moving!"

Ogilvie looked. It was a brief look but enough. All of a sudden there was a curious flowing of the surface, like the living quality seen on water under a moon. As the R.S.M. had said, the very ground seemed to be alive—alive with squirming, wormlike bodies. Ogilvie addressed the bugler sharply. "Sound the alert," he ordered.

The harsh notes cut through the night. Behind the group of men soldiers and officers came rudely awake, reached out for rifles and revolvers, manned the ten-pounders and the Maxims. There was a clatter of equipment. At the same time the pattern ahead changed as the native force, realizing now that they had been spotted, got up from their stomachs and came on at the run. As the Maxims went stuttering into action, Ogilvie ran towards the Colonel to make his report.

"A force of native infantry, Colonel," he said breathlessly, "attacking from ahead."

"Yes, I see them. Thank you, James." The Colonel's voice rose. "Spread the men out on a wide front," he called. "All rifles will hold their fire till ordered otherwise."

More orders were called as the company commanders took over, spreading out their men across the pass and up the hillsides, using what little time they had to get into position as the old-fashioned muskets of the attackers opened up. Ogilvie, his responsibilities as guard commander now ended, was running to join his company when he heard the order passed for the rifles to open and join the fire of the Maxims. The leading natives were only thirty yards away when the rifles of the battalion smashed the first volley into them. Wave after wave came on, disregarding the steady fire. There seemed to be no end to them; as fast as men went down, more took their places, materializing from out of the night along the pass to the westward, their naked bodies, oiled for slipperiness, gleaming in the moonlight. They cut through the front rank of the British soldiers, plunged into the centre, cut the battalion in half. The men swung their rifles, firing point-blank into the attackers' flanks. Already one of the Maxims had jammed and was silent. Then, from the rear, the mountain battery opened up in smoke and flame and fury, cleaving into the rear of the advance, which began to waver. The effect was like the blowing of a bridge, cutting off the native support. At the same time the British front rank was ordered to close across the line, which they did; part of the native force, caught in the centre now and surrounded, was cut up by a murderous short-range fire from the rifles and, once again, by both the Maxims. With the artillery still depositing shells between the British and the attacking force, the natives beyond the shell-bursts began to scatter to north and south, and then Ogilvie heard the British bugles sounding the cease fire. Hard upon this came a shout from the Colonel: "Fix bayonets and charge!"

As the order was repeated by company commanders and platoon sergeants, Dornoch, mounted now, spurred his horse towards the running men, trampling over bodies, and swept down on their rear with his broadsword lifted. With wild yells and cries the Royal Strathspeys charged behind their gleaming bayonets. Ogilvie, attempting to lead his half-company, was overtaken by the rush of men and practically trampled under foot. Bemused and uncertain, but feeling in himself a strange lust for battle now, he disengaged himself from the men as best he could and stormed along the pass with his sword in his hand, running like a deer. In point of fact most of the natives, unencumbered by heavy equipment and knowing their terrain, got clear away; but the Royal Strathspeys overtook some of the stragglers and at one point Ogilvie saw a bloodstained, bulky figure ahead of him lift a Highland broadsword, fitted with a cross-bar guard, above his head with both hands and bring it down with a vicious sideways slash at a running Afghan. The sword flashed in the moonlight and took the man's neck, and the head jerked a little in the air and then fell to the ground and rolled horribly. For a few seconds the legs kept on running, the body stayed upright, and then it crumpled and fell and as the portly victor of that particular duel puffed on for another kill, James Ogilvie recognized his father. He knew in that instant that his father had done something for which he would long be remembered and honoured, that the men would mightily approve of the General Officer Commanding the Division being in the thick of the fighting; but he felt also that it was an alarming and appalling thing to see one's father in the act of slicing off a man's head.

The dawn came up soon after and showed the full extent of the British casualties: fourteen men, three N.C.O.'s, one subaltern—Syme—dead; fifty-eight assorted wounded, some serious, others slight. Four more men died of their wounds whilst the cooks were preparing breakfast. The *bhisties*, the water-carriers, were kept busy, as were the medical orderlies under Surgeon Major Corton, who was himself wearing a bloodstained head bandage. But the enemy had gone, the pass was clear, and once again they were able to bury their dead in peace. Ogilvie saw his father talking to the Colonel; Sir Iain's right arm was bandaged and in a sling, with his sleeve cut away, but he looked calm and serene enough, and confident too. He was laughing as his servant brushed down his uniform and then clipped carefully at the ends of his moustache and brushed again. The night's events, it seemed, hadn't disturbed him in the least. Ogilvie wondered how many years of service he would need to see before the same would be true of himself. Possibly such detachment would never come to him. Possibly there was too much of his mother in him.

Breakfast over, Lord Dornoch had the men fall in along the pass, then called his officers and senior N.C.O.'s together. He said, "We mustn't discount the possibility of further attacks, gentlemen, but we have only one more day's march on our own. If the situation has not changed for the worse outside Jalalabad since the last reports via the field telegraph, I expect to be met at dusk by scouts from the main body of the Division. When they meet us, at least we'll have established contact. From then on we'll be in direct touch with Division and on the assumption the lines of communication are secure, I expect little more trouble. You'll pass the word of this to the men." He nodded at Hay. "That's all, Major. Report when ready to march, if you please."

Briskly he returned the salutes. Ogilvie saw him staring sombrely along the pass towards the cairns where the dead lay buried. There was a sadness in his face, a reluctance to march away and leave them. Ten minutes later the battalion was once more on the move behind the pipes and drums, which beat bravely into the still, clear day. The men marched now even more wearily than before, more sadly for their numbers were depleted, more soberly because they had had a taste of real action and were beginning to realize what the north-west frontier was all about.

One of the men who had died was Private Storr—Jamie, whose girl had come to Portsmouth so many weeks before to try to stop him sailing in the *Malabar*. Jamie Storr's company commander in life had been Captain Graham. Ogilvie wondered what Graham would find to say when he wrote that difficult letter to Jamie's girl, or Jamie's parents. Something about his having died well for the Queen-Empress and the Empire? Or to the greater glory of the 114th Highlanders? It wasn't going to help Jamie's family very much, though no doubt, like everyone else, they revered the old Queen in Windsor Castle and might be proud to feel Jamie had died to help keep her there. But if Private Jamie Storr had died sheltering in fear behind a boulder —which for all anyone knew, he might have—the flow of tears would be exactly the same back in Invermore.

Black came riding down the line, eyes roving, seeking out faults. *"Mr. Ogilvie!"*

It was all formality now. "Sir?"

"Your men are shambling along—not marching. Mr. Ogilvie, this is the 114th Highlanders, not a supply and transport column."

"Yes, sir." Better, perhaps, to have taken the bull by the horns and answered: "This is the Khyber Pass, not the parade at Invermore," but Ogilvie couldn't quite get around to that today. And really there was no point in giving the adjutant any openings. One of the difficulties of the situation was that the men of his half-company were going to be made to suffer for his sins *vis-à-vis* Mary Archdale. Ogilvie sighed and turned to the platoon sergeant behind him. "Smarten the men up, if you please, Sergeant."

"Sir!" The sergeant stepped out of the line, marched backwards, brought his rifle to the slope, slammed his right hand in to his side, and roared out mechanically, "Snap oot o' it, lads, swing those arms, lift yer feet don't drag 'em . . . look like soldiers of Her Majesty, not railway guards!" Plainly, the sergeant didn't approve; you didn't drill men through the Khyber, you let them march at ease if you had enough sense to fit into a cat's navel, and you helped them along. Not that young Mr. Ogilvie could help it, of course. It was that bastard, Black, and he alone. Sweating in the day's mounting heat, the sergeant turned and, doubling ahead, resumed his place in the column. Ogilvie heard Black chivvying the following companies along as well. When the adjutant had trotted back up the line again, some singing came from the rear. It had an ironic sound about it. Back came Black, his face crimson and furious. "Stop that damned devil's orchestra!" he shouted. "We're in the Khyber Pass, not on a route march through the Speyside villages." Black was strong on comparisons. He wheeled away again as the singing died and soon after that Ogilvie saw the Colonel talking to him, quietly enough, but Black wasn't looking happy. The singing started again after a twenty-minute halt when the battalion fell out for a rest, and this time Black kept well up in front of the column and pretended he hadn't heard.

It was a little before dusk when the section that was scouting ahead sent a man back to report that troops, believed to be British, had been spotted. The pace of the column quickened in anticipation but the sharpshooters became even more alert and the word was passed from Lord Dornoch to be ready for action if the newcomers should turn out to be unfriendly, unlikely though this in fact was. And within the next half-hour their friendliness was proved when two British officers, one of them from the General's staff, rode up with a headquarters detail to make contact with Lord Dornoch and the newly-appointed Divisional Commander. Later that evening they were joined by the main body of the contacting force and that night the battalion made camp along with the 96th Mahratta Light Infantry in company with another battery of mountain guns. The presence of those extra guns were comforting; all night their muzzles stared out along what was left of the Khyber Pass and over the next two days trundled comfortingly along with the Royal Strathspeys, clear of the pass now and across the plains of Ningrahar, to join up with the Division laying siege to the town of Jalalabad by the Kabul River, near the junction of the Kunar flowing from Chitral.

One of the officers who had been sent out to meet the Divisional Commander turned out to be none other than the Brigade Major of the Mahrattas—Major Archdale, Mary's husband. He was a whiskered, tubby, red-faced man with grey hair and protuberant blue eyes, a fussy, self-important manner and a loudly demanding voice. When he knew this man's identity, James Ogilvie studied him with some considerable interest. He didn't look like the killer his wife had said he was; more a buffoon. But in any case he and Mary Archdale seemed poles apart. The Brigade Major was accompanied by a curious item of equipment. It was an article of furniture, apparently, and looked like a commode, but an exceptionally large commode of unusual construction. It intrigued Ogilvie; and evidently it intrigued Sir Iain as well, for next morning, in James Ogilvie's hearing as it happened, the General mentioned the article to Lord Dornoch.

"What the devil's that feller got with him?" he demanded.

Dornoch said, "It's his field lavatory, sir."

"Field *what*?" Though in fact the General was no stranger to commodes accompanying the more fastidious officers on active service, he was in a difficult and fractious mood. "*What* did you say, Dornoch?"

"Lavatory."

Sir Iain exploded. "Well, I'll be damned. *Field lavatory!* As if we hadn't enough clutter already to haul to Jalalabad! Can't he manage the same as the rest of us?"

Dornoch said tactfully, "I'm told not, sir. He suffers from chronic constipation, and—well, the situation is, he generally *needs* this specially constructed—er—apparatus. I gather it's a case of comfort. He can't be parted from his own field lavatory, it appears."

"Who told you all this?"

"A British officer of the 96th M.L.I." Dornoch coughed, kept a straight face but didn't meet the General's eye. "The apparatus is attended by a *havildar* of the 96th...a man referred to, I'm told, as the Brigade Major's bum-*havildar*."

"God give me strength," the General said.

If the cantonments at Peshawar had been very different from the barracks at Invermore, the encampment outside Jalalabad was also very different from peaceful Peshawar. Here the whole Division apart from the many sick was at its war station and urgency was in the air, all fit personnel were on a continual semi-alert in case of attack, with details standing-to all along the perimeter, and there was an expectancy of a foray in every moment of time. The British were drawn in their circular formation on the plain and around the hills overlooking the town; Ogilvie could stare down on the fortress occupied by Ahmed Khan, its gaunt towers reaching up like lances threatening the very sky. North of that fortress lay the Kafiristan mountains and west lay the gap in the British circle, the gap that was heavily defended on the hilltops at either side by the rebels, the gap that kept the fortress and town supplied—the gap that the Royal Strathspeys had to close and then to hold; and once that had been done the grand assault on the fort itself would be mounted. The 114th's lines were next to those of the Mahratta Brigade, so Ogilvie wasn't far from Major Archdale, a fact which he found kept bringing Mary into sharp focus in his mind's eye. Shortly after the battalion had made camp, all the officers were called together by the Mahrattas' Brigadier-General to be given a summary of the current situation. The Brigadier-General came straight to the point. "You'll all be well enough aware," he said, "of the overall position. Ahmed Khan is very strongly entrenched in his fortress. We have to eject him. It sounds simple. If we had the necessary superiority in numbers, it would be. But we haven't. Nevertheless, we shall achieve our objective, of course. It won't be the first time British troops have won the day against seemingly insuperable odds. We all know that." He paused for effect. He was a small, perky man like a belligerent sparrow, and he stood with his hands held tightly behind his back and his shoulders drawn very far backwards. He went on, "The 114th is to be brigaded with us, so you have now come under my orders, gentlemen. I may say I'm glad and proud to be associated with you. I much admire the Scots regiments, and their aggressive fighting spirit. There's nothing like them anywhere." Ogilvie glanced at his Colonel; Dornoch's eyes were downcast, his mouth slightly pinched as though he felt the Brigadier was laying it on a shade too thick. "I think you already know that our *special* task — what you have joined us for — is the closing of the gap — the supply line from the Hindu Kush which is still open to Ahmed Khan." He turned and pointed with his stick, using the terrain itself as his blackboard. He indicated two high craggy peaks in the foothills to the west, some twenty miles away as the crow flies and directly beyond Jalalabad. The peaks, which were both south of the Kabul River, were very clear in the still air, clear and brooding and dangerous. The Brigadier said, "Between those peaks there is a wide defile, the entrance to a valley running through to the Hindu Kush — where Ahmed Khan has a powerful following and an equally powerful arsenal, also a more than adequate supply of food, crops and so forth, to enable him to withstand a siege of almost any length — so long as that route remains open. We face defeat," he added, in contradiction to his earlier words of patriotism, "if it does remain open." He looked up intently into the officers' faces, his eyes beady and bright and earnest. "To close the rebel's supply route, gentlemen, is going to be a devilish tricky business — *devilish* tricky, let me tell you! You see the peaks.

79

Both have excellent lines of communication to Jalalabad, both are well defended with the rebel artillery. Our task in the Brigade is to take the southern one. At the same time as our attack is mounted, the northern peak will be assaulted by another infantry brigade, all home troops, from the lines on the far side of the perimeter—over there." Again the stick was brought into play and waved towards the other side of Jalalabad. "Once we have both those peaks in our hands, we shall then command the defile. This may in itself be enough to prevent the passage of any supplies or reinforcements. But, in order to ensure the complete closure of the route, I have been ordered to extend across the defile and hold the line there, being joined by the northern brigade of course. After that, the whole Division will close in in preparation for the kill. The kill will come once the rebel is reduced for lack of supplies. It is our hope that this will be done before this terrible curse of sickness cuts our own strength further. Now: intelligence reports reaching us in the last few days from political officers operating between here and the Hindu Kush indicate that a supply column—ammunition, men, foodstuffs—is expected to reach the defile within the next twelve days from now. It is vital—quite *vital*—that the closure is most fully effective by then, for the safe arrival of the column at Jalalabad will be most serious, gentlemen—I stress this again. It is also important that we mount our attack with the element of surprise in our favour. Thus, we shall advance around the perimeter only during the hours of darkness, and keep in cover, and rest, throughout the day. Three nights will be allowed for the two brigades to complete their march. That should be more than enough and is, indeed, generous. You will have tonight only, gentlemen, to rest before that march begins. I suggest you and your men take the very fullest advantage of this. There will be no guard or picket duties required of the 114th or their attached artillery in the meantime. Incidentally, you will leave your own artillery behind to reinforce this end of the line and will pick up the assault batteries en route. That is all for now, gentlemen. Detailed orders will be issued tomorrow, together with maps of the southern peak and the entry to the valley."

There was a buzz of talk as the officers dispersed. Ogilvie's eye was caught by John Hay. The second-in-command said quietly, "You'll not find the assault any worse than the Khyber, my boy. A little more concentrated — but the total strain won't last so long."

"No, Major. Not if the attack's successful, anyway!"

"It will be, boy, it will be." John Hay gave Ogilvie a steady look from under his shaggy, good-dog's eyebrows. "Now just remember you came well through the Khyber. The Colonel's pleased enough."

That was all Hay said before he turned away towards Lord Dornoch, who was waiting for him with a touch of impatience; and he had said it diffidently and awkwardly enough. There was nothing new in it; the same thing had been said, Ogilvie supposed, to every young man before his first taste of real battle. Yet it helped him quite a lot, for there was a quiet sincerity and a kindliness about Hay that spoke more for him than his tongue was able to utter, and he had, as it happened, spoken as if by instinct at precisely the right moment of time. Ogilvie was feeling, more than in the Khyber itself, the strange remoteness of Afghanistan and was finding it a frightening experience. Civilization such as he knew it lay now beyond the Khyber, way back in India, through fifty miles and more of largely hostile country that no man could cross in a hurry. Here outside Jalalabad, between those Kafiristan hills and the vast 14,000-foot high snow-line of the Sufaid Koh, he was utterly cut off, the Division to which he now belonged was out on its own, away from base, from comfort, from help, and was dependent wholly upon the whim and good sense of its Divisional Commander who, out here, ranked more or less with God. It was little comfort that God happened this time to be his own father, that man of blood and iron and unpredictable temper. The fact certainly didn't make him into God the Son . . . Ogilvie was feeling lost and helpless and very aware of both his own deficiencies and of the responsibilities he was to bear for his men's lives in action. Thus Hay's fumbling words had brought comfort.

Ogilvie walked away to the Royal Strathspeys' lines, where his servant had pitched his tent and laid out his gear. On the way he passed other regimental lines and the sick lines, and he saw how full the latter were at the expense of the former. A few convalescents moved about, helping the medical orderlies. They looked wan and thin and only half alive. This sector of the line had been hit by dysentery, serious enough but, thank

81

God, not the scourge of cholera. Not yet. Cholera had hit other sectors of the line and it could come here. Ogilvie halted outside his tent, looked across the far horizons to the foothills and beyond to the great mountains of the Hindu Kush. Over all this savage, vast spread of territory British soldiers had fought and died to protect the Raj way back in India beyond the passes. Here was the very outpost of Empire—the outer bailey, in a sense, of all that Windsor Castle itself stood for, the farthest-flung part of the perimeter of the Queen's Majesty, the last bastion of all that British life meant, the guardian outpost of a whole way of life. On what happened here, to a very large extent at any rate, depended the might and the wealth of Great Britain, the future of her peoples, of her steel mills and her shipyards and her workshops, her ships and her mines, of the Stock Exchange in London, even of sterling itself . . .

Later, after Ogilvie had had a wash in the basin provided by his servant, and after an evening meal from the field kitchens, he watched the magnificence of the going down of the sun behind the western hills that lay under a spreading, darkening mantle of gold and deep blue and purple and green. And in this he was joined by Colour-Sergeant MacNaught, in shirt sleeves and without his pith helmet. MacNaught had been walking past the end of the officers' lines and Ogilvie had caught his eye and he'd stopped. He moved towards Ogilvie and came to attention.

"Stand easy, Colour-Sarn't."

"Thank you, sir."

"Anything you want, Colour-Sarn't?"

"Not really, sir, no, thank you all the same." MacNaught added quietly, "It makes a man think deeply, up here, sir."

"What about?"

MacNaught hesitated, screwing up the sun-browned flesh round his eyes, then said simply and sincerely, "It's very close to God, sir. Closest to heaven in a physical sense a man'll ever get until the day he dies."

"Or until he climbs Everest."

"Aye, sir. And that's not as likely as death, begging your pardon, sir."

Ogilvie thought again about the soldiers who lay in their shallow graves or their cairns of stones—or at the bottoms of chasms or gorges, their bones picked white and clean by the filthy carrion birds that even now were circling in their grisly way over the regimental lines — waiting, probably, for the sick to die. He said something of his earlier thoughts to the Colour-Sergeant.

Slowly MacNaught said, "Aye, it's true, sir. True enough."

Ogilvie brought out his cigarette-case. "Smoke?"

"No, thank you, Mr. Ogilvie. I don't fancy them things at all. I've my pipe, if you don't mind?"

"Go right ahead." Ogilvie lit a cigarette, passed his lucifers to MacNaught when the pipe had been brought out and filled with strong stuff, not so fragrant as MacKinlay's. MacNaught said, "As to what you were saying, sir. There's little thought given in some circles to the value of what we do on the frontier. But mind you, Mr. Ogilvie, we're the outpost for a hell of a lot of other things as well."

"Such as?"

MacNaught puckered his eyes again, staring into the distance, then shook his head. "I'd doubt if I need to tell you, sir, if you think about it. There's the rich people, right enough, but there's also the filthy, stinking slums of Glasgow and Edinburgh to name one thing. I've been in tenements in Edinburgh, not a stone's throw from the Castle, where there's been fifteen persons to a room. *Fifteen*, Mr. Ogilvie! And babies being born, and men and women dying, and making love too, in the same room. There's the men who cannot find work and their women-folk and bairns suffering from real starvation and lack of clothing and lack of any warmth in winter. I've known families who haven't seen a lump of coal or turf or a log for many winters together." There was a bitterness in the Colour-Sergeant's voice. "There's the Highland families trying to exist in the crofts in isolated sheilings and not having much of a time of it at all." He sighed. "They're a far cry from London town and Windsor Castle."

"But not all that far from Balmoral."

"Sir?" MacNaught looked puzzled for a moment, then said, "Oh, aye, Mr. Ogilvie, I see your meaning. Aye, and that's true. The old Queen herself has a soft spot for Scotland right enough. It's just a hell of a pity some of the injustices can't be righted, sir, that's all."

Ogilvie laughed good-naturedly. "You sound like one of these Socialists, Colour-Sarn't!"

83

"God forbid that I should ever be that, Mr. Ogilvie. They're a dirty bunch, sir, a dastardly lot and they make me sick to my stomach to hear them rant. I'm as loyal to the old Queen as the next man, as loyal as the Colonel himself." He paused, looking again towards the distant hills now vanishing in the darkness. "It's just that my father . . . an old man, sir, one of the crofters I was speaking of, a man who worked hard the whole of his days . . ."

"Yes?" Ogilvie prompted.

"The field telegraph has just brought news from Peshawar, sir, that the old fellow's died. My old mother'll be needing me now, sir. That's all. It's set me thinking."

Ogilvie said awkwardly. "Of course. I'm sorry, Colour-Sarn't."

"That's all right, sir, there's nothing you can do about it, Mr. Ogilvie, and I know you would if you could. If we were quartered in England, say, I'd be asking for compassionate leave, but there's no leave from beyond the Khyber." He said no more, but stood very still, watching the last of the sunset, listening to the sounds of the tethered horses, their nostrils steaming into what was now a chilly night. "I'll be wishing you good night, then, Mr. Ogilvie."

"Good night, Colour-Sarn't."

"Sir!" Once again MacNaught stiffened to attention, thumbs held against the sides of his kilt, then he turned about smartly and marched away back to the N.C.O.'s lines. He was a good soldier, dependable through and through. He had made Ogilvie think a little more deeply than before, too. The Empire was a solid and good force, with noble aspirations to follow upon a glorious past, but mostly it had been built on human misery and blood and poverty. But how, Ogilvie wondered, could it be any other way? How could you iron out the differences between men? Men were *not* equal. It was inevitable that some should rise and others fall, some grow rich while others spent their lives close to the breadline. You couldn't, indeed, have the one without the other; they were complementary—the sons of Mary and the sons of Martha. MacNaught himself, when he became a time-expired soldier, would have little future. He might keep himself in tobacco with his pension, but what of the rest, if the little Highland croft couldn't keep him and his old mother, to say nothing of the wife and three children Ogilvie knew he had

84

left in Scotland? He might possibly, if he was lucky, become a postman, or a commissionaire, or something in a gentleman's household. It wasn't really much of a prospect after a life of giving orders and seeing them obeyed smartly. But—again—what other way could it ever be? If you cut out the city slums, if you clothed and fed and warmed all of the people all of the time, the country would very quickly go bankrupt. Then there would be nothing for anyone and there would be an end of the Empire. There were no two ways about that. You couldn't have an Empire supported on this new-fangled Socialist theory; the two were incompatible. And to have a well-ordered society in a well-ordered world, you had to have the poor to do the work. Fortunately, with the exception of a few hotheads—men like Keir Hardie, for instance, and a fellow called Shaw, an Irishman who wrote plays or something, and temporarily saddened and embittered men like MacNaught, who would recover in a day or two—apart from such, the poor didn't mind. His father had always maintained that and he was right—they were proud to feel that so much depended on them, that they were an essential cog of Empire. And there was nobody in the realm who would say a word against the good old Queen. They hadn't been subjected to her tea-time stare at Balmoral . . .

At such an irreverent thought Ogilvie smiled to himself. He admired the old lady tremendously in actual fact; she kept a very tight rein on the politicians and she was proud of her soldiers, which was as it should be. And she had no time for Gladstone . . . As the sound of a lone bugle blowing Last Post broke the silence from outside Divisional Headquarters—the tent which his father would use as an office—and died away, Ogilvie went inside his own tent and turned in. He lay wakeful for a while and soon heard some singing from the men's lines, a song from the American Civil War:

"Bring the good old bugle, boys, we'll sing another song,
Sing it with a spirit that will wake the world along,
Sing it as we used to sing it, fifty thousand strong,
While we were marching through Georgia . . ."

And tomorrow night the brigade would be marching to close the gap on Jalalabad but they wouldn't be fifty thousand strong, only a little over four thousand, plus their artillery when they picked it up. And the bugles would be sounding out Last Post

85

for many dead after the brigade had reached its objective and joined battle.

All next day the 114th were kept on the move, exercising with their new brigade comrades. They were, they knew, constantly under the distant observation of the rebels in Jalalabad, but the movements, if spotted, would be unlikely to convey any useful information to the enemy. Some kind of small local movement—redeployments on account of sickness as it struck different sectors of the perimeter, or on account of casualties from the sporadic forays—had been going on continually since the British siege force had taken up its positions; and although Ahmed Khan would realize well enough that the arrival of a fresh battalion must signify an attempt ultimately to close his supply route, he would still not know when the attack on the defended peaks was to come.

During that day the detailed orders for the march and the assault were promulgated to the Colonels, each of whom thereafter briefed his officers separately and took them painstakingly through the maps of the objective area and its approaches. The Royal Strathspeys were informed by Lord Dornoch that, while the Mahrattas would form the spearhead of the attack following the artillery bombardment, they themselves would in fact be in the thick of it the moment the assault was under way and it would be their task to take the rebel guns while the Mahrattas mopped up the warring tribesmen. So far as the march itself was concerned, the essential point was to keep well in cover throughout the daylight hours, and the hope was that the advance would not be spotted until the artillery bombardment began. The final leg of the march would be timed so that their arrival at the attack position would be during the hours of darkness on the third night.

Sir Iain Ogilvie himself rode up alone to the brigade lines shortly before dusk. He was not coming with them; his task was to remain at Divisional H.Q. for the time being. He wished them well in his loud, gruff voice. Momentarily, James caught his father's eye. Its gaze seemed to linger on him, though briefly, and the son was baffled by the expression. It was the penetrating look to which he was well accustomed, the look of the man of action summing up an officer, but there was something else there as well: doubt, and a fleeting anxiety. James

86

Ogilvie found himself wondering whether the anxiety was for his safety as a son, or whether it was an apprehension lest he should bring any discredit on the father and the family name.

Once it was full dark, with so far little moonlight, the brigade moved off. They moved with the pipes and drums silent, in as much anonymity as was possible for a brigade on the march, with its attendant train, and they moved on foot — no horses now, not even for the Brigade Commander, Brigadier-General Hewlett. There were no pack animals either, and the assault artillery, which would be waiting for them nearer the end of the march, at the extremity of the British lines, would be drawn on by manpower. They stole through the night, away from H.Q., pressing on fast and without talking, making around the circle for the peaks, moving behind the sickness-depleted siege units spread out so pitifully thinly along the perimeter. Later the moon came out from its cloud cover, high and bright, sending shafts of silver across the Ningrahar plain and the snows of the Sufaid Koh behind. The bayonets were scabbarded, rifles held low so as to reflect no light. As usual Black was in evidence for a good deal of the time, making his way up and down the Royal Strathspeys' column, criticizing, cursing, exhorting. Occasionally he was accompanied by the Brigade Major, and once Ogilvie heard them talking together, discussing Peshawar — and, in the course of this, Mary Archdale very briefly.

"Girl has a damn dull time of it, I sometimes think, when I'm away from the station," the Brigade Major said, but he spoke off-handedly, as though he didn't really worry about it much. Then they moved on, and Black didn't answer — at any rate not in Ogilvie's hearing. Mary Archdale was, in fact, much on his mind as he went forward through the night. He admitted the shock he'd felt when she had said Archdale had no interest in, or ability for, sex; it was not quite the way to speak. Women — ladies, rather — were not supposed to enjoy the act of sex in any case. Nevertheless he wanted to see Mary again, though he realized there could be no future in such a relationship. Indeed, though he had no intention of being unduly inhibited by Andrew Black's tirade *en route*, he knew that it could become impossible to meet her except in the course of the formal social round. He would not be returning to Peshawar until Jalalabad was taken, and when that happened and the battalion marched east again into India, the whole force would presumably return with them, and after that Major Tom Archdale would also be in Peshawar. Life in cantonments would become a strain. No doubt Black had been right and he'd been remarkably foolish. The girl had been a ship passing in the night, and he should leave it at that.

He made an effort to force Mary Archdale out of his mind, but he succeeded only when some while later there was a sudden diversion: a heavy sliding sound came from somewhere off the track, followed by a spatter of falling stones and simultaneously with the latter a human cry, a cry of terror, fairly near at hand at first, then very quickly becoming fainter.

Ogilvie halted his men. He drew his revolver. Behind him —he had given no order as perhaps he should have done—he heard the sound of rifle bolts being worked. Urgently he called, "No firing!"

"What is it, sir?" a hoarse voice—MacNaught's—asked.

He said, "I don't know. Stay where you are, all of you. I'm going ahead for a look."

Keeping low, with his revolver ready, Ogilvie crept forward towards where he fancied the sounds had come from, moving off the track to the left. There was still that cry of fear, strangely muted now, seeming to come from quite a long way off. The company ahead, not hearing it apparently, had gone on unheeding. Ogilvie made for that cry. He stopped suddenly when he reached a crevice in the dried earth of the plain, a crevice some twenty feet off the track and invisible until a man stumbled right on it. Then he heard the cry again and realized it was coming from the crack in the earth and that a man was trapped there.

He slid forward on his stomach and put his head down. He called, "Who's there?"

A cry of stark terror came up. "I'm trapped, Ogilvie, I'm trapped and I can't move anything except my arms. James . . . for God's sake . . . get me out!"

Ogilvie lifted his head, then stayed motionless. It was Black's voice. He sweated with a curious fear of his own, a fear of his own weakness. They were alone; no one else knew what had happened. In all sorts of little ways Andrew Black had done his very best to make his life a misery, would continue to do so until one or other of them left the regiment, presumably. One day Black might well be his Colonel if he remained on, and one day too Black might carry out his threat in regard to Mary Archdale. And now all he had to do to settle the thing for good and all would be to crawl back to his company and report that he had found nothing. Black's voice wasn't carrying back anything like that far now, and it would grow weaker if he, Ogilvie, wandered around a while to waste a little time, and when the adjutant's absence was eventually noted it would be much too late to find that crevice. But Ogilvie was horrified that he could ever have been visited by such a thought and in fact the hideous idea of murder held lodgement in his brain for no more than a fleeting second of time.

Badly shaken now, he called down, "Hold on — don't move — I'll be back with help as fast as I can."

He dragged himself backwards, then got to his feet and ran back to the waiting men, gasped out what he had found. A ragged laugh, quickly suppressed by the N.C.O.'s before Ogilvie could himself react, went up from the men and a private muttered, "Leave the bastard where he is, why not!"

"Get a rope!" Ogilvie snapped.

"I doubt if there'll be such a thing in the whole column," MacNaught said briskly, "that is, not until we join up with the mountain batteries. How far down is he, Mr. Ogilvie, and what state's he in?"

"I don't know," Ogilvie answered, his voice shaking.

"Then we'll go and find out, sir," MacNaught said. He rounded on the men. "You and you and you. Come with the officer and me. The rest of you, stay right where you are and keep your eyes skinned. You," he jabbed a finger at a fourth man, "you'll act as runner, Mathieson. Report to Captain MacKinlay what's happened, and the Brigade Major if you meet him on the way. Now, Mr. Ogilvie."

The men detailed followed Ogilvie to the deep earth crack. As they came up they could hear the adjutant still calling out for help, his voice high and panic-stricken. Colour-Sergeant MacNaught crawled to the edge and looked down. He called,

"D'you know how far you fell, sir?"

"No, damn you, how can I tell that! *Get me out!*"

"We'll be doing our best to do that, sir," MacNaught answered, then got to his feet. He said, dusting himself down, "I have the idea he's not all that deep, Mr. Ogilvie, and he's not in such a desperate situation as he seems to be thinking. I believe we can raise him by a human chain. It'll be necessary for a man to go down head first, with his feet held from up here, and grip the Captain's hands. With luck—if his feet are not caught—a strong pull should lift the both of them clear. Shall I call for a volunteer, sir?"

Ogilvie shook his head. "No, Colour-Sarn't, I'm not asking any man to go down there."

"But it's not—"

"I'll go myself." He spoke abruptly. He had had those terrible thoughts and they had to be expiated. He was the man for the job from another point of view as well: he was the tallest available, and he was as slim as Andrew Black. Another man might stick fast too. He it was who would have the best chance. He said as much.

"Are you sure that's wise, Mr. Ogilvie?" MacNaught's voice was oddly urgent.

"What d'you mean by that, Colour-Sarn't?"

MacNaught hesitated and when he answered Ogilvie had the feeling he wasn't speaking what was really in his mind. The Colour-Sergeant said, "An officer's life is reckoned to be of greater value than that of a private soldier, Mr. Ogilvie, and we are marching into action. I know well what the Colonel would say, sir."

"The Colonel isn't here," Ogilvie said. He looked around at the others. "I'm going down now. Stand by to grab my legs and for God's sake don't let go."

He got down again on his stomach at the lip of the crevice. Black's weak voice came up to him, beseeching now, whining. He called, "It's all right, I'm coming down to you. Reach up as far as you can and take my hands the moment they touch yours." He edged forward, head down into the bare, open earth. Stones fell around him, spattered down on Black's head. The adjutant gave another terrified cry. Ogilvie himself felt the fear of the unknown as his body slid down faster. For one horrible moment he felt himself fall free, and then he felt the grip tighten around both his ankles, felt his body lifted clear of the sides and held vertical.

Down he went, slowly now, grabbing at the sides as he was lowered. He could almost smell the animal fear emanating from the trapped adjutant. Blood filled his head till he felt something

90

must surely give. He heard the heavy breathing of the men above, the men holding him, heard the sobbing cry from below — and now something else: the sound of turbulently rushing water a long, long way down, a subterranean torrent, tearing along somewhere beneath Black's body.

A hoarse voice reached him from the top: "We're at full stretch now, sir. Can you make it?"

He groped around. He knew Black couldn't be far beneath him now. He called, "Try to come down a little more if you can, up there." His voice sounded muffled in his own ears, muffled by that pounding blood. He felt his body ease downward a few more inches — and then one of his hands contacted Black's outstretched fingers. At once that hand was gripped as if by a vice. Wincing, he reached around with the other until that, too, was gripped hard. Black was never going to let go now. The adjutant was whimpering out a mixture of obscenities and drooling gratitude.

"You're a good fellow, Ogilvie — James. I've often said as much to the Colonel. I'll be a good friend to you. You're going to get me out . . . oh God, please, I beg of you, James, don't let me go now! I'll be your lifelong friend. God, man, James, you can't let me die in this dreadful pit . . ."

He was babbling.

"Shut up," Ogilvie said distinctly and with a touch of venom. "Shut up — and push with your feet!"

But the terrible babble went on. Ogilvie called desperately, "Heave away up top, there! I have him now."

The men on the surface wasted no time after that. Ogilvie felt the tug on his ankles, on his arms. Black didn't move. Ogilvie's body stretched as though on a rack, he felt that his limbs were being drawn from their sockets. Black was babbling still and a moment later began crying like a baby. Ogilvie felt a furious loathing of the man he had come to rescue, but he couldn't have let go now if he had intended to, for Black's grip would never be shifted. The adjutant would drag him down to join him in his death before he would let go of his only lifeline.

Ogilvie began cursing — cursing Black, cursing the men who were doing their best. Dimly through the pounding blood he heard MacNaught shouting, probably calling up more men to tail on to the others and heave. The pull increased and he felt every sinew come to full agonizing stretch. Then he felt a movement, and heard loose earth dropping, and Black moved a fraction. After that it was all over very quickly. Another strong pull from above freed the adjutant completely and as the resistance stopped both men came up with a rush and a jerk. Soon Ogilvie felt the fresh air reaching his face and felt the hands of the soldiers on his body as he was brought up and then guided to the ground and set on his stomach. Men tried to free his hands from Black's grip, but failed. Black, his uniform filthy, his contorted, staring face muddied with tears and earth, was still holding tight to salvation. Twisting his body and looking into that broken face in the light from a shaded lantern, Ogilvie realized that the adjutant had passed out. Colour-Sergeant MacNaught, his face expressionless, lifted his heavy boot and crashed it down on the adjutant's left wrist, a few inches from where Ogilvie's hand was gripped. The fingers opened on a kind of reflex action and MacNaught repeated the process on Black's other wrist.

Ogilvie got unsteadily to his feet as three medical orderlies came up.

MacNaught said evenly, "I'd be obliged if you'd not say a word to anyone as to how you were released from yon bloody yellow-belly, Mr. Ogilvie, sir. Never in all my service have I had to be a witness to such a terrible exhibition from an officer."

Ogilvie didn't answer. He felt a rush of faintness, and he staggered a little, but was all right when he sat down for a spell, and he needed no attention from the medical orderlies beyond a welcome swig at a brandy bottle. Ten minutes later the march was resumed, with Captain Andrew Black being borne along by cursing stretcher-bearers.

Soon after this episode the column was halted as the first streaks of the dawn came across the eastern sky, and they bivouacked out of sight from the rebel fort, behind the siege lines, had a welcome meal, then slept. When they resumed the march at full dark that night Black walked down the line for a word with Ogilvie and his half-company — or those of them who had assisted in the rescue operation. He seemed to have recovered his equilibrium, though he was still deathly pale and his wrists were bandaged. Stiffly he said, "Thank you all. You did well. As you can see, I'm little the worse. It was a small enough affair, of course."

Then he turned away. But before he went Ogilvie saw his face and read the truth in it plain — and realized, in a flash of understanding, just what it was MacNaught had tried to warn him of the night before. Captain Andrew Black, adjutant of the 114th Highlanders, The Queen's Own Royal Strathspeys, had been seen by a subaltern as it were with his pants down around his ankles, having given way to abject panic and crying like a two-year-old. And for that he would never forgive James Ogilvie. It would be a long-term affair and he would bide his time, but there would come a day when he would even the score. For, as his face was now proclaiming, he had a very twisted mind.

When the brigade halted on the second dawn a curious incident took place that brought a welcome touch of lightness to such of the men as witnessed it. Major Archdale, with much distant hauteur, was seen by Ogilvie to march off the track into some handy scrub preceded by his irreverently named bum-*havildar* bearing in his arms the Brigade Major's field lavatory. The procession vanished from sight and a few moments later the native sergeant retired to a respectful distance and waited. After some ten minutes there was a splintering sound, followed by a sharp cry and an oath; the *havildar* sprang into action with a look of great concern. He disappeared again, then returned with the Brigade Major, who was scarlet in the face and blowing out his moustache angrily, and the field lavatory, now broken. As a British subaltern of the 96th Mahrattas later said to Ogilvie, now the Brigade Major had bust his apparatus, he would probably cement right up.

Five

BY two o'clock in the morning following the third leg of the march, the brigade was in position for the assault, having now been joined by its attack artillery drawn by sepoys. So far, all had gone entirely to plan. Ahmed Khan's men appeared to have no knowledge at all of the movements that had been taking place. And now every man was watching for the signal from the supporting column, the brigade that was to attack the peak on the farther side of the valley's entrance.

The 114th Highlanders were spread out around the lower slopes leading to the point of attack, hidden in clefts and gullies and behind boulders, with the screw-guns of the mountain batteries in rear of them. James Ogilvie lay at full stretch on the bare earth, his revolver in his hand. He was aware of the heavy breathing of his men behind him, of the tension as they waited for the word to go. Though close to him, he could scarcely see their faces when he looked round, except as vague whitish blurs in the darkness. The brigade's advance had melted into a sector of the hills where they were right out of the moon's light; but when the assault itself began they would be moving right through that moonlight and would be as nakedly visible as in daylight. It was bad luck but was just something they had to put up with.

Ogilvie was looking for what he guessed must be the hundredth time at his watch when a rocket streaked up from the far side of the defile, trailing stars of red and green and white. Ogilvie noted the time precisely as 2.43 a.m. and felt his stomach loosen. Close upon the first rocket another went up from their own side and at the same instant the batteries behind them went into action. Shells whistled like express trains over the heads of the Royal Strathspeys and the Mahrattas, who were spread out in front of the Highland line. A similar artillery action had started on the other side of the valley. Bursts of light appeared around the peaks ahead, the whole air seemed to fill with vibrancy from the din of the double bombardment. Fragments of rock and shrapnel flew—but there was no return fire. Thirty-five minutes precisely after its commencement, the artillery barrage was lifted from both sides and Ogilvie, his head reeling from the racket, heard the orders being passed to the Mahratta regiments to get up and charge with bayonets fixed. Ahead of him a long, triple line of native soldiers scrambled to their feet and ran forward, belting up the hill, holding their fire until the orders came to shoot. The Indians were yelling like devils as they charged up the difficult, rock-strewn terrain. The moon made them fully visible now from the British ranks behind, and they must have been equally so from above, but there was no firing as yet, and no sign of the defenders either. Ogilvie felt a sense of alarm; there was the smell of a trap about this. But he had only just formulated this thought when the defenders came suddenly and dramatically to life. Heads appeared over boulders, over redoubts farther up the hillside, over the ridges at the summit of the peak itself. A withering rain of fire came down from the long-barrelled muskets, a fire that was supported by a simultaneous barrage from the rebel artillery, now at last in action. Once again the British artillery started up. The Mahrattas went down like skittles in all directions, rolling in their blood. For a while the advance was sustained; then it wavered, and finally it halted, stunned by the murderous gun-fire. As the artillery shells burst before and behind him, Ogilvie heard the cries from the 114th's ranks. Then, as some of the Mahrattas took shelter behind the boulders, others broke and began streaming to the rear, running in panic down the slope again as the rebel bullets and shells smashed into them.

Away to the right Ogilvie saw a tall, kilted figure run ahead into the moonlight, waving a broadsword. He recognized the Colonel and a moment later, as there came a lull in the barrage, he heard Dornoch's voice, strong, defiant: "The 114th will advance, officers and pipers to the front. Men, it's up to us to stop the rot now. God be with you all."

Lord Dornoch turned about and dashed up the slope. As the British guns kept up their fire, the battalion's pipers, led by Pipe-Major Ross, moved through the ranks of the Royal Strathspeys, blowing wind into their instruments. Even above the renewed firing the men heard the brave notes of Cock O' The North playing them on. They came out from the shadows as one, line upon line of yelling, cheering Highlanders filled with

95

the blood-lust, advancing at the double behind the bright, moon-silvered steel of bayonets, their rifles firing as they came on behind Lord Dornoch. They met the running Mahrattas and forced them back into the attack. The slaughter was wicked; men fell, screaming, all around Ogilvie, but the line held and the advance went on as the fighting-mad Scots charged blindly. Ogilvie himself felt the terrible urge of the blood-lust, the over-whelming urge to get to grips with the enemy and kill—kill—kill. He saw men go down ahead of him and he ran over them; he saw a corporal's head vanish as though removed by magic as, presumably, an artillery shell smashed through it, saw the body run forward a few steps just as the tribesman's body back along the Khyber had done that night after his father's sword had sliced off the head. He saw Colour-Sergeant MacNaught stagger with half a shoulder gone, and then fall screaming to the ground. That, perhaps, shook him more than anything else could have done. He thought of Company Serjeant-Major Apps back at Sandhurst. Senior N.C.O.'s were not associated in his mind with screams. He ran on doggedly, so far completely untouched himself, leading a group of men. He scarcely knew where he was leading them, except that it was ahead, and up-wards, towards the redoubts and, apparently, into the very muzzles of a thousand guns. He had lost sight of the Colonel, of all the other officers as well by this time. Somewhere the pipes still played, though the volume of sound had dropped as the pipers were picked off by the rifle-fire. A bullet snicked through Ogilvie's right sleeve, grazing the flesh of his arm and giving him a burning, stinging sensation that in fact he scarcely noticed. All around was the stink of cordite. He ran past the open side of a redoubt unscathed, saw in passing that some men of the battalion had taken that redoubt, and plunged on. Soon he found that he had come upon a high, almost sheer rock face. Tribesmen looked down upon him, firing as he flattened his body against the rock, concealing himself beneath an overhang. He was out of breath and panting. Then, looking about his position wildly, he saw the track leading around the base of the rock face to the left, and he ran along this, continuing the up-ward climb. The men behind him followed blindly, trusting their officer. Then, as he climbed, he saw a heavy figure running from his right and as this man puffed up he recognized Bosom Cunningham. The R.S.M. shouted, "Careful, Mr. Ogilvie. The brigade as a whole has run into a trap, that's obvious — the tribesmen knew we were coming. You'll do no good where you're going and —"

"I think this track may lead to the summit, Sarn't-Major."

"And that's just what I mean, sir. It'll be well guarded. If it doesn't appear to be, then it's another trap."

"We'll have to chance that, Sarn't-Major."

Cunningham didn't answer. He looked behind once, then seemed to make up his mind, and advanced with Ogilvie and the men along the track. There was no sign of life here but they heard the firing as heavy as ever from their right, and below them now, while the defenders answered from above. The track wound and twisted upwards steeply; they stumbled and scrambled, with bleeding hands and knees, up over the rough, boulder-strewn ground. Ogilvie felt that if only he could reach the top and attack the high-mounted guns from the rear, he just might give the main body of the brigade their chance. After a while the track flattened out and when they came around a rock outcrop Ogilvie saw that they had indeed reached the summit. It was a big, flat hilltop and, as he had hoped, they seemed to have worked their way round behind the defensive artillery positions. A battery of big guns, ancient enough pieces, was pounding out its shells along the edge, sending them down into the still advancing Highlanders.

Ogilvie lifted his revolver. "Charge the guns!" he shouted. He ran forward as he spoke, then he saw a body fall from the lip of the rock wall that had been shielding them. The body came down square on Cunningham, carrying him to the ground, and fingers went round his throat. As Ogilvie turned with the intention of killing the native, more and more bodies came over the top, silently, accurately dropping down upon the British. Ogilvie himself was flattened beneath a huge robed body with a bandolier slung across the chest. As the fingers reached for his throat he fought back desperately, lashing out with his legs, scrabbling with his hands, trying to pull the death grip from his windpipe. It was a useless effort; he wondered, as he struggled, why the tribesmen hadn't shot them down as they came along the track, and the answer came to him only as he felt his consciousness going: Cunningham had been right, this was another trap; and Ahmed Khan wanted hostages.

* * *

97

When he came round again he found that his hands were roughly but adequately tied behind his back and his body, which was as limp as a rag doll, was being carried along between two men so that every now and again his bottom was bumped and scraped along the ground. They were moving fast, moving down the hillside with the sure-footed swiftness of the hill tribes. His head ached abominably and he felt sick and weak, but he was able to look around him in the light of the moon. Several such burdens were being borne down the track; the sounds of battle were far off now. He had no idea what the outcome of that desperate advance might have been. Whatever it was, he supposed hazily, it would be unlikely to affect his own future much. He knew that the Pathans always killed their prisoners — in the end. They didn't kill them cleanly or tidily, either. He shivered, felt all his courage draining out of him. He had faced action and he hadn't been as afraid as he had feared he might be; but action was a different thing from certain and protracted death. Not a word was spoken during that first descent of the hillside, not a word when they reached the valley. The bound soldiers were carried into a wide hollow at the foot of the slope, a hollow that was surrounded on all sides by high rock with a narrow exit to the east. Here there were horses waiting, and more wild-looking Pathans, and more rifles. The prisoners were carried to the horses and laid across their backs in front of the riders, and the moment the last man was mounted the cavalcade moved through the narrow exit and out into the eastern extremity of the valley, directly along Ahmed Khan's supply route. As each horse came through it was ridden ahead hard, and the men went like a rushing wind out of the valley, their heads low across the horses' necks, pounding along towards Jalalabad as the fighting continued on the heights behind; and within a few minutes they had passed through an advanced line of the rebel infantry, and more guns, from the fort.

Not long after this they came into the area of the walled fortress-city of Jalalabad with its bastions and curtains constructed from sun-dried bricks and chopped stones. They passed first through derelict gardens and orchards and vineyards, past decayed old tombs of old-time noblemen, overgrown irrigation cuts and clumps of poplars and high, ever-shifting sand-hills; it was no wonder the town was said to be hard to defend, though Ahmed Khan didn't seem to be doing too badly in spite

98

of that fact. Inside the walls the stinking, narrow streets were lined with people; it seemed as though the whole population had turned out to watch the disgraced British soldiers brought in. There was laughter and jeering, and waved fists, and worse insults—Ogilvie, helpless across the horse, felt a stream of saliva, black and horrible with chewed betel-nut, smack into his neck and drool down his uniform—not once, but many times. Fists beat at him, curses were called down upon him. The insults came from women and children as well as from men. The riders made their way through the thronging mass haughtily enough, for they were warriors and thus contemptuous of the rest of the population, but they behaved indulgently and rode without hurrying so that all could join in the sport. It was another half hour before the calvalcade reached the gates of the fort itself to be admitted by the quarter-guard. They passed by the gatehouse and into a long, wide courtyard filled with armed men and horses and stocks of weapons and ammunition. The prisoners were taken across this courtyard towards a part of the high surrounding wall. The horsemen halted outside a heavy, iron-studded door where to the left a long iron plate was set in the ground, for no reason that Ogilvie could fathom. The British were lifted from the horses and dumped on the ground, well covered now by the rebel's guns. One of the Pathans brought out a long knife and cut the ropes.

"On your feet," he said in good English.

The Scots obeyed; some more quickly than others. One private remained on the ground, sitting with his hands linked around his knees, smiling disdainfully up at the man who had spoken. He said, "I'll get up when told to by my own officer. Not by a dirty nigger."

Ogilvie saw the lifted gun and said urgently, "On your feet, Grant, for God's sake!" but he was just too late. The bullet took Private Grant between the eyes and his forehead split. Brain-matter poured down into his uniform. Ogilvie felt horribly sick, and even Bosom Cunningham's blood-red face turned a greenish white in the lanterns shining down from above the iron-studded door.

The Pathan said calmly, "A lesson to you all in how to behave." He turned away, said something in dialect, and a man opened up the heavy door. "Now go inside, all of you, at once."

They filed through into total darkness.

Immediately inside was a steep flight of worn stone steps. The first two men plummeted to the bottom. Thus warned, the others went down with more circumspection and made it without falling. Cunningham and Ogilvie went down last, and then the door was shut and bolted behind them. They were in a dank, stinking cellar with no outlet to the fresh air. Someone made the inevitable comparison with the Black Hole of Calcutta. Just as Ogilvie reached the bottom of the steps and began feeling around with his outstretched hands, the door from the courtyard was opened again and there was a thumping, scraping sound and something took him hard on the back of his shoulders. He fell flat with this weight spreadeagled across him and as he struggled clear he felt the uniform and the brass badges and the buckle and he knew that the almost decapitated body of Private Grant had been thrown down the steps to join his comrades.

On the peak where the 114th, together with all that was left of the Mahrattas, had finally carried the assault and had by now consolidated their position with the aid of a hastily-summoned company of British infantry from the end of the defence perimeter, stock had been taken of the casualties. These had been heavy. Graham, D Company's commander, was dead; so were eleven more officers including the Brigadier-General himself; and eighty-seven men. Three hundred and sixty-two of all ranks were in various degrees wounded. Colour-Sergeant Mac-Naught was dying of his injuries and so, in spite of all Surgeon Major Corton could do, were around one hundred and fifty others. The three Mahratta battalions that formed the rest of the brigade had lost some fifteen hundred dead and wounded. A full muster of the living, the wounded and the dead of the Royal Strathspeys had failed to produce any evidence as to what might have happened to Second-Lieutenant James Ogilvie, the Regimental Sergeant-Major, and twenty-three junior N.C.O.s and men. A second muster brought no more evidence, neither did an exhaustive combing of the gullies and the boulders of the slopes up which the battalion had charged.

Black, conferring with an anxious Colonel, now acting Brigadier, and the Brigade Major, was looking sardonic. He said, "It would appear they must have been taken prisoner. I cannot understand the R.S.M., Colonel . . . but maybe young

Ogilvie hadn't the stomach to be . . . shall I say, *overly* resistant. After all, he's young and totally inexperienced."

Dornoch drew in his breath sharply and stared at the adjutant until the man's gaze fell away. "What are you suggesting, Andrew?"

"Why . . . nothing at all, really, Colonel."

"Then if I were you, I'd restrain myself from any further speculation, I think! In any case, I've never myself subscribed to the view that to be taken prisoner is any disgrace." He gave a sound like a snort. "In the meantime, I'll want full casualty lists reported back to Division."

"A runner, Colonel, of course?" The lists were large for the field telegraph to tap out.

"The detailed nominal lists can go by runner, certainly, but the numbers by rank and regiment must go via the field telegraph. And one other thing, too. Whatever your private opinion as to the motive for the General's appointment, Andrew, the fact remains that he's Ogilvie's father. A runner would take too long, so you'll use the field telegraph to report his name."

"Very good, Colonel." Black sounded highly disapproving. He coughed. "What, specifically, shall I report in the case of Ogilvie and the other missing men?"

"Simply that they're missing," Dornoch answered. "That's all. It's all we know for certain, isn't it? If they've been taken prisoner, we shall undoubtedly be informed of the fact by Ahmed Khan, and we must wait for that."

He turned away abruptly and stared into the sunrise at the distant town below the heights. It was an unpleasant position to be in, to be the Colonel who had lost the Divisional Commander's only son to the enemy—especially bearing in mind that James Ogilvie could prove a far more dangerous hostage than most subalterns.

Six

THE prisoners were left without food or water, and unvisited, in that total darkness, for what seemed to Ogilvie an age. He had been dazed and bewildered; horrified by the unseen proximity of Private Grant's body. He was thankful for the sturdy, phlegmatic presence of the Regimental Sergeant-Major, whose first action, unbidden, after the door was finally shut, had been to carry out a muster of the men and to ascertain what injuries had been caused by the fall down the steps. These, along with Ogilvie's flesh wound sustained in the assault, turned out to be not serious. The twenty-three junior N.C.O.'s and rank and file—reduced now to twenty-two—included a corporal named Brown; a lance-corporal; and Private Jock Burns. Burns was already making a blistering attack on generals, an attack that was nipped in the bud smartly by the thunder of Bosom Cunningham's voice. Ogilvie was grateful both to Cunningham and Burns. Together they had brought a touch of the ordinary, a touch of the barrack-room and the square to this hell-hole; indeed the very matter-of-factness with which the R.S.M. carried out his count of heads—or rather voices—was a help.

When he had finished Cunningham called out briskly, "Mr. Ogilvie, will you please indicate your whereabouts again. Sir!"

It had sounded like an order and despite his worries Ogilvie grinned to himself. "Over here, Sarn't-Major. I've not moved."

"Very good, sir. Thank you." The R.S.M. moved across, stumbling into the men as he went. A minute later Ogilvie said again, "Here, Sarn't-Major," and he was aware of Cunningham groping around and then lowering his body down on the bare earth beside him. Cunningham said in a low voice, "This is a pretty kettle of fish, Mr. Ogilvie."

"I know. And I'm afraid it looks like my fault, Sarn't-Major."

"You've no reason to think that, sir, no reason at all. You did your duty, Mr. Ogilvie. You carried out your orders, which were, to reach the summit of the hill. That is all."

Ogilvie said, "You warned me, Sarn't-Major. You warned me about a trap and you were right."

"I think we'll say no more about that, Mr. Ogilvie. If I may say so, more experienced officers than you have been ambushed before now, and many times too. You have nothing to reproach yourself over." The R.S.M.'s voice became brisker. "It is profitless to worry about what's done, sir, begging your pardon. We need now to consider the future, and what our action should be. I've no doubt you've already given thought to that. I'd say it's already in your mind to break out at the first opportunity."

"Yes," Ogilvie agreed untruthfully. He had been too shaken to give any constructive thought to the future at all, and frankly he doubted if any opportunity of escape would be given them. But he appreciated the tactful guidance of the R.S.M. nevertheless. He had been given a lead now; he must respond to it. The men had to have a leader, and that leader had to be him. He had been pitchforked into sole and total responsibility of command. This was what he had been commissioned for, was broadly what Sandhurst was supposed to have prepared him for, even though, in point of fact, he had never felt less prepared for anything in all his life. Bullet wounds, death even, he had conditioned himself to expect and face. Never had he considered the idea of being taken prisoner and thus, to some extent at any rate, disgraced. Whatever Cunningham had said, it was not expected of officers that they should lead their men into ambush and capture by a band of ruffianly brigands, mere irregulars. Soon his sense of pride began to feel the affront, and with his resurgence of pride came a return of spirit.

He said, "Yes, you're right, Sarn't-Major. It's our duty to break out and rejoin the battalion."

"Aye, sir." Then came the old soldier's word of caution. "But of course — not foolishly."

"How d'you mean?"

"An attempt should be made only when there is a likelihood of success, Mr. Ogilvie. To do otherwise would lead to an unnecessary loss of life, and nothing gained in the end. If I might make a suggestion, it would be this: if we hold our hand a while and do not rush into too quick an attempt, it is possible that in the meantime we may learn something of Ahmed Khan's plans for the future, and of the state of this fort. All such information will be of value to Division, Mr. Ogilvie."

"Yes." Ogilvie hesitated, then said in a low voice, "I'd give a good deal to know what my father's thinking now!"

"Nothing adverse to you, would be my guess, sir. The General's experienced in frontier fighting."

"And in frontier ways. He'll have a pretty good idea of what we might be in for, won't he?"

There was a brief hesitation. Ogilvie wondered if the same thought was in Cunningham's mind as in his own: there might be no time for waiting to garner useful information before the rebel leader had them put to death — or worse. Then the R.S.M. said, "I'd not be at all surprised, sir. Aye, he'll have a shrewd idea. But I have a feeling that wasn't quite what was in your mind, Mr. Ogilvie, when you spoke of his thoughts about you."

Ogilvie gave a rather high laugh. "Damn it, Sarn't-Major, it wasn't."

"Then what was, sir?"

Ogilvie said bleakly, "I was wondering, actually, if he'd order out a punitive expedition from Brigade."

"To rescue you, sir?"

"And all of us," Ogilvie said quickly.

"Of course, sir. Now, you'll know your own father well enough, so I think you can answer that for yourself."

"Not well enough even to try, Sarn't-Major."

"Is that so, sir? Well, then, I'll try myself, for I know him quite well enough. I served many years under him as a corporal and platoon sergeant when he commanded the 114th, Mr. Ogilvie, indeed I've served under him up here on the frontier itself. Sir Iain'll not be sending any expeditions from Brigade or anywhere else, sir, and it's my guess he'll give specific orders to the Colonel that he is not to take it upon himself to do so either. He will put out of his mind that you are his son. If you put yourself in his position, Mr. Ogilvie, you'll see he has no other course open to him."

In the darkness Ogilvie nodded without giving an answer. Cunningham was right; he always was. To Ogilvie it seemed that he himself could prove an incubus to his comrades in captivity — if the fact was that his father *would* have ordered out a force to get them back had his son not been one of them. But further reflection told him that *any* rescue operation was in fact highly unlikely. No small force could hope to penetrate as far as this fort, and anything more ambitious than a sortie would have to wait for the main assault, the final tightening of the circle. Twenty-odd lives could not be allowed to disturb the overall strategy of a campaign.

Cunningham's voice broke into his thoughts. The R.S.M. said in a whisper, "It's going to be a race against time, sir. I do not myself believe that the rebel will have any ideas of a quick end for us. He means to make use of us first. If we're lucky — and on the assumption Brigade has taken the peak — Division may tighten the circle and come in for the kill before he's made that use of us."

That, Ogilvie knew, was designed merely for comfort; even Cunningham couldn't believe his words really. As soon as Ahmed Khan got wind of any tightening circles, he would almost for a certainty despatch his prisoners. But Ogilvie played along and said, "It'll be up to me to dream up all the delaying tactics I can, Sarn't-Major."

"Aye, sir, that's about the sum of it, and in the meantime we can no' but wait and see what happens."

After that, Cunningham moved away and spoke to the men, doing what he could to keep their spirits up. Ogilvie tried not to think about Private Grant. There was a renewal of the foul-mouthed whining from Burns, who was once again silenced by Cunningham. The R.S.M. threatened him with all manner of punishment as soon as they got back to the British lines. This effectively put a stop on Burns, at any rate for the time being; the regiment and its iron-hard discipline was still too close a thing to be disregarded. Ogilvie found himself wondering how long that would hold. It was action that held a body of men together; action was excitement and lust and even a kind of fulfilment once you had the enemy in your sights or beneath your sword. Captivity led to lack of hope, and if hope should go, discipline would follow at once. It was Ogilvie's task to keep the hope in being, to act as Commanding Officer while Cunningham fulfilled his traditional role of ramrod to maintain the discipline. But Ogilvie wondered, too, how he himself was going to face the kind of death the Pathans dealt out and how he would react in the waiting period.

From beyond the thick door, dimly, they heard sounds after a while. Those sounds were of shouted orders and of the jingle of harness, and the heavy roll of limber wheels along the court-yard above. To Cunningham's experienced ear the sounds were those of elephant-drawn guns, the heaviest of all batteries. A little later there came the sound of tinny drums and trumpets, and after that gunfire sounded in the distance. No one could tell what it might mean but Cunningham made a guess that the British had taken the peaks and either Ahmed Khan was mounting his counter-attack or Brigade had sent out an exploratory sortie to test the fort's offensive spirit.

They all wanted to believe the R.S.M.

The news had begun as a ripple, but, ripple-like, it spread. First of all to Division, where it was quickly reported to Sir Iain Ogilvie by his Chief of Staff that both the peaks had been taken with heavy losses to the British and Indian units, but that it had not been possible to extend across the entry to the valley, which was very heavily held by rebel forces; and that twenty-five of the Royal Strathspeys could not be accounted for. There was the faintest twitch of a muscle in the Divisional Commander's face, following a tug at the heavy moustache, when his son's name came up; and that was all.

Sir Iain said evenly, "I'm damn sorry about the casualties — it's bad, bad! Hewlett gone — poor Hewlett! His wife'll take that hard. He didn't appear to have the strength of a flea in his body, but he kept that rapacious woman well satisfied whenever he was close enough to do so . . . Confirm to Lord Dornoch he's to regard himself as acting in Hewlett's place temporarily, without extra rank or pay of course. That feller Hay can have the 114th on the same terms for the time being, though he's a damned old woman in my view. Like someone's maiden aunt." He blew his nose loudly. "Got a sister like him myself. Congratulate the Brigades on both peaks on the successful outcome of the assault itself — and add that I expect the defile to be closed as soon as possible. Tell Dornoch, I'm to be informed immediately when it's known what's happened to the missing officer and men. The loss of the Regimental Sarn't-Major is especially to be regretted."

Not a word about the son until the Chief of Staff prompted gently, for there were aspects of that relationship to be considered. The Chief of Staff said quietly, "I'm very sorry, sir, about your son."

"Hey—hey? Of course—thank you, Trevelyan. I assume they've been taken prisoner." His hands clenched on the table-top that he was using as a makeshift desk. "Only hope to God the boy has the wit to try to conceal his identity—that's all!"

"You have the possibility of hostages in mind, sir?"

"I have!" Sir Iain snapped. "Haven't you? If you haven't, you damn well ought to have. I'd have thought it obvious enough ... when that damn rebel finds out he's got his filthy hands on an Ogilvie, he may well consider he has an ace, Trevelyan."

"Yes, sir." Brigadier-General Trevelyan, late of the Sappers, spare, sallow, thin-faced and, in his General's rancid opinion after a few days' experience of him, too clever by half, was out of his depth; he had not encountered such a situation before. "I'm sorry, sir."

"Sorry you may well be, blast you, and so am I! It's confounded unfortunate—*damned* awkward." Sir Iain got up abruptly from the bare table and stood with his back to the Headquarters tent and the Chief of Staff. Using field glasses, he stared for some moments towards Jalalabad, churning over the unwelcome fact that he was unable to report to the Commander-in-Chief in India that the rebel's supply route had actually been cut. Lowering his glasses sharply he ordered, "Send Brigade's report through at once to Peshawar and add that I want the 88th to join me soonest possible. They can damn well *double* through the Khyber! Those casualties were too damn heavy, Trevelyan."

"Yes, sir."

"Can't you find anything else to damn well say, except 'Yes sir,' like a damn parrot?"

The Chief of Staff sighed inwardly. "I'm sorry, sir."

"Oh, God give me strength!" The General lifted his arms, let them drop again. He had a feeling he might be needed at Brigade in person, but if he went, he would go with only an *aide-de-camp* and leave the rest of the Staff behind at H.Q. He preferred to deal direct with his field commanders, the real fighting men. "Now I'll have my breakfast. Where's that blasted servant of mine—hey?" He swung away and as an after-thought added over his shoulder, "Trevelyan, there's one other thing ... my wife. She'll have to be told, and before the damn Press gets hold of it, what's more! I'll add a personal message before you send the signal to Peshawar."

And so the news went out to Peshawar and on to Northern Army H.Q. in Murree. From there it reached the Commander-in Chief India and went on via Calcutta by urgent cable to Whitehall and then to Fleet Street. All over Britain in due course the newsboys called it from the street corners. The country, though it was growing tired of the continuing Afghan involvements, was disturbed. To be sure, Afghanistan was far, far away and the valorous taking of a couple of peaks in the foothills of the Hindu Kush was a small thing and no more than was expected of British soldiers; it scarcely affected the lives of the butcher, the baker, the candle-stick maker; but John Bull was affronted because British soldiers were languishing in some stinking rebel stronghold in the lee of those distant alien hills — *The Times* newspaper and other journals published small maps that indicated the geography—and this meant somebody had to do something about it, fast. If the military couldn't or wouldn't, then the politicians should prod them into it. James Ogilvie became national news, became of national concern. The Prime Minister himself saw the Queen, hurrying by train to Windsor where a brougham from the castle met him and his bag of documents. Her Majesty expressed her wishes in the matter contradictorily: the soldiers must be got out but the overall campaign should not be compromised in the doing. An officer must not be subjected to indignity, especially since he was the son of a lieutenant-general wielding the personal authority of the Queen-Empress in his district of action. Her Majesty ended by saying, acidly, that perhaps more common sense might prevail if everything was left strictly in the hands of the military on the spot; and in vain Lord Roseberry pointed out that political considerations—especially *vis-à-vis* His Imperial Majesty the Czar of All the Russias—were involved on the frontier and that the military themselves had asked for guidance. When he returned again to Downing Street the Prime Minister was suffering badly from dyspepsia brought on by the Royal tea-scones. The Duke of Cambridge left the sanctuary of the Horse Guards and waited upon him in something of a ferment, managing when admitted to talk garrulously in a series of short, sharp, military barks while his face grew redder. When Lord Roseberry spitefully suggested that the best way out might be to relieve Sir Iain Ogilvie of his division, at any rate for the time being, His Royal Highness almost burst a blood-vessel.

"Damn fool!" he was heard to mutter thickly. "There's not a blasted General Officer of suitable seniority in all India from Murree to Ootacamund that's damn well capable of lifting his blasted backside from an easy chair, let alone take over from Ogilvie!" He ruminated for a moment, chewing his lips. "Damn good mind to suggest to Her Majesty that I go out myself."

The Prime Minister stared at him in alarmed dismay, then gave a sardonic snort after which he terminated the interview as briskly as was compatible with tact.

Below those distant Kafiristan hills the prisoners heard, at last, the sounds of a key being turned in the lock of the door and the bolts being withdrawn. Daylight came down the steps, daylight and fresh air to dispel the stench to which, in fact, they had become accustomed by this time. As a figure appeared Ogilvie called sharply, "No one move!"

The figure in the doorway said something in his own language. Ogilvie answered, "I do not understand you."

"He's speaking Pushtu, Mr. Ogilvie," Cunningham whispered. "He says to come up singly. You first, sir. Do as he says. I'll be behind you."

Ogilvie got to his feet. As the man at the top moved back, sunlight came down in a broad band. Flies rose in a swarm, coming from Grant's body. The sun shone on the faces of the men; they were unshaven, drawn, tired and anxious. But that of the Regimental Sergeant-Major was like a rock still. Ogilvie moved slowly for the steps, and climbed. He emerged into the courtyard, blinking in the strong sun, feeling the day's tremendous heat strike through his uniform in sharp contrast to the dank fug of the cellar. The man who had opened the door stood waiting. He was a massively-built fellow, a Persian Ogilvie fancied, not an Afghan, with a bare chest and baggy trousers of scarlet looped at the ankles, and he carried a long leather whip in his right hand. In front of the cellar entrance a dismounted guard was drawn up, wearing uniforms that were at once filthy and splendid — splendid in their lavish colourings and ornaments, but worn and soiled. They carried curved swords, heavy ones that reflected the sun, and they wore turbans of sapphire blue. An order was given in Pushtu. One man left the guard and, marching up to Ogilvie, placed a sword against his neck so that he could feel its cutting edge nick the skin above his adam's-apple. Nothing more was said, but as each of the British prisoners came up, another man moved out of the line and held him at sword point. When they were all up from the cellar the native guards moved around behind them, placing the swords against the backs of their necks. Another command was given and the swords pressed, the British were urged ahead in file, with Ogilvie in front following the bare-chested Persian who had unlocked the cellar door.

They were led across the courtyard towards a battlemented strongpoint, a tower set in the farther wall and coloured rose-red, across bare dusty earth trodden by many men and animals into an almost stone hardness. Around the courtyard there were many trees, a dusty, sun-drenched line of green, and beyond the wall they could see the tops of more trees, but apart from this splash of faded greenery the place was as military and utili-tarian as the British lines themselves. The men were marched towards a flight of stone steps rising from the courtyard towards a doorway into the tower, and once inside were led down a long passage. Ogilvie felt a sinking in his stomach, was, as ever, glad of the presence somewhere behind him of Bosom Cunningham. At the end of the passage a spiral staircase, also of stone, twisted steeply upwards. This the soldiers were made to climb. Eventually they emerged on to a wide, flat surface, heavily guarded by more tribesmen and surrounded by the battlements they had seen from below. A tall man turned as Ogilvie came through from the staircase, a man with a thick black beard and a light blue turban with a great diamond glittering in its front, a full-faced, full-blooded man of obvious vigour and strength. This man came towards Ogilvie, smiling.

In perfect English he said, "Good morning, Ogilvie sahib."

This was startling. Ogilvie asked, "You know my name?"

The man's smile became broader. "Of course, my dear fellow. I, also, have a field telegraph system – if it is not of quite the same kind as your British one, it works equally well insofar as it sends me the information I require from time to time, and so I happen to know that the General's son is missing... *et cetera!*" He shrugged. "It is really a very simple matter, though I confess it is nothing but my good luck that it was *you* my men captured."

"You mean you have spies in the British lines?"

"Spy is an unpleasant word, Ogilvie sahib. Shall we call them . . . political officers in reverse?" The smile was very mocking now. "Your country has no monopoly of misleading titles, my good young friend."

Ogilvie flushed. He asked, "You are the rebel, Ahmed Khan?"

"That is absolutely so, Ogilvie sahib. I am the man your father is under orders to destroy, am I not right?"

"I don't know what my father's orders are, Ahmed Khan. But to the best of my knowledge no one has orders to destroy you, only to eject you from Jalalabad and to return the town and this fortress to the Amir in Kabul —"

"The Amir in Kabul? I am glad you make the distinction! I, you see, am the Amir in Jalalabad!"

"But not for much longer," Ogilvie said. "The orders will be carried out, Ahmed Khan, you can be very sure of that."

The man gave a low, insulting laugh. "You are very British," he said. "Also, very stupid. You must not believe that British soldiers always carry out their orders successfully. You should read your history books a little more carefully, Ogilvie sahib, you really should! The frontier is signposted by more British defeats than British successes. Allow me to prophesy that Jalalabad will be one more defeat for your British arms." He reached out and put a hand on Ogilvie's shoulder. "Come with me now, and look, and then use your mind, and think."

He led Ogilvie across towards the battlements to the west, and handed him a pair of field glasses. "Look," he repeated.

Ogilvie did so. At such range — it was around five miles, he remembered, on the maps — he was not able to see much detail on the peaks, but he did notice some considerable movement on the plain across the entry to the valley, where a large force seemed to be positioned. Ahmed Khan, beside him, said, "Allow me to explain, Ogilvie sahib." He paused, studying his prisoner's face for a moment. "The British have been quite successful in that they have taken the hills on either side of my supply route. They fought well, and this I concede, and I willingly admit defeat thus far. But it is only a small defeat. The

British will not command the valley for long. Already, as you can see, a strong force has gone out from here, and indeed has for some time been deployed across the entry—since before your soldiers had consolidated their positions enough either to stop them or to close the gap themselves Out there, my young friend, I have cavalry and infantry, sappers, much heavy artillery drawn by elephant trains and supported by lesser guns. In due course, my men will infiltrate to the rear of the peaks and recapture them. Even should they not succeed in this—and failure is most unlikely—my military presence in the gap between the peaks will ensure the entire safety of my supply column, for my soldiers will keep the British very well occupied, and already my artillery is starting to silence their guns, so that there will be none to fire on the supplies. This column is expected quite shortly, and once it is through, the British may as well fold their tents, Ogilvie sahib, and steal softly away before I catch them up! The column brings me many thousands of fresh men, and very many more guns and foodstuffs—but this perhaps you know already. There is something I think you do not know, however, and it is this: the Amir in Kabul is willing to treat with me. If I am able to conclude an agreement with him, and I believe sincerely that I am, then you British will be fighting on wholly alien ground, Ogilvie sahib."

Ogilvie lowered the glasses. What Ahmed Khan had just said, if it were true, put a very different complexion on the whole affair. The British would probably have to withdraw at once—indeed, would be bound to do so if thus requested by the Amir; their ground would be cut from under their feet and all the casualties would have been in vain. As to themselves, prisoners here in the fort . . . well, no doubt their disposal would be part and parcel of any agreement between the Amir and the rebel, but if anything other than handing back to their regiment was on the cards for them, then presumably the situation would alter yet again and Army Headquarters in Murree would press for a punitive expedition. But, in the execution of it, they would have the whole area, including the Khyber, against them. Such might well mean the effective end of Ogilvie's career, or at least of any promotion beyond the rank of major; for no government was likely to look favourably upon an officer who, almost single-handed if not voluntarily, had stirred up an extension of the conflict, made it in effect into an Imperial war, by the stupidity of having allowed himself to be captured . . .

Ahmed Khan went on, "In the meantime, Ogilvie sahib, I have a use for you and your men. It will have occurred to you already that I had ordered the taking of prisoners for use as hostages?"

Ogilvie nodded; smiling, Ahmed Khan took his arm and led him on a perambulation of the rooftop. The native said, "But now there is a difference. I have been most exceptionally lucky. As I am sure you can see, the fact of your name, of your birth, makes this difference."

"A squeeze on my father?" Ogilvie gave a rather shaky laugh. "That won't work, Ahmed Khan! My father is a soldier, a British officer of the old order, and a man well used to the ways of India and the frontier. He'll never be moved an inch by any relationship."

"Yes, this I understand," Ahmed Khan said quietly. "I know you are right. The General sahib is as you say — I know this — and would do his duty no matter what should happen to his son, as I myself would also, in similar circumstances."

Ogilvie was puzzled. "So?"

Ahmed Khan smiled again and let go of his arm. He stood back. "You are not the only hostage, as you know. There are — let me see — twenty-three more, one of them your own *havildar*-major. I shall leave you to think about this, Ogilvie sahib. For now, I have said enough. I shall speak with you again shortly."

He nodded at the Persian, and turned away himself, walking back across the space to watch again from the northern battlements. Once more the escort surrounded the prisoners with their drawn swords and ushered them back down the spiral staircase. When they reached the passage Ogilvie found a young man waiting, a slim young man, an Indian, in white with a brilliant blue cummerbund. This man halted the escort, approached Ogilvie, bowed, and said in English, "Excuse sahib . . . come this way please," indicating a door leading off to the left.

"Why?" Ogilvie asked.

"The orders of His Highness Ahmed Khan, sahib. As a British officer you are not to be put in the cell."

Ogilvie's face hardened. "I prefer to be with my men," he said.

"An officer, sahib —"

113

"Here we are all prisoners. I don't want any privileged treatment. My duty's to my men. I insist on being accommodated with them."

"I am so sorry, sahib." The young man clapped his hands and the door opened. Four men with curved swords came through and formed a close escort round Ogilvie. He shrugged, caught Cunningham's eye and said, "I'm sorry, Sarn't-Major, but there's nothing I can do about this."

"That's all right, sir." Cunningham slammed to attention, disregarding the sword at his throat. "Keep your chin up, Mr. Ogilvie. I'll see to the men."

"The *havildar*-major also will receive the treatment of his rank," the young man said in his sing-song, Bombay-Welsh voice. Ogilvie was marched away by the new body of guards, but not before he had heard some choice and very bitter comment from Private Burns.

It was, of course, though James Ogilvie didn't fully realize it, an old gambit, as old as the war game itself and played by all contestants. Chivalrously treat the officers and senior N.C.O.'s according to their rank and you automatically separated them from the men. It was, though perhaps no British officer would admit this, a rough-and-ready form of the 'divide and rule' principle. The men lost their leadership, the officers lost their support, escape became virtually impossible, at least in the circumstances of a frontier war. No officer was going to break out and leave his men behind and it was highly unlikely that the men would leave their officer either. Quite apart from considerations of honour, everyone knew only too well what would happen to the unlucky ones. Even taking the lowest view of human nature, everyone knew equally well what would happen when the me-firsters reached their own lines, if ever they did. They wouldn't be the lucky ones any more.

After Ogilvie had been taken over by the slim young Indian and the new set of guards, he was ushered politely into a long room, beautifully furnished, with a gold-draped divan bed at the far end. There was a thick Persian rug on the stone floor and the ceiling was ornately decorated with many-coloured tiles depicting what appeared to be scenes of debauchery from about the time of Ghenghis Khan. There were three windows opening on to a terrace, but these were heavily barred and outside two armed men marched up and down. And, naturally enough, the door through which Ogilvie had come had been locked and bolted once the Indians and the escort had withdrawn and more regular footfalls spoke of yet another sentry-post.

On a beautifully inlaid table beside a Western-style armchair was a bottle of Scotch whisky, tumblers, a siphon of soda water, and a carafe in an ice-bucket. There was a solid gold canister containing cigars and cigarettes. As Ogilvie drank the water thirstily, he smiled to himself at the thought that he had far more comfortable quarters than even his father had, out there in the British siege lines. It was an odd situation; and it was also highly dangerous. Ogilvie walked up and down, up and down, trying to work out what could be in Ahmed Khan's mind. If the pressure was not to be put on his father, who *was* it to be put on? Ogilvie scarcely presumed to imagine his personal fate would be of very much moment to Her Majesty's Government in the comfortable seclusion of Whitehall, or indeed to the Government summering in Simla. Lord Elgin would hardly be disturbed to any great extent. And why, in any case, did Ahmed Khan bother with hostages at all if he were about to treat with the Amir? Was it just a form of insurance, in case the Amir wriggled out from under the negotiations? And again, what had Ahmed Khan meant by remarking so particularly on the fact that he was not the only hostage?

The rebel leader had left him to ponder this very point, but from whichever angle he examined it, he could find no ray of light.

He sat down at last in the armchair, his head in his hands. Then he looked at the whisky. That whisky could be one of Ahmed Khan's ways of softening a prisoner up; a man who had taken drink might well speak of things that were better kept inside his own head. But by this time James Ogilvie had learned his capacity for alcohol and he hadn't been long enough on Indian service to have a dangerous disregard for that capacity. He could trust himself. He was about to pour a couple of fingers of whisky, and light a cigarette, when he heard the bolts going back on the door and half a minute later a lithe, nubile girl in a flimsy veil came sinuously into the room.

Seven

"I've no doubt ye heard," came Private Burns' voice from the darkness of the stinking cellar, "what yon Ogilvie was sayin' to the Sar-Major earlier on . . . before he was removed to a life o' luxury in the harem?"

Corporal Brown said, "Shut your mouth, Burns."

"I'll do no such thing," Burns answered back indignantly. "You can try an' make me if you want! This isn't the British lines. We're all equal now . . . except the bloody officer and *Mister* bloody Cunningham." He hawked and spat viciously. "I asked you, did you hear what Ogilvie said? If you didn't, then I'll tell you: he said the General wouldn't be sending out an expedition to get him out o' here. Well, now, I reckon he's right. The General won't be wantin' to have it said that he ordered men out to bring in his laddie, will he? Now, from that fact I make a deduction, Corporal, and it's this: yon Ogilvie is stoppin' us bein' rescued—if he wasn't here at all we'd be in a better situation, d'ye see—so it follows we'd be better off without him. And you can bet your stripes on that!"

"I told you to shut your mouth," Brown said. He listened to the dry scurry of rats in a corner of the cellar and felt his flesh creep. "If you don't, Burns, you'll be talking yourself into clink the moment we get back, and—"

"We'll not get back," Burns shouted in a high voice, "while Ogilvie's alive to prevent it, so you'd all do better to listen to what I say!" He failed to hear the movement of Corporal Brown towards him and he went on ranting till he felt the Corporal's hands slide around his neck. Then he shrieked. Brown's hands pressed and cut short the shriek. Brown said savagely, "You'll keep your thoughts to yourself from now on, you bloody little worm, or so help me God . . . I'll have you on a drumhead court martial charged wi' mutiny just as soon as we rejoin the battalion. Which we are going to do! But only if we hold together and not try to get at Ogilvie behind his back." He eased the pressure on Burns's throat. "I'm in charge down here now and in charge I intend to stay. If anyone thinks differently about that, just let him say so, and I'll smash his face to a pulp."

There was no answer; Brown was a big man with something of a reputation as a boxer. He flung Burns from him bodily, caring nothing for the man's comparatively advanced years, and got to his feet, stood for a moment breathing hard through his nose, then, realizing there was nowhere else to go, he sat down on the earth close to Burns; closest to where the most likely trouble lay. Meanwhile there was nothing he could do but sit and think and listen to the busy rats, and one of his thoughts was that thinking was all the others could do as well unless he could keep them occupied. Thinking was dangerous; thoughts could easily run along the lines already so bluntly planted by Private Burns, and most of the men in the cellar were young, inexperienced, frightened, and impressionable. They could prove an all too fruitful nurturing ground for mutinous thoughts. Brown himself had to admit there was a grain, a tiny grain certainly but still a grain, of truth in what Burns had said, and the grain could grow to such an extent that it could fill the horizons of them all. Brown racked his brains, tried to think what the R.S.M. would find for the men to do in the circumstances. He could think of only one thing, the good old stand-by of British troops in difficult times, and he said with a show of heartiness, "Come on, now, lads, let's have a wee bit of a song to keep us going, eh?" And in a strong and not untuneful bass he began, himself, with an army song of many years before when the ragged Highland regiments had come back to Glasgow after too long on foreign service:

> "March past the Forty-second,
> They were Hielan' laddies braw,
> March past the Forty-second
> Comin' doon the Broomielaw . . ."

In no time he had them all at it, bellowing out the verses, the final words a roaring crescendo of sound in the constriction of the cellar:

> "March past the Forty-second
> March past the Forty-four,
> March past the bare-arsed buggers
> Comin' frae th' Ashantee war . . ."

Temporarily at least, the subversion of Private Burns had been overlaid. Up top in the courtyard four Afridi tribesmen, on guard with their long-barrelled rifles, stared and listened and shook their heads in wonder at each other. Truly, the British were quite mad.

From the high roof where Ogilvie had had his meeting with Ahmed Khan, a heliograph winked in the sunlight, directing its reflections in dots and dashes towards the peak captured by the Royal Strathspeys. A signaller on the peak read and took down the message on a pad, tore the sheet off, and ran to the adjutant. Black scanned it briefly and took it direct to Lord Dornoch. It confirmed that the missing twenty-five men had been taken prisoner. It gave no other information beyond the fact, the potentially dangerous fact, that the identity of Second-Lieutenant Ogilvie was known to the rebels.

"I don't like this," Dornoch said briefly, his face drawn and anxious.

"Nor I, Colonel, nor I." Black pursed his lips, and looked away towards the distant fort, whilst at the same time looking obliquely at Dornoch. "It seems a pity Ogilvie should have admitted his identity . . . the General will not be pleased at that, Colonel."

"I know that."

"I wonder . . . I wonder how easily they got that information out of him, Colonel? The boy would surely have had the common sense to realize what he was admitting, what he was handing to the scum?"

Dornoch said, "If he had that, he would also know what he was letting himself in for by the admission, wouldn't he? Do you see any gain to himself in that?"

"No, no, indeed . . . but I was wondering, d'you see, Colonel, if there's to be some . . . shall I say, some *co-operation* on the part of young Ogilvie?"

Dornoch drew in his breath, sharply. "You're suggesting he might have cracked to the point of turning traitor?"

Black shrugged. "Oh, I wouldn't care to make such a concrete suggestion as *that*, Colonel."

"I think you would be well advised not to, indeed!" The Colonel's stare was hard and his eyes level. Black flushed and looked away. "If you make the slightest suggestion of such a thing again, or make it to anyone other than myself at any time, I shall ask for you to be relieved of your duties and sent back to Division. Is that clear, Black?"

Black inclined his head. "Very clear, Colonel. It will not be said again."

Dornoch turned his back and walked away without another word. He was furiously angry, and had only with the greatest self-control prevented himself from committing the utterly unforgivable military crime of striking his adjutant. He had absolutely no doubts in his mind that young Ogilvie had acted with entire innocence. He was a very sound young officer and entirely loyal—that went without saying, of course—and no coward, even though he was young and inexperienced and, because of this, apt perhaps to commit errors of judgment. Such as this. Dornoch gnawed at the ends of his moustache. Oh yes, it was undoubtedly an indiscretion—damn foolish! But no more than that. And yet . . .

God damn Black!

Black with his insinuations—insinuations the man was only too clearly glad to be able to indulge in. It had not been lost on Lord Dornoch that the adjutant had had it in for Ogilvie in particular these last few days. Well—he would see, he would see.

The Colonel halted and turned and looked back towards the fort beneath the sun, across the dusty dry heat of the burning Afghan plain. These were a cruel and ruthless people, currently with much at stake. Ahmed Khan would scarcely be the man to hold back on brutalities and no man could say how another man, or he himself even, was going to behave when under the kind of duress the Afghans were capable of inflicting. The Colonel's mind went back over the years and he saw again some of the results of persuasion he had seen along the frontier in the old days. Men horribly beaten, maimed, mutilated. Some things they got the women to do . . . on the plains of Afghanistan a regiment never, never left its wounded behind, whatever the military situation. If they did that, the Pathans sent out their women . . . and far better not even to think about what the regiment would find when they marched back over the same ground again.

And again God damn Black, who had started such thoughts going.

Fifty miles away, beyond the Khyber Pass in Peshawar, Mary Archdale had heard the news that the British columns had taken the peaks, and that the 114th Queen's Own Royal Strathspeys, along with the rest of her husband's brigade, had been badly cut up in the taking of one of them. And a little after that, having made a formal enquiry as to her husband's well-being and having been informed that his name had not so far appeared in any of the casualty reports, she went shopping in the market attended by a native servant and a dismounted trooper of the Bengal Light Horse. Mary Archdale bought her provisions carefully, and always personally because you simply couldn't trust the native servants not to rook you; and with a due regard to her husband's army pay, which was his sole means of support. Without private means, life for an army wife could be hard indeed. This morning she was much concerned with the price of such vegetables as were available, and she gave little thought to the goings-on outside Jalalabad until she happened to meet, quite by chance, an acquaintance, another wife who also lived on a husband's unaided pay.

"Why, Mrs. Archdale," the acquaintance said gushingly. "How very nice to see you. I expect you've heard the news from Jalalabad?"

Mary said, "Yes," and smiled.

"I do hope Major Archdale is safe?"

She said, "Oh, yes, he is, thank you, Mrs. Ffoulkes."

Mrs. Ffoulkes, who knew the facts of the Archdales' married life well enough, smiled happily and said, "I'm *so* relieved, I've been thinking about you *such* a lot. I hear the Mahrattas were simply splendid, but very badly cut about I'm afraid." She edged away from a bespectacled, clerkly Indian who in his turn was agitatedly trying not to be touched by another Indian, a man of lower caste. "These *filthy* natives! I can't wait to see England again, I keep telling my husband he simply *must* press for a posting back as soon as possible, but you know what the army is." She broke off. "Mrs. Archdale, I've heard a rumour, and it is only a rumour, but my husband says it's pretty certain to be substantiated, though he won't say why, that poor Sir Iain's son is missing."

"Sir Iain?"

"*Ogilvie.*"

"Oh—yes. Yes, of course." Mary frowned attractively.

"You danced with his son at the ball at the palace," the woman said with a curious inflexion in her voice.

Mary recognized the inflexion at once and was infuriated by it. "Oh, I've no doubt I was seen by some busybody," she said tartly. "If you can so much as blow your nose in bed without all Peshawar knowing about it by breakfast time, you're a lot cleverer than me, Mrs. Ffoulkes. His name is James and he's a very nice boy — and if what you say is true, then I'm very sorry."

"Well, I just thought I'd tell you."

"Thank you," Mary said, and, lifting her skirt from the ground with a gloved hand, moved away. She *was* sorry about young Ogilvie; she was wise enough in the ways of the frontier to know what 'missing' meant and wise enough, too, to know what could follow. He had been a nice young man — terribly callow, of course, and terribly repressed, the gauchest young man, in fact, she had ever met. But he had also been honest and sincere, with no guile in him at all, and very good-looking, and had an impetuosity that had appealed to her. She smiled inwardly, then felt a touch of sadness and regret. He had made it so obvious that night that he'd wanted to toss her into bed, she had felt his urgency, she remembered, like a physical force reaching out to her. It would have been an act of the sheerest kindness and it would have been so easy really to have given him what he wanted. But she had also had an odd feeling that when it came to the point he would have been scared stiff.

In any case, it was too late for regrets now.

She gave a small shrug and went on with her buying till the servant and the Bengal Light Horseman were loaded to capacity, and then she went back to quarters and found, as the day went on, that she couldn't quite get James Ogilvie out of her mind, though until now she had scarcely thought about him at all since he had marched away through the Khyber Pass.

Later that day more news reached Peshawar from the siege lines outside Jalalabad and by nightfall the whole garrison was laughing itself sick. Brigade Major Archdale's specially-built field lavatory, it was reported, had become a casualty of war. Not only had it been damaged accidentally by its owner, but it had subsequently been totally destroyed by a rebel artillery concentration. The Medical Officer had made urgent representations to the acting Brigadier-General, Lord Dornoch,

that for the sake of the Brigade Major's health and efficiency—
for without his apparatus Major Archdale was as bound as an
egg—a new commode should be constructed and sent through
the pass with the 88th Foot, the Connaught Rangers, when
they marched to reinforce the Division.

Blood pounded through Ogilvie's head still. He wondered
just how many kinds of a fool he had been. He was lying now,
face down, on that luxurious divan bed and he was alone. The
girl had gone at last when she had seen that he was adamant in
his refusal of her. She had been young and slim and her body
was as mobile as a kitten's; she had been none of Feroz Khan's
Peshawar hags. Her eyes, pools of darkness in a peach-soft
light-brown face, had given him looks of genuine desire. She
had come to him gently, and at first modestly, and had simply
taken his hand, leading him towards the bed. She had pressed
her body against his and then she had unbuttoned his khaki drill
tunic and slid soft hands inside to roam over his chest.

He remembered other things, among them her nakedness
when she had lowered her veil and then shrugged off her
flimsy clothing. It had been then that he had got up suddenly,
and moved away across the room, leaving her standing by the
divan. She had pleaded with him but he wouldn't give in, even
though he believed she would suffer at the hands of Ahmed
Khan for her failure to seduce the British officer. He had refused
to give in partly because his whole upbringing had conditioned
him against casual sex relationships and had rendered it almost
impossible for him to break through the barriers even when they
were down upon the other side. But also partly because he had
felt that he must not be guilty of trading with the enemy, must
never allow himself to be suborned by Ahmed Khan, who
would be wanting something in return for favours given and
received.

But—now that the danger was past and temptation overcome—he, like Mary Archdale, was facing his regrets and
finding them much more painful than she. Someone, he
recalled, had once said that a man's greatest regrets were always
for what he has *not* done—not for what he *has* done. Ogilvie
was pondering the truth of that when the door of his apartment
was opened up once again and Ahmed Khan himself entered,
alone. Smiling, he walked slowly across towards Ogilvie, who

122

sat up. Ahmed Khan said, "I have apologies to offer, Ogilvie sahib. I am told you sent the girl away, and—"

"You mustn't blame her," Ogilvie said quickly. "It was no fault of hers."

"Have no fear, I understand very well and the girl will not be punished. My apologies were not on her behalf, but on my own. I insulted you, by the implied suggestion that you would take my favours. I see now that you will not. You are a loyal young man, Ogilvie sahib. For this, I respect you."

"Thank you."

Ahmed Khan gave a slight dip of his head and moved over to one of the windows. He stood there looking out for a moment, then Ogilvie saw him give a hand-signal, probably to one of the two sentries. He turned away and said to Ogilvie, "I have other distractions which will perhaps be more to your liking. You shall hear."

A minute later Ogilvie heard. He heard, and heard with keen nostalgia, the familiar sound of wind being puffed into bagpipes and the tramp of marching men. He got up in surprise and looked out of a window. Some thirty men, Afridis, were marching up and down. As he watched the music swelled: they were playing Will Ye No Come Back Again. They played well and they marched smartly. Ogilvie felt tears pricking suddenly at his eyes. Once, his mother had taken him to St. James's Palace in London to watch the guard-changing ceremony. The Scots Guards, the Old Guard, were being relieved by the Coldstream. The slow march of the Scots off parade had been impressive and had engendered a fiercely patriotic fervour in the schoolboy. This outlandish march in the shadow of the Kafiristan hills was poignantly reminiscent, even to some extent in its setting, of that day when the music of the Scots Guards had beaten off the old walls of the enclosed courtyard of St. James's.

Ogilvie caught Ahmed Khan's sardonic eye. "Where did you get the pipes?" he asked.

"They were taken in battle by an uncle of my cousin on his mother's side, during the mutiny in India. They are old now but they are lovingly maintained as a trophy of war, and they play well, would you not agree, Ogilvie sahib?"

"Admirably. I congratulate you on the ability of your pipers, too."

Ahmed Khan bowed graciously. "The music they are playing," he said after a while. "If I may be mawkish for a moment, I suggest it is germaine to your own thoughts and wishes?"

"In what way?"

"You would wish to come back again—or rather, *go* back again, to your own land—the land that gave that music birth?"

Impatiently Ogilvie said, "Of course."

"Yes, indeed." Ahmed Khan looked gravely into his eyes, a brown hairy-backed hand trifling with a chain of gold hanging from his neck. "For myself, Ogilvie sahib, I see no reason why you should not do so."

"I thought prisoners were always killed, Ahmed Khan?"

"Yes?" The rebel seemed surprised; he lifted his eyebrows. "Then you are a brave man, Ogilvie sahib, for you have given no hint that you thought this." He added, "It is true, of course—I do not deny this—but there can always be exceptions. You have a saying in your country that the exception proves the rule. Perhaps, Ogilvie sahib, you can prove the truth of the saying."

"Oh?" Ogilvie looked him in the eyes. The pipes were still playing. "I've no intention of helping you, if that's what you're offering—safety in return for help."

"I see." Ahmed Khan shrugged, raised his hands, let them fall again to his sides. "This is, of course, what I am offering. Allow me to say that life can be made very uncomfortable for those who refuse to do as I wish. As a soldier, you will understand this?"

"I suppose so—in Afghanistan."

"Not only in Afghanistan. The British are not too squeamish at times, Ogilvie sahib. But I shall let the point pass. You do not change your mind?"

"No, never."

Ahmed Khan laughed. "I can always put that to the test, Ogilvie sahib—and I prophesy that it would be I who would win!" Suddenly he clasped his hands in front of his body and moved away, pacing the floor. After a while he swung round on Ogilvie again and said, "But I have no liking for uncivilized measures. Indeed I regret that it was necessary for one of your men to be shot so soon after your arrival here. Contrary to what I understand is said about me in British India, I am a civilized man, Ogilvie sahib. Had I not been, I would scarcely have bothered to learn the English tongue. It would be of little enough use to me were it not for the fact that I appreciate English literature, and English music also." He laughed again. "I dare say I am better read than you, Ogilvie sahib. British officers are not a reading class—it is considered women's entertainment, is it not? How foolish they are! What a lot they miss! I have read all the works of John Bunyan, Geoffrey Chaucer, Sir Walter Scott to name but a few. Shakespeare, of course, and Marlowe and Alexander Pope. And your great Charles Dickens, from whom I have learned an immense amount about the English character. You should not allow your novelists to reveal so many useful secrets! I would like to say that I have much admiration for many facets of the English character. As a race you are brave and mostly chivalrous, and to a large extent honest—except when it comes to dealing with the natives as you scornfully call us. You are an industrious nation and a conscientious one, and you do not lightly break treaties with powers as strong as yourselves. You also guard the little ones that do not much matter, and this gives you a reputation for fair play. All this is good so far as it goes. But oh, my dear young man, you are so stupid a nation, so very, very stupid, and at the same time the length of your arm of conquest is equalled only by the length of your prodding nose. Let us sit down, Ogilvie sahib, and discuss your stupidity without heat. I shall be obliged if you will pour me a glass of whisky—which is another British custom I have grown to like!"

He sat cross-legged on a large cushion and gestured Ogilvie to the armchair. Feeling a little foolish, Ogilvie said stiffly, "I'd rather not."

"You are also a demonstrably *polite* nation, Ogilvie sahib. What you really wish to say is, 'I damn well don't want to drink with a filthy native who is fighting my country', but this you will not say. Thus you are also a hypocritical nation." Ahmed Khan's dark eyes mocked him. "Come, sit down and we shall talk, and you shall drink. Do not behave like a spoilt little boy, Ogilvie sahib! Already you have magnificently fought one temptation. Do not martyr yourself by fighting them all, for they are really quite harmless."

Ogilvie scowled, then with a gesture of irresolution, sat. He was bewildered by this man. He poured the whisky, passing a tumbler to Ahmed Khan, who asked abruptly, "How much do you know of the quarrel between the Amir in Kabul and myself?"

"Only that it's hardly a quarrel. You've rebelled against him and seized this fort."

"That is all? You do not know the reason why?"

Ogilvie shook his head. "No."

"You do not concern yourself with reasons? They do not matter? Reasons are for the politicians, not the military? The military caste simply carries out the orders of the politicians?"

"Broadly, yes."

"And in detail yes, also!" Ahmed Khan gave a throaty chuckle. "I understand your system. We do things differently, Ogilvie sahib! That is the first thing for you to learn. The warriors make war, and when they win, they appoint the little scribblers, the officials, the men in offices. It is the military caste that runs affairs and gives the orders and makes the laws. That is the way we have always wished it, and we seek no change. Nor do we wish to have the interference of your country in our own affairs—"

"Then you should not act rebelliously, Ahmed Khan."

There was a light laugh, and a twinkle in the rebel's eye. "Oh, my dear young man, you show so very clearly that you do not understand! In effect, what I am rebelling about, as you put it, is quite simply the fact of British interference. This interference comes through our illustrious Amir in Kabul, to which city I am most heartily glad his influence is largely confined. The Amir, as you are no doubt aware, is friendly with your Government, he is its lackey, its lickspittle. Because I am not these things, I have a very large following. As the leader of that large following in Afghanistan, I must achieve their wishes for them. I wish no man harm, Ogilvie sahib; but you and the British must try to understand that I am a patriot who means to set the people of Afghanistan free of an unwelcome influence. Think, Ogilvie sahib—think, if your country had been invaded by the French again, subsequent to the invasion by William the Norman—in recent times—would you not resent any French influence thenceforward in the conduct of your affairs?"

"I suppose I would," Ogilvie answered guardedly. He recalled that Mary Archdale had said something similar in Peshawar.

"Of course you would, and such a resentment would be very

126

natural and proper. And would you not resent it if, in those circumstances, your Queen made agreements with the French, some of them secret agreements which even, let us say, her Prime Minister knew nothing of, and that because of those agreements your people suffered, and lost their independence?" Ahmed Khan made a sweeping gesture. "Of course you would —I need not ask the question at all really. And that, you see, is the precise counterpart of the position here in Afghanistan. Our people cry aloud—to me, Ogilvie sahib!" He smote himself on the breast, "To me—to depose the Amir and then to ask the British to be so good to leave Afghanistan alone. You must see the similarity between my hypothetical case in regard to your country, and the actual one in regard to my country. You cannot, except by the exercise of hypocrisy, resolve a conflict in your mind by saying that we in Afghanistan are merely filthy natives. We also feel pain and sorrow and joy, we also have wives and brothers and sons and fathers, we also die when shot, bleed when wounded—and we also have pride in our independence. Why is it wrong for us and yet right for you?"

"That's something I can't answer," Ogilvie said, and added curiously, "Why are you telling me all this, Ahmed Khan?"

"Because I prefer to reason with men rather than to kill them or torture them, though these things can become necessary. And for another reason also: I wish, as I have said, for your help, but it must be willing help. Do you understand?"

Ogilvie said, "I'm damned if I do! All I have gathered is, you intend to make use of me in some way—and I'll refuse to co-operate whatever you say or do."

Ahmed Khan bowed his head. "Well spoken, Ogilvie sahib," he said. "You have my respect. Your father would be proud of you—your Colonel also. But—it is not much I ask of you, and you may be able to be of great service to your own country. Do you wish to hear more?"

Ogilvie made a weary gesture. "I can't stop you talking, can I?"

Ahmed Khan got to his feet and stared down at Ogilvie. He said, "Ogilvie sahib, I wish for you to meet your father, man to man. I wish you to go out from here under a flag of truce, and talk to him, half way between my advanced line and the British positions. You see, I have things to offer him and I prefer the personal approach. When I have your word that you will go, and go willingly—for as I have said, that is most important—I shall send a message that will reach your father. Now do you understand?"

"I don't know if I do or not." Ogilvie bit his lip. "What if I refuse?"

Ahmed Khan's eyes seemed to glow at him. "In my possession I have two documents," he said slowly. "Agreements, the existence of both being unknown to the British. One, made as I have already told you with the Amir in Kabul, grants me my terms, namely, that he abdicates in my favour with ample financial recompense and full guarantees for the safety of himself and his family and servants. Because he knows my strength, he is willing to sign this document—*provided the British agree*, for he fears a punitive war against him if he acts without their approval, and I know he is right to have this fear. As for me, once I am in Kabul, I shall deal with any British demands or threats. In the meantime, the British must agree, if agree they do, to the treaty precisely as it stands and they must seek to attach no strings to their approval. In return they will be assured of a peaceful neighbour on this side of the Khyber Pass. Now—I realize very well that the British will in fact be certain to *refuse* their approval . . . unless, Ogilvie sahib, *you* can persuade them, through your father, that it would be wiser to give it."

"*Me?*"

"Yes, Ogilvie sahib, you, for—"

Ogilvie broke in with a jeering laugh. "Really, you do overrate my influence, you know! I might just as well save you the bother of preparing horses!"

"You are the General's own son—"

"Certainly, and so . . . look, Ahmed Khan, I think there's an awful lot you don't know about the British! Fathers don't often listen to their sons—and certainly don't take orders from them, or even advice! My father would simply laugh and—and ride away!"

"Not, I think, this time," Ahmed Khan said, shaking his head. "I have not yet told you of the second agreement. This is with the Imperial Russian Court in St. Petersburg, and it provides for me to overthrow the Amir by force with Russian help and then to admit the main Russian armies to march through Afghanistan to the Khyber. Do you understand what this means, Ogilvie sahib?"

Ogilvie had gone white. But he said, "I understand that this would hardly be the *freedom* you seek for your country, Ahmed Khan."

Ahmed Khan smiled. "It would not be the alternative I would choose, certainly, but if you should force me to choose it, let us say simply that the Russians would not be permitted to interfere in our affairs as the British have been permitted by our present Amir, indeed they would not seek to interfere—provided we allowed them free passage through to India! Or," he added with something like a twinkle in his eye, "if you prefer to think this of us, let me say simply that it is sometimes possible for other countries to be as two-faced as the British themselves. In any case, if the British will not give their peaceful consent to the one, then I, Ahmed Khan, effective Amir in Jalalabad, will sign the other immediately. You are a very young man, Ogilvie sahib, and a very junior officer in your army, but you have the great honour now of being the only representative of your Queen-Empress with whom I am able to treat personally. You may say, why do I not send my terms direct to Calcutta by means of the telegraph wires, but I would answer once again that I prefer the personal approach. Telegraphed terms would be no more than cursorily considered and then rejected. I wish you to convince your father that I mean all I say and am able to carry it out. The future of the Frontier lies very largely in your hands now. I urge you to consider this matter deeply, and quickly, for time is running out and my people are becoming restless."

Throughout, he had spoken quietly and sincerely and with emphasis. When he had finished he bowed and turned away. Soon after he had left the room Ogilvie heard the pipers' music fading. His mind in a whirl, he went over to a window and looked out. The light was fading as well now, in time with the dying pipes. He saw the pipers halt outside a wooden door in a part of the thick courtyard wall that extended from the outer part of the tower block, and then go inside. A few minutes later they came out, having evidently stowed their instruments. They marched away. They looked a well-disciplined body of men. If all his forces were like that, Ahmed Khan could probably put his threat into effect and, in giving free passage to the Russian armies, imperil the whole delicate balance of the North-West Frontier. And that, having its repercussions inside India, could even lead to another mutiny.

Ogilvie felt almost sick with the weight of decision that had fallen upon him. On the face of it, there was really no reason why he shouldn't agree to going out under a flag of truce; but to plead the rebels' cause was going to strike, not only his father but also the ultimate command in India, as a somewhat curious act for a British officer.

Eight

OGILVIE passed a largely sleepless night. All through the dark hours he heard the rumble of the guns in the distance, the guns that would be firing against the British positions. His thoughts were with the battalion, and no less with the men who endured their captivity in lesser comfort than he. Vicariously he shared their ordeal in that dungeon cellar, knowing too well what they were having to endure; knowing, too, how mutinously Private Burns would be reacting to his own preferential treatment. Burns had applauded him that day off Aden when he had stood up to Andrew Black, but he would not be applauding now. That irresolute moment of weakness might come home to roost in this present situation; men like Burns, as Ogilvie was beginning to understand, often despised lack of firmness in an officer more than did the loyal soldier. It even, in some odd way, exacerbated their class-war instincts—perhaps because it gave point to the notion that officers gained their commissions by birth rather than by ability; a hard argument to refute. And men like Burns were something new to the army—or rather, it would be more correct to say that authority's reactions to them were new. Every regiment had always had a handful of similar characters but in earlier years they had been tamed by the lash. Men like Andrew Black knew how to deal with them far better than he . . .

Restlessly, Ogilvie paced his splendid apartment, for hour after hour, listening to the guns, wondering when Ahmed Khan would come for his answer, wondering what he should do when he did come. And as he thought and worried and paced, he was startled to find subversive ideas creeping like dangerous snakes into his own head. Looked at objectively, a British presence in Afghanistan simply couldn't possibly be represented to the native rebels as a good thing. They would not be won over, and the peace that would come after a British victory by force of arms would be an uneasy peace. Ahmed Khan's reasoning, from his own viewpoint, had been right and proper enough,

131

if one disregarded the fact that he was acting against his own legally-ruling Amir. And even that was far from being a unique situation. Oliver Cromwell had rebelled against the King of England, not that Ogilvie approved of that; and the army had subsequently restored the Monarchy by what in a sense had also been an act of insurrection. Many English kings, indeed, had gained the throne by rebellion, mostly in the name of the people, whether or not the people cared. Anything done in the name of patriotism was all right. And Ogilvie had a definite feeling Ahmed Khan was a patriot. There was no doubt at all about the fact that the British presence was the sole cause of the lengthy fighting and the killing, in the sense that they had thrust themselves into a family quarrel in order to gain their own ends; and Ogilvie found himself wondering if the holding of the *status quo* was justification enough for the deaths.

In the morning, by which time Ogilvie, succumbing at last to exhaustion, had slept a little, Captain Andrew Black, in the British lines, happened upon an untoward occurrence that made his blood run cold. He had risen early, very soon after the sun had crept in blazing splendour over the eastern horizon to bathe the plain and the hills in gold. He had taken a walk by himself and coming from a hollow a little way down the hillside in front of the defences, he had happened to catch a curious and alarming flash as of a mirror reflecting the sunlight.

He sank back behind a boulder and kept very still. Again he caught a flash; and then again. Somebody was signalling, and although there were no answering flashes so far as Black could see, it was fairly obvious that whoever was flashing was doing so towards the enemy lines spread across the defile. Black swore to himself. He was unable to read the message, for he was seeing only occasional flashes, as the spy so used his mirror from time to time as to bring it within his vision. He came out from behind the boulder, went fast but silently back the way he had come, and found the Sergeant of the Guard. Quickly he told his story; at once the Sergeant and two file of men set off down the hillside and closed the hollow. They made their capture as the man was coming away. Before breakfast the Divisional Commander, who had now joined the Brigade on the southern peak — minus what he referred to as 'the damn Staff' — had been informed and had dealt with the matter. Before the spy, having been closely but vainly questioned, was shot upon his personal order, Sir Iain sent for the Brigade Major. When Archdale reached the H.Q. tent he found the General beside himself with rage.

"You have the damned impertinence to bring what in effect amounts to an unauthorized article of equipment with you, and then cause the cluttering-up of the field telegraph with a damn silly request for a new one after you've been damn fool enough to allow it to be destroyed by enemy action. You then cap this with a total lack of appreciation of the need for security . . . by appointing, as what I'm told is called your bum-*havildar*, a man who's in the pay of the blasted rebel! You've been harbouring a spy in your monstrous damn commode, Brigade Major—a damn spy! I won't have it, d'you hear me—I won't *have* it!"

An immense breakfast was brought to Ogilvie; having little appetite, he merely picked at the dishes so as to keep some strength in his body. After the meal had been removed, Ahmed Khan came to him again, accompanied this time by a bearded officer of his cavalry. "Good morning, Ogilvie sahib," he said. "I trust you have passed a pleasant night?"

"Thank you."

"Also that you have given thought to my proposal."

"Yes."

"And your conclusion, Ogilvie sahib?"

Ogilvie said stiffly, "I await further clarification, Ahmed Khan."

"I would have thought my words clear enough already. However . . ." Ahmed Khan shrugged, smiled somewhat enigmatically and walked across towards a window. The cavalry officer remained by the door, his face impassive. Ahmed Khan stared thoughtfully out of the window for some moments, then turned suddenly and said, "Ogilvie sahib, you will no doubt have heard the artillery fire during the night?"

Ogilvie nodded.

"It was a very sustained bombardment, Ogilvie sahib, and most of it was concentrated on the *northern* hill—the one, you will remember, that was taken by another brigade, not your own. I fear the casualties will have been quite exceptionally heavy. The same may occur tonight, but directed towards the hill held by your own regiment."

"And your own men, Ahmed Khan? The British did not fire back?"

Ahmed Khan shrugged again. "There were casualties, but they were light enough not to cause me concern. I understand that quite early in the engagement, your British marauders lost many of their guns—"

"We're no marauders, Ahmed Khan—"

"No, Ogilvie sahib?" The native gave him a long, cool look, his heavy eyebrows lifted. "What other name would you give yourselves, then?"

Ogilvie flushed, glared. "I don't think this is getting us very far, Ahmed Khan."

"No farther than military action against me is getting your soldiers, perhaps?" There was no response from Ogilvie and the Afghan smiled obliquely, catching the eye of the bearded soldier by the door. "Allow me to introduce Major Faiz Gheza, who commands my cavalry squadron in the fort."

The Major bowed; Ogilvie returned this with a stiff nod. Faiz Gheza said in a deep, rumbling voice, "Ogilvie sahib, I am happy to make your acquaintance."

Again Ogilvie nodded, but said nothing. Ahmed Khan went on, "Faiz Gheza will command the cavalry escort that will take you to the meeting place with your father. You see, Ogilvie sahib, I am assuming you will agree to my proposals, and agree as willingly as I require." He lifted a hand as Ogilvie started to speak, and his voice grew harsher when he went on, "You will please allow me to finish. I do not wish an impression to be given that you are under duress. I wish you to see my point of view as already explained to you, and to put this convincingly to your father. I am wise enough to know that you British do not treat with anyone until you see an advantage to yourselves —or until you have been made to realize that the alternative to treating is certain defeat for yourselves, even if that defeat will come only in the long term. I think you will do your best to be as convincing as I want you to be."

"What makes you think that?"

"Because of what will happen if you fail to convince your father of the absolute need to make urgent representations to your High Command, your Governor-General in Council—or your Government in London, perhaps, if necessary—to order the withdrawal of all your soldiers."

Ogilvie said, "I asked you last night, now I'll ask you again: what happens if I don't do this?"

"You mean, of course, apart from the putting into effect of the agreement with the Czar of All the Russias?"

Ogilvie's lips felt dry. "Yes," he said.

"If you refuse to go out under a flag of truce, Ogilvie sahib, or if, upon your meeting, your father refuses his co-operation, a good deal of unpleasantness will be suffered by . . . not by yourself, Ogilvie sahib, but by your men now in my dungeon. This, I believe you will be unwilling to permit as a result of any act of omission on your part. I am a good judge of character, Ogilvie sahib, besides which I have been informed as to your demeanour when you were told yesterday that you were to be accommodated more comfortably than the rest of my prisoners. My conclusion, Ogilvie sahib, is that you will not wish to bring trouble upon your men through no fault of their own. Am I not right?"

Ogilvie took a deep breath and said, "You're right that I wouldn't want to. But if necessary . . . they'll do their duty, they'll understand why it is they have to suffer."

"Understanding will not make it any easier to bear, Ogilvie sahib, nor will it, I suggest, lessen your own feelings of responsibility. But now, I think, you have a full awareness of what is required of you, and of what will happen if you do not do as I wish. May I have your formal word of agreement that you will go out to meet your Divisional Commander? You see no harm in this, surely?"

Ogilvie hesitated; *ipso facto*, there was indeed little harm in a meeting. It was the implications that might be read into his action, as he had feared during the night, that worried him. But had he the right to consider his own future against his men's present? It seemed to him that he had not, and after a few more moments' thought he said in a low voice, "Yes. Yes, I'll go."

"I congratulate you. You have made a right decision, Ogilvie sahib. I shall leave you now, and soon Faiz Gheza will return for you, and you will ride towards the British position. You see, anticipating your agreement, I had already sent a message to the British and have had their answer. Because I quoted your name and because it is known prisoners were taken, they have agreed to a meeting, though at this stage no mention has been made of the fact that you will bring terms. As it happens, your father is already with the soldiers holding the peak." He turned away and, with the cavalry officer, left the room. He was back within an hour, again with Faiz Gheza and this time with two dismounted troopers as well. Ogilvie was led from the room, back along the passage and down the steps into the courtyard. Here all seemed quiet; the gunfire had ceased some while earlier, no doubt to clear the air, as it were, for the two truce parties to meet in what for the time being would be a no-man's-land between the lines. Ogilvie followed Ahmed Khan across the courtyard towards the guarded entry to the dungeon where the British soldiers were being held. The air was very still; there was a tenseness, an expectancy. Ogilvie's and the escort's footfalls echoed out across the dusty space. Ahead an order was given and two of the men who had been standing on either side of the door into the cellar turned to open it up and then stood with their rifles ready as the soldiers were ordered out.

Led by Corporal Brown, they stumbled up from the pitch darkness. They blinked in the strong sunlight. They were haggard, unshaven, dirty—but they came up like men, like the Scots soldiers they were, with heads high and shoulders straight. Ogilvie's heart swelled. No one, not even Private Burns, was going to let the regiment down today. Brown, who had seen Ogilvie as he reached the courtyard, waited until the rank and file were in line and then slammed to the salute, fingers quivering at the brim of his helmet. "Ten and a half file of the 114th Highlanders present and correct. Sir!" He was grinning sardonically, but he remained at attention as though awaiting orders.

Ogilvie was about to speak when Ahmed Khan cut in. He gave a sharp command in Pushtu and the native guards, using their rifles, pushed the soldiers back until they were standing against the wall above the dungeon. There they waited. A few moments later Ogilvie heard marching feet and when he turned he saw the Regimental Sergeant-Major being brought along from the right, and, behind him, a squad of rebel infantry all armed with the long-barrelled rifles.

Cunningham, like Corporal Brown, saluted as he was marched past, his kilt swinging as though on parade at Invermore. He was lined up with the others. After this Ahmed Khan took a large, curiously-shaped iron key from the folds of his clothing and held it out to Faiz Gheza, who took it, turned about smartly, and marched towards the wall where the men were standing. He reached up, pushed the key into a small hole in the stonework, a hole that Ogilvie had not noticed until now, and turned it by means of an iron bar which he picked up from the ground and thrust through its ring. As he turned the key, the iron sheet set in the ground immediately to the left of the line of men — the iron that Ogilvie had seen earlier — began moving. A gap formed in the ground, grew larger as the cavalry-man, sweating at the key, moved the iron plate back towards the wall. Faiz Gheza was a man of powerful physique but the effort taxed his strength visibly. Soon, as the iron moved away to slide right under the wall amid a cascade of sandy dust and grit, Ogilvie looked down into a shallow trench, some thirty feet long and six feet wide but no more than perhaps eighteen inches deep. Faiz Gheza stopped his work at the key, turned to Ahmed Khan and said in Pushtu, "All is ready, Your Highness."

Ahmed Khan nodded. He said, "Into the trench, all of you. Lie flat, with your feet towards the wall. Quickly!"

Brown, Cunningham, all of them stood staring, unable, it seemed, to believe Ahmed Khan could have meant what he said. There was a total silence for a moment then Ogilvie said, "You can't do this, Ahmed Khan. It is . . . uncivilized, horrible!"

"Your people regard us already as uncivilized, Ogilvie sahib."

"Then I would have thought you'd want to prove them wrong."

The rebel shrugged, folding his hands inside his clothing. "Afterwards, yes. For now, it is necessary to use all methods to bring about the results I wish."

"If you put the men in that trench," Ogilvie said, "I'll not go out under any flag of truce."

Ahmed Khan merely smiled patiently. "Oh yes, you will," he said. "Because they will be put down there whatever you do. Only they will not be released until you have gone, and have come back again to this fort with your mission completed and with a favourable answer — do you understand?"

Ogilvie sweated; he was in a cleft stick and he knew it. Cunningham and Brown and the others were watching his face; the R.S.M. made a slight movement of his jaw, seeming to set it firmer than ever beneath the great moustache whose points, now unwaxed, were drooping on either side of his lips. His eyes were hard but strength-giving as they stared into Ogilvie's. Once again there was a silence. This time it was broken by a movement from the British ranks, a surge forward, an almost involuntary movement of the whole made as one. Ogilvie and Cunningham shouted at them to stop and move back, but it was too late already. There was a single shot from Faiz Gheza's revolver and one of them fell dead. At the same time four rifles swung to cover Ogilvie and Ahmed Khan called, "Remain still or your officer will die."

Burns looked like saying something, his mean, peaked face savage, but he was prevented from uttering by a roar from the Regimental Sergeant-Major. Cunningham said, "We'll do as the rebel says, lads. All of us. We'll leave this to Mr. Ogilvie. I for one believe he'll get us out of here and honourably too — and he's the only one who can. If we let the officer be shot, then it'll all be up with the lot of us. You'll all now follow my example. That is an order."

It was, Ogilvie thought, almost grotesque. Cunningham moved away from the native soldiers forming his escort, came across Ogilvie's front, halted, turned left, saluted. Formally he said, "Permission to carry on. Sir!"

"Yes, thank you, Sarn't-Major."

Another salute, smartly returned by Ogilvie, and the R.S.M. turned about, swinging his kilt grandly around his legs. Then, stiff and straight, he marched towards the shallow trench, halted, removed his pith-helmet, placed it carefully on the ground, and lowered himself into the trench, lying flat on his back with his arms down his sides. The remainder of the prisoners, white-faced, shaken, muttering, urged on by the rifles, did likewise. When they were all lying still Ahmed Khan nodded at Faiz Gheza, who turned back to his key, inserted the iron bar again, and slowly closed the metal cover, sliding it back across the chests of the men. There were cries and gasps as the iron rasped over their uniforms, over their bodies, closing out the air and the light of the day. Ogilvie was watching Cunningham. The R.S.M.'s face was expressionless, the mouth firmly clamped, eyes stoically open to watch the progress of the coffin-like lid. It cleared that massive chest by no more than a quarter of an inch, then moved on over his face and settled back in its slots with a slight but audible clang.

Ogilvie looked at Ahmed Khan with bitter loathing. He said,

"I suggest we don't delay now. If you allow those men to die, there'll be no peace in Afghanistan until you've been taken through the Khyber and hanged as a common murderer outside a civil jail in India."

Ahmed Khan looked furious for a moment, then waved a hand.

"Words, mere words," he said. "However, we shall not delay. I am as anxious as you are for speed." He called to Faiz Gheza to mount his squadron. Faiz Gheza acknowledged the order, returned the key of the trench to Ahmed Khan, and despatched one of the infantrymen, who doubled across the courtyard. Within the next few minutes Ogilvie heard horses' hooves. Eight cavalrymen with tall lances came up at a walk, two of them leading saddled mounts, big black stallions both. Faiz Gheza took the reins of one of these and swung himself up agilely. Ogilvie was told to take the other animal, which he did. When he was mounted Ahmed Khan looked up at him and said, "A word of warning, Ogilvie sahib. Major Faiz Gheza speaks English equally as well as I myself. He will be listening carefully to all you say to your father. You will confine yourself strictly to what already you know you have to say. You will say nothing else, you will answer no questions not pertaining strictly to the terms you will be offering, you will in fact volunteer nothing whatever. You will make no mention of my punishment trench. If asked, as no doubt you will be, about your men, you will say that all the soldiers are safe and well and that naturally they and you will be released at once when my terms have been accepted by your Government and your armies are removing themselves through the Khyber Pass. You will make no mention of my source of information in the British lines. Is all this quite clear, Ogilvie sahib?"

"Quite clear."

Ahmed Khan nodded at Faiz Gheza. The order was given to move out. Ogilvie rode towards the gatehouse, his kilt rucked up uncomfortably around his waist, the back of it trailing over the stallion's rump. He must look a curious sight, he thought. With the squadron in close escort around him, he rode past the quarter-guard and out into the stinking alleys of the town, past the mud walls once again, past the bastions and out into the shifting sand-hills, heading west towards those distant peaks held by the British and Mahrattas, towards the line of rebel troops which with their artillery were waiting to keep Ahmed

Khan's supply route open against the time, soon now, when the replenishment train would move through the valley.

The courtyard of the fort grew intensely hot as the sun climbed a clear, metallic sky. There was little wind, no more than a gentle zephyr to ruffle the rebel standard flying from the battlements. Quite soon the iron cover over the trench began to absorb heat, acting as a kind of kettle in reverse, warming that restricted area from above instead of from below. The effect was no less wicked. The stale air grew staler and more foetid, more sweat-laden. The men beneath the cover could scarcely find room to move a hand or a foot. Insects crawled over them, over the exposed areas of their skin, and they were powerless to brush them away. Flies gathered, buzzed and bit, moved unimpeded over lips and into nostrils. Small scuffles and cries indicated the presence of rats. R.S.M. Cunningham was thinking that if ever they were released they would surely have the plague upon them after this. He had tried to lend the men strength by talking to them, but even his voice didn't seem to carry properly in that enclosed dead atmosphere and so he had stopped, feeling thoroughly dispirited himself in any case. Soon he felt the burning heat of the iron pass into the metal pieces on his uniform — to say nothing of the fact that his chest and stomach, when he breathed, made direct contact with the cover. He lay there as inert as the others, trying not to hear Private Burns, who was next but one to him in the line, keeping up a continuous low whining dirge of fear and of hate against everybody in his universe.

Under the white flag fluttering like a guidon from the lance of the right-hand man of the leading pair of riders, Ogilvie and his escort moved across the desolation of the plain, coming up behind the rebel line thrown across the valley. There was no sign of life from the hilltops on either side, but as they neared the advanced rebel position Ogilvie saw a mounted party cantering out from the mouth of the valley under a large white flag. He was surprised to see cavalry, since the brigade had brought no horses, but supposed this was his father's personal escort as Divisional Commander in the field. A couple of hundred yards from the rebel line, the British party halted. There were four officers and eight men — the same size escort as their antagonists. As his own party came through the line and neared the British riders, Ogilvie watched the square figure of his father in the centre. An A.D.C. was alongside him; no General Staff officers. On either side of the pair were Lord Dornoch and Andrew Black. The cavalry escort, he saw, were men of the Guides. His own party slowed as they approached the British group, halting ten yards away. Faiz Gheza saluted; Sir Iain Ogilvie returned the salute punctiliously, then without any preamble snapped, "Well, sir? What do you wish to say to me?"

Faiz Gheza said, "General sahib, I represent my leader, His Highness Ahmed Khan, Amir in Jalalabad—"

"Amir in fiddlesticks."

"As you please, General sahib. May I ask, General sahib, to whom I have the honour of speaking?"

Gruffly Sir Iain answered, "The Lieutenant-General Commanding, 9th Indian Division."

"I may take it, General sahib, that you represent your High Command?"

Sir Iain seemed to rise in his stirrups and said haughtily, "You may take it that I represent, for all present purposes, Almighty God—through the person of Her Imperial Majesty Queen Victoria, Empress of India, good friend and ally of your ruler, the Amir of Afghanistan. I repeat, what do you wish to say?"

Whilst this exchange had been taking place Ogilvie had been studying the British officers. His father's face was stiff and formal and at the same time hot with anger and disdain; he clearly had no liking for any parleys with the enemy, with rebels, and especially with a subordinate, a mere commander of a cavalry squadron. Ogilvie was as certain as he could be as to what his father would answer to the terms—at least as to the content of that answer. The language he would use was the only matter for surmise, and even that wouldn't be much of a guess. Yet Ogilvie knew he had to convince him, both on account of the men below the courtyard at the fort and because he felt in his bones that the acceptance of the terms meant the only hope of lasting peace. He looked at the other officers. The Colonel, he felt, was more concerned with Ogilvie himself than with the formal establishment of the status of the opposing representatives. Dornoch was studying his face as if trying to assess his conduct in captivity and to read his mind. It made Ogilvie feel uncomfortable, and he looked at Black, but Black was withdrawn and sardonic and was refusing to meet his eye. Ogilvie didn't like anything about this meeting.

Faiz Gheza answered his father's question: "I come with terms, General sahib."

"Terms?" The General started, glared. His face went purple, seemed to swell over the top of his collar. "I have neither the authority nor the intention to discuss terms with a rebel!" Then he added, "What, pray, are these . . . *terms*?"

"General sahib, your son will tell you this." Faiz Gheza moved his horse a little aside, giving Ogilvie room to move past.

Sir Iain snapped, "My son — hey? Why — why him?"

"General sahib, he wishes himself to do so, because he believes them to be worthy of acceptance."

"The devil he does!" Sir Iain was thoroughly put off his stroke, that was obvious. "What the devil does he know about it?" He opened his mouth again, but Dornoch leaned across to him and whispered in his ear and he said ungraciously, "Oh, very well! Let Ogilvie speak for himself, then, but no damn nonsense, Ogilvie, mind that!"

Ogilvie said, "Sir, I wish to — "

"Wish? Wish? Don't you mean you're *commanded* — commanded by that damn rebel — hey?"

Ogilvie hesitated for a second, felt himself going red, then said firmly, thinking of his responsibilities towards the men in the fort, "No, sir. I *wish* to put Ahmed Khan's terms to you. May I have permission to do so?"

Sir Iain seemed incapable of speech. He glanced fractionally at Lord Dornoch, then at the A.D.C. He opened his mouth, shut it again, then nodded his head wordlessly. Ogilvie said, "Briefly, sir, Ahmed Khan's terms are as follows. If the British forces are withdrawn, there will be peace — "

"Peace! *Peace*, in which the rebel will defeat the duly authorized ruler of his country?"

Ogilvie, very conscious of Faiz Gheza's close proximity, broke out in a sweat. He would never, never bring this off successfully, never make his father understand. He said hoarsely, "No, sir, I don't believe that will happen. I believe Ahmed Khan is sincere. Certainly he wishes, and so do his people, to depose the present Amir. That is part of the terms offered. I gather the Amir is regarded as—as a British puppet, and—"

"May I remind you, sir, that you are, or have been, fighting on the Amir's behalf?"

Ogilvie nodded. "I know, sir. I know how all this sounds, but I believe we have to face the facts. Ahmed Khan has a very strong following—"

"So *he* says."

"Yes, sir. But he has already drafted an agreement which in fact the Amir is ready to sign—"

"I know nothing of this!"

"No, sir," Ogilvie said patiently, "no one does, except Ahmed Khan and the Amir. But the Amir is willing to abdicate in favour of Ahmed Khan, peacefully, provided the British Government agrees and does not try to mount a punitive expedition against his country. For his part, Ahmed Khan will maintain the peace afterwards."

"You say this agreement exists already?"

"Yes, sir."

"You've seen it?"

"No, sir."

"Then what the devil are you talking about, boy? This is bluff—sheer damn bluff!"

"I don't think it is, sir. I believe what Ahmed Khan has told me. It all sounds—logical."

"Logical, does it? Ha! What the devil's *logic*?" Sir Iain's mouth was a thin line like a trap. "Well? What's the alternative to all this—this damn fiddlemetits?"

Ogilvie said, "The entry of Russian troops into Afghanistan, sir, and their march on the Khyber."

Sir Iain said, "Good . . . God." Ogilvie could see the amazement and the consternation and the fury in his father's face. The effect on the other officers was equally electric. There was a hurried, whispered conference. Black was apart from this, a superior and sardonically bitter smile twisting his lips as, at last, he looked straight at James Ogilvie. Meanwhile an argument was developing, and Sir Iain was tending to bluster; the A.D.C. was looking worried, as well he might; so was Dornoch, who seemed disapproving of something the General had said. Then suddenly Sir Iain looked across at his son and raised his voice. He said coldly, "I want some clarification of the threat regarding the Russians. You needn't bother to go into the overall political situation for my benefit, Ogilvie. I think we're *all* well enough aware the Czar would welcome Afghan co-operation in pushing his forces to the Khyber. What else is there?"

Ogilvie said, "Ahmed Khan has another agreement in his possession. This is with the Czar. It permits a full-scale entry into Afghanistan . . . that is all I can say, sir. Except that they'll clear the country of our forces and then garrison the passes to keep us out. And if that's allowed to happen, it means a war."

"I've worked that out for myself already, thank you!" Sir Iain gnawed at the ends of his moustache. "It means a war all right — bloody war. The immediate committal of all troops in the Murree and Ootacamund commands — and massive drafts from home, which'll take time to arrive. Too much damn time!" His father stared at him keenly. "Why does the rebel think *you* can persuade me to recommend his terms be granted?"

"I've said already, sir . . . because I think he means what he says. He has persuaded *me*."

"Of what?" The voice was like a whiplash.

"That a great deal of bloodshed would be avoided by accepting the inevitable, sir."

"*Accepting the inevitable?*" The General's whole body seemed to quiver. "Now you listen to me, boy! There's never been any damn inevitability about the British Army — except that it's always going to win a victory! We shall win this one too!"

"Perhaps, sir. But with a colossal loss of life if the Russians come through. I believe Ahmed Khan when he says he has the support of the vast majority of his people, that it is only the British that are keeping the Amir on the throne. And what is to be gained by winning a victory for a people who forever after must be kept subdued by force? Why should we do this?"

This time Sir Iain did stand in his stirrups as he shouted, "Because your Queen and country order us to — that's why! As a reason, it's good enough for me. It should be that much the better for a damn subaltern! What's that man done to you, boy? Turned you into a damn traitor — or a eunuch for his pleasure?"

Ogilvie started as though hit with a bullet. "Father!" he said, going crimson.

"No damn father — your Divisional Commander, to whom you have the impertinence to speak treason!" Sir Iain, with obvious difficulty, took a grip on himself. "*My* father would turn in his grave to hear you talk like this! Now—let me tell you a thing or two. You're still wet behind the ears—all damn subalterns are! You're a baby—a baby in military matters. You don't know a thing, not a damn thing, about fighting, or about the Frontier. You're not alone in that, of course. None of the damn Staff in Whitehall know a damn thing about the Frontier either! They sit on their arses and talk, and have the effrontery to tell *us* what to do and how to fight our troops. Damn popinjays, the lot of them, strutting up and down outside the Palace, going to garden parties and doing their fighting in bed with the wives and daughters of the peerage! Meanwhile, I'm in command out here before Jalalabad and I take my orders from Sir George White in Calcutta and no one else. Now listen to this: whatever strength the rebel may think he has in the rest of Afghanistan, he's powerless unless he can get it through to him *here*, because if it doesn't come through, we're going to crush him and then it'll be too late—hey? We've ringed him in—except for that gap behind me." The General waved an arm to the rear. "That's our job—our one and only job, d'you hear me, boy?—to close the gap and complete the circle. *Then* we have him! This campaign depends not upon terms, but on one thing and one thing only: the stopping of that supply column. After that, Jalalabad is as good as fallen to my Division. Understood?"

Dully Ogilvie said, "Yes, sir."

"I hope it is," his father snapped. "Behave as a man now! Go back to Jalalabad—tell the rebel all I've said. Tell him I reject his terms out of hand, that I'll have no trading with him—"

"Sir," Ogilvie broke in with desperation, thinking, as he had been thinking all along, of the men in their plight beneath Ahmed Khan's courtyard. "You'd not consider passing his terms on to Calcutta?"

"Certainly not," Sir Iain answered promptly. "His terms are sheer impertinence, designed only to cause a division of opinion among the politicians—which will have the immediate effect of weakening our whole military effort. The next thing I knew, I'd be ordered to hold my troops back—even let that damn supply column through, I shouldn't wonder—while they thought the matter over! So the answer's no!"

Ogilvie tried to reach his father through his eyes and his

expression, to make him understand that he had other reasons, reasons that he could not express, for being so insistent; but it was too late. Already the General was turning away with an air of finality. Ogilvie tried once more. He called out, "Sir, I would appreciate a word with my Colonel, if I may."

Sir Iain stopped his horse. He waved an arm. "If Lord Dornoch's willing, *I* see no reason why not," he said distantly.

Dornoch rode forward.

His eyes seemed to search Ogilvie's face as they had done earlier. His own face was anxious as before, and he was frowning, and there was a willingness in his expression to read and learn, as though all along he had felt something had been left unsaid. "You must not worry about your situation, Ogilvie," he said simply. "You were taken in battle. There is no dishonour attaching to that."

"Thank you, sir. I . . . I think my father has been a little hasty, sir."

"Oh?"

"I think Ahmed Khan's terms should be referred to Calcutta."

Dornoch studied him closely, frowning still. "You are very insistent, James," he said at last. "Is there anything you wish to add to what you have told your father?" There was no answer, but he could read in James Ogilvie's eyes that there was indeed more and he had a fairly good idea as to what it was. He asked, "How have you been treated, James? You look well enough."

"I am well, sir."

"And Mr. Cunningham—and the men?"

There was a slight pause, a meaningful one to Dornoch, then Ogilvie said, "They are well too, sir."

"Not badly treated—no rough measures?"

"No, sir."

"I see. You will, of course, bear in mind, James, that even if they had been, and I believe you when you say they have not— it would not be possible for that to be taken into account?"

Ogilvie's face fell, though he nodded and said, "Yes, sir." Dornoch had understood, at least; but he had rebuked him. A commander could not allow a campaign to be altered, much less abandoned, for the sake of a mere handful of soldiers. They would be avenged later, naturally, but for now they had ceased to exist in the military mind. He should have known, of course; and in fact at the back of his mind he did, but had been hoping for a miracle; further, he had gone rather more than half way in quite genuinely seeing Ahmed Khan's viewpoint. Now his mind was a muddle and he felt that his father might be right and he'd been a traitor and a fool as well. He hung his head; Dornoch stared at him a while longer then turned his horse and walked the animal back towards the waiting British group. There was a longish conference, and his father seemed at first angry, then more amenable. Ogilvie caught a word or two here and there: a mention of there being no option, that terms had been proposed and could not be rejected out-of-hand . . . things like that. It all took some time. Ogilvie brooded, conscious all the while of the presence of Faiz Gheza and the native cavalry, of the guns in the native lines behind and the concealed British artillery on the heights. Soon now those guns would be in action again, more men would die or end their lives as helpless cripples selling matches in the streets, begging, playing music-hall songs to the crowds in Piccadilly for the contemptuously-tossed halfpennies. The Imperial arrogance of the old lady in Windsor Castle; the inflexibility of parliament; the stupidity of generals; the 'patriotism'—vengeance might be a more appropriate word—of the British man-in-the-street—all these would be the really blameworthy things, but no one in Britain would in fact blame them. They would blame Ahmed Khan, of course. He was a native. But this, after all, was Ahmed Khan's land, its own peoples' land, and this was a stupid war. An agreement honourable to both sides might well bring more lasting peace than any number of campaigns such as this one. Fighting would break out again and again if they did not sign a treaty. Surely a soldier's job was finished when he had reached the point of possibility of a negotiated peace formula?

At last the conference ended and Lord Dornoch rode towards the rebel squadron. Sir Iain had pointedly turned his back and was now staring towards the British-held hills, but Ogilvie had caught sight of his face and had seen a gleam of something like triumph in it, and a kind of slyness too, which wasn't like him. Reaching him Dornoch said steadily in a loud voice, "The General orders me to say that Ahmed Khan's terms will be forwarded to higher authority, but he offers no guarantee of a quick answer," then, without another word, he turned and rejoined the others, and the party retreated at a gallop towards the British position. Faiz Gheza gave orders to his own squadron and they swung round for Jalalabad.

"They'd be rejected out of hand," the General said contemptuously as he spurred his horse, "if White was allowed his way! Trouble is—he wouldn't be! He'd *have* to forward 'em. That's when the trouble starts—the weak-kneed vacillation, the insidious thoughts that perhaps peace is better than war after all. Damn buggers! There's only the one thing for it, Dornoch."

"Yes, sir?"

"I've agreed to forward 'em, therefore forwarded they must be, of course. Some day. I didn't say *when* I'd forward 'em—did I?"

"I don't think I quite understand, Sir Iain?"

"Don't you, my dear fellow? Then I'll explain. The field telegraph is needed for urgent messages and can't possibly be cluttered up with long signals detailing terms. Neither can I possibly spare a detail to ride back through the Khyber. A little delay, Dornoch, a little expedient delay—until we've wiped out that confounded supply column!"

"I don't think I can approve of that."

"Not approve?" The General looked sideways, face set. "Who the devil asked for your damned approval? I didn't! I gave an order. And who are *you* to disapprove, man? Damn it all, when I commanded the 114th you were a damn company commander! Confounded impudence!"

Dornoch cleared his throat. "Then let me put it differently, General. I'm not sure it's wise."

"Wise—hey? Fiddlesticks. I'm not an academic man, Dornoch. Never read a book in my life, except military history. Wise—ha. I have to make *decisions*, all too often on insufficient knowledge, I agree. I distrust wisdom—damned if I don't!" He pulled at his moustache. "Why don't you think it's *wise*?"

"I'm thinking of those men in the fort. As I said, I'm convinced they're being made to suffer, and probably atrociously. That was what Ogilvie was wanting to tell us. When Ahmed Khan sees no results from his talk with you—they'll suffer more."

"I know. I think of the men too, Dornoch. I'm not entirely insensitive to the fact my own flesh and blood's there with 'em."

148

"I'm sorry, sir."

"No need to be sorry, or to feel you have to apologize. It's your privilege to consider your men, Dornoch. I no longer have that privilege. I often wish I were just a battalion commander again. No, my job's to accept the sacrifice when I think it necessary for the good of the majority. My brother, the one who went into the Navy, can't think why, once served under a Captain on some hell-hole of a foreign station—West Africa. I remember him telling me . . . some man asked for a posting home because the climate was killing him. Medical Officer backed this. But d'you know what the Captain said, Dornoch? He said he would willingly send any man to his death if he thought it was for the good of his country. That's what he did. He didn't grant the request and the man died. That's all. I may be in the same position as that naval Captain."

Ogilvie and his escort rode back into the fort, past the quarter-guard. The sun was high now; the time was past noon. The courtyard sweltered in the grip of that sun. Men moved about lazily. There were no guards on the dungeon or the trench outside it. Ogilvie fancied he saw a shimmer of heat rising from the metal plate.

Faiz Gheza gave the order to dismount outside the cellar entrance. Stiffly, Ogilvie climbed down from his horse. He dreaded what he must see when Ahmed Khan gave the order for the trench to be opened. As he looked around he saw Ahmed Khan approaching, on horseback now, from the direction of the battlemented tower. Mounted, the man appeared more imperious than ever; he made a very striking figure, and he was looking expectant. Nearing Ogilvie, he reined in his horse and looked down, raising his eyebrows. "Well, Ogilvie sahib?" he asked.

"My father will forward the terms."

Ahmed Khan glanced at Faiz Gheza. "This is correct?"

"It is correct, Highness."

"Good, excellent!" Ahmed Khan's keen gaze swept Ogilvie again. "Your father will keep his word—you have convinced him that what I have said about the Czar is no bluff?"

Ogilvie said, "My father is a British officer, and will keep his word. He understands that you're not bluffing about the Russians. He knows the politics of the Afghan borders, Ahmed

Khan. But I am bound to add that he can offer no guarantee that an answer will come quickly." He paused, expectant himself now. "Well, as you can see, I've done what I agreed to do. Will you now do your part?"

A slight smile on his face, Ahmed Khan produced the key of the trench-cover. He held it aloft. "Ogilvie sahib, you have carried out your part of the bargain as you say. I also am a man of honour. The men will be released, but remember this, if there is no sign from the British that my terms are being favourably considered, it will be easy to return them to the trench again. For now, Ogilvie sahib, you will release your soldiers yourself."

He reached down with the key, a mocking look in his eyes now. As Ogilvie took the key Ahmed Khan said, "I believe the British will treat with me rather than risk the Russians. While you were parleying, Ogilvie sahib, a runner reached me after making his way through another part of your British line, a lightly-held and hilly sector through which he passed with ease. I am informed that my supply column is approaching and will move through the gap between the hills, under cover of the darkness . . . not tonight, not tomorrow night, not the night after that—but the following one. This is a little sooner than I expected. From that time onward, this fort will no longer be under any serious threat. With the replenishment of arms and food and men, I shall, if I wish, be able to break out and force the British line virtually wherever I want, and once that line is cut, your regiments will be decimated. This, your high command will know. Now—release your men."

Ogilvie turned away with the key. Faiz Gheza handed him the iron bar. He walked around the trench-cover, pushed the key home into its hole, felt it engage over a metal spigot. He inserted the iron bar through the ring, and began turning, using all his weight in the effort. He felt the tremor of the ground beneath his feet as the heavy cover began to slide away under the wall. It took him ten minutes. When the key jammed at full open he let go of it and turned about, looking down into the trench. He met blank stares from puffy, sweat-streaked faces. There was little strength left in the soldiers; all energy had been sweated out of them and the lack of air had had its effect as well. Cunningham was the first to move. He reached out an arm, felt vaguely for the lip of the trench, and pulled himself to a sitting position. He was soaked with sweat and he moved stiffly, like an animated corpse. His face set, Ogilvie went towards him and knelt by his side, reaching out to give him support.

"This is damnable, Sarn't-Major," he said.

The voice was a whisper and Ogilvie bent closer to catch it. "I have a stronger word for it, Mr. Ogilvie. If it happens again, however . . . Mr. Ogilvie, I would like a word with you if it can be arranged—the bastards are watching now. Help me out, if you please, sir."

Ogilvie did so; held him for a while till he could stand on his own, then went to the assistance of the others. Some had taken it more easily than their comrades and were able to help the less fortunate. One man lay still. Ogilvie went to him and bent to run a hand beneath his tunic, feeling for the heartbeats. The man was dead. One by one, his small force was being whittled away. He felt a terrible sense of foreboding and helplessness. It was unnerving, but he fought it down. He straightened, and walked away from the trench towards Ahmed Khan. Standing by the rebel's stirrups he said, "Ahmed Khan, you have killed three of my men since we have been held prisoner. I—"

"This is war, Ogilvie sahib. It is not a war of my own making —that is to say, your British involvement was never sought by me. This you know. I regret the deaths, but you must think yourselves lucky you are not all dead."

"I know this is war, Ahmed Khan. Facilities for decent burial are also a part of war. You would wish your own men to have proper burial. I now ask the same for mine."

Ahmed Khan stared down cynically and gave a short laugh. "When you kill my men in battle, Ogilvie sahib, do you always give *them* proper burial?"

Ogilvie flushed. All he could find to say was, "Your ways differ from ours. We do not always know what sort of burial a man of the hill tribes would consider proper and fitting."

"Therefore you take the easy way, and leave them to the vultures, who alone along the frontier welcome the British, for providing them with their meals." Ahmed Khan regarded him critically and in silence for a while, then shrugged. "I shall not have it said that Ahmed Khan was guilty of any lack of magnanimity in approaching victory. You shall have your decent burial, Ogilvie sahib. I shall give orders to that effect and you will be informed when it shall be—but you will excuse me from personal attendance," he added sardonically. "I have other affairs that need my attention." There was a sudden change in his tone then, and he looked grave, almost kingly, as he went on, "Do not think, however, that I have no respect for your dead. I have no personal approval for my countrymen's customs in regard to enemy dead. I always respect a soldier who has fought well, whichever side he is on. Perhaps, after the acceptance of my terms, such bloodshed will cease to be necessary . . . though I have no doubt but that the British will find other peoples upon whom to sharpen their swords!"

He swung away before Ogilvie could say anything more, riding at a walking pace back towards the tower. Ogilvie called after him, and he turned. "Yes?"

Ogilvie asked, "May I have permission for my men to attend the burial, Ahmed Khan?"

"No, Ogilvie sahib. You alone shall go."

"May I take my sergeant-major, Ahmed Khan?" Fresh sweat broke out, running down his face and body. "He'll want to be present."

There was a pause. Then Ahmed Khan gave a wave of his hand, a dismissive gesture before turning away again, this time finally. "Very well, then, your sergeant-major, no one else."

Ogilvie waited while the released men filed down the steps into the cellar and the guard was re-set — and he recalled that both the iron-covered trench and the cellar door had been unguarded on his return. That could be worth bearing in mind. Ahmed Khan evidently felt his trench was secure enough in itself. Ogilvie could find no use for the knowledge but he had had the idea Cunningham was on to something, and every chink in the fort's armour was worth thinking about. When the men had been locked in again Faiz Gheza snapped an order and four of his squadron formed up, two on either side of Ogilvie and Cunningham, who were marched back to their respective quarters. Soon afterwards Ogilvie had a meal brought to him, but he still had little appetite and once again ate only so as to retain his strength. He was extremely worried now; his situation seemed utterly without hope. In three nights' time Ahmed Khan's supply column would arrive, would probably catch the brigade on the hop since it was so far ahead of schedule, and would quite likely break through and join Ahmed Khan's advanced line thrown across the valley. Then, since there would hardly have been time for Åhmed Khan's terms to be considered and acted upon, the real holocaust would start. Ogilvie knew his father would press home an attack on the supply column even as far as the gates of Jalalabad itself. Ahmed Khan must know that too, and was apparently not worried. No doubt he had his good reasons for that! Ogilvie was also very conscious of the fact that he might well be the only Briton who knew with certainty when the column would come down through the valley—he could not assume that the political officers operating behind the rebel lines would find it possible to get any messages through from now on; which left him in the position of being in duty bound to get word through himself. But how could he? A breakaway from the forthcoming funeral party might be a possibility, if an unlikely one, but in any case he still had his men to consider. Or should he be considering them now? He knew well what both his father's and his Colonel's answer would be to that question. And he was under no parole. His clear duty was still to rejoin his regiment at the first opportunity; the fact of the flag-of-truce meeting earlier made no jot of difference to that, and no more would it be altered by the fact of terms being under offer. He paced his apartment restlessly, hour after hour; and his head was aching with the concentrated effort of trying to find his way clear when Faiz Gheza came into the apartment just as the sun was going down the sky.

The native officer said, "All is ready for the burial of your dead, Ogilvie sahib." He stood erect beside the door. "You will come, please. His Highness has given orders that all respect shall be shown, and it is desired that you yourself should commend them to the mercies of their God according to their own belief."

"Thank you," Ogilvie answered. He moved for the door and went out in front of Faiz Gheza. Descending the great steps he made his way down the courtyard and saw the burial party drawn up near the gatehouse. There was a handcart with two loinclothed and turbaned bearers in the shafts, and three humps under—of all things—a tattered Union Flag that Ahmed Khan must have taken in battle in the past. Six of Faiz Gheza's cavalrymen were mounted in rear of the handcart, six more in front—too strong an escort altogether to make a break from. The Regimental Sergeant-Major, as smart as paint, was standing at attention immediately behind the handcart.

Ogilvie fell in beside him.

Cunningham said no word but remained looking straight ahead. Cunningham was thinking of Invermore. There at the depot of the Royal Strathspeys, under the lee of the Monadhliath Mountains, a Scottish soldier would have gone home to rest to the beat of muffled drums, sad drums swathed in black crêpe, and the pipes of the battalion playing Flowers of the Forest, and then the volley over the bare grave, and finally the quick-march back to barracks, the lively music from the band that would take the thoughts of the men away from death and its corruption . . . but the black-hearted bastards of heathen tribesmen would not be understanding all *that* . . .

But they understood some of it, it seemed.

As Faiz Gheza gave the order to move, there was a jingle of harness, the men in the shafts started dragging the cart forward, bumping it heavily over the rough surface towards the gates, where the dismounted quarter-guard was brought to attention — and then as they moved out past the gatehouse they heard, from ahead of the cart and its forward escort of mounted men, an old Highland lament, played falteringly and thinly on the pipes of a solitary piper. It was a nice gesture on the part of Ahmed Khan. Ogilvie took a sideways look at Cunningham. The R.S.M.'s face had gone a deep purple and there was a suspicious sparkle in his eyes, and he was holding himself, if possible, straighter than ever. The pipes played the cortège through the ramshackle, smelly streets. Flies buzzed, descending in loathsome swarms upon the humps beneath the flag. There were murmurs from the crowds and some fists were shaken, and some men spat. But Ahmed Khan's cavalry was not to be trifled with. At a word from Faiz Gheza the escort drew their sabres and that was that. The crowd fell back from the horses and the hard, thrustful faces of their riders; they followed distantly, as the cortège moved on beyond the mud walls and out into the sand-hills, leaving the Kabul River away to their right as Ogilvie's truce party had done that morning. Darkness was falling swiftly now and the bearers lit lanterns on the handcart; but despite the darkness any attempt at a break-out would be fated from the start. The mob behind would turn into a savage hunting pack, directed on to their prey by the cavalry. An evening exchange of artillery fire was starting to the west. To the accompaniment of the rumble of the fire and the distant flashes from the opposing guns, the remains of the three soldiers were lifted from the handcart and shallow graves were excavated in the sand by the bearers. Without the aid of a prayer-book, Ogilvie murmured a few words over the bodies and Bosom Cunningham threw down handfuls of sand, the graves were filled in and the outlines marked with boulders with the British Flag planted on a staff at their heads.

Then the cavalcade started back for the fort.

There was a shake in Cunningham's voice when he said, "My God. What motivates the rebel, Mr. Ogilvie? I swear I could have cried like a bairn when the pipes started up!" The R.S.M. was more shaken than Ogilvie had ever dreamed of seeing him.

"Don't ask me to explain, Sarn't-Major," he said. "It's beyond me. He's half good and half bad—like all of us, I suppose."

Cunningham nodded. It was full dark by this time, but they were fitfully lit by the flickering cart-lanterns. Ogilvie said, "You wanted a word with me, Sarn't-Major. Now's the only chance we shall get."

"Yes, sir." The R.S.M.'s lips seemed scarcely to move and he kept his eyes front and his voice low. "When we were in the trench I felt a crumbling with my feet. I reckoned the wall was imperfect. There might be a way out to the dungeon for what it's worth. I couldn't try it myself. Avoirdupois—I'm too fat! A thin man could maybe do it. Then this evening I was sent for to the dungeon, to supervise the preparation of Atkinson's body. The niggers provided a lantern and I had the time to look around. The wall by the trench is definitely crumbling all right—right up by the top of the dungeon, Mr. Ogilvie. It could be worth remembering."

Ogilvie whispered back, "Thank you, Sarn't-Major," and then they were coming back through the town. Soon they were at the gatehouse and once again they were separated each to his own quarters.

Ogilvie remembered once again that the dungeon had been left unguarded while the men had been in the trench. If only they could all come together, something might be done . . .

From a window Ogilvie watched the native piper, the man who had played for the burial. Idly, he watched the man go into the doorway opposite and come out without his pipes, and then make off in the general direction of the quarter-guard. After he had disappeared Ogilvie went on staring from the window, thoughtfully, as the sentries passed and re-passed. Something, some vague and ill-formed notion, had begun to stir in his mind. That man had walked in and out of the doorway easily enough—he had unlocked no locks and had left the door unlocked when he had come out. If only he, Ogilvie, could break out from his sumptuous prison, that store might perhaps provide a useful if temporary hiding-place . . .

He shrugged, wondering what the point would be. But it was just a thought, possibly useless in itself.

He turned away.

The sentries were far too alert—far too conscious, no doubt, of what would happen to them if they allowed their prisoner to escape. The watch was changed every two hours, day and night. No man was permitted to grow weary. There was no escape that way, nor by way of the solid, equally well guarded door leading to the passage.

But the pipes were calling to James Ogilvie as he tried to find sleep that night. Those pipes, Ahmed Khan had said, had been taken years before and obviously they had belonged to a Scottish regiment; perhaps they could be made again to play their part in war! The notion grew, but was still unformulated, and Ogilvie knew still that he could do nothing unless and until the whole British party was together again and able to act as a unit. But time was not on the side of the British; no delay at all could be afforded—if there was to be action, it had to be taken before Ahmed Khan's supply column reached the siege perimeter. Ogilvie's thoughts circled, round and round in his head throughout that night. Again, and almost continuously now, he heard the distant artillery bombardment. The British losses would be growing, the British reserves of ammunition would be becoming depleted and they too had their urgent supply problems, to say nothing of the sickness. There were other worries also that weighed upon Ogilvie, personal anxieties as to what the battalion would be thinking of his pressing for terms on behalf of a rebel. He had seen the contempt in his father's face and his father's words had hurt cruelly. By now his father may well have regretted his language and his sentiments, but it had been said, and had been overheard by Andrew

Black into the bargain. But perhaps Black had been right. Perhaps he hadn't been officer material from the start. Certainly he had had no commission so insistently to propagate the cause of the rebel, the Empire's sworn enemy. His father had been right as well: he had known nothing whatever of frontier ways. Ahmed Khan had made rings round him.

A pageant, an unreal parade of the past went through his head. Stories he had heard from his father, from his father's friends, in childhood days seemed to come alive for him as he lay sleepless, hearing the tread of his gaolers outside the windows. Stories, some of them, that went back to the days even of the old East India Company, the days before the mutiny had led to the establishment of the formal British Raj in India, the taking over from the traders and soldiers of John Company in the name of the Empress of India. He saw in his mind's eye the regiments attempting to stem the flood-tide of rebellion as that mutiny got under way, their colours marching before them or going down in a welter of blood and gunpowder and the hideous cries of tormented, dying men. He saw the glorious defence of Delhi by General Wilson following upon the gallop to the Delhi Fort of the mutineers of the 3rd Light Cavalry; their assembly below the Musamman Burj; the murder of Captain Douglas of the 31st Bengal Native Infantry; the blowing of the Kashmir Gate by the British relieving column. He heard the pipes of Havelock calling the bearded Highlanders on to the relief of Lucknow . . .

The gallant blowing-up of the Kashmir Gate, even though it was an act from outside and not inside, remained in his mind to torment him with his own inadequacy. If only he could do something like that, if only he could blow this fortress's gatehouse and then overpower the quarter-guard . . . if! *If* he had the gunpowder, *if* he had weapons, *if* he could release his imprisoned men, *if* they all bore as many lives as a cat—then they might break out; but to do what, after all? They couldn't hope to reach the British lines through five miles of alerted hostile country.

In the morning Ogilvie had a blinding headache and his eyes were red-rimmed with lack of sleep. After breakfast Faiz Gheza came to him.

"You will accompany me to His Highness, Ogilvie sahib." he

said. "At once." He led Ogilvie from the room, and towards the spiral stone staircase leading to the battlements. Once again Ahmed Khan, surrounded by his lieutenants, was scanning the distant British line through field glasses. As Ogilvie was brought up he turned and lowered the glasses.

"Good morning, Ogilvie sahib," he said. "I think there is another matter in which you can assist me."

"I'm giving you no help, Ahmed Khan."

"But you have done. so already! To refuse more help is only to split hairs, Ogilvie sahib, is it not?"

Ogilvie shrugged. "Give it whatever name you choose. Taking your terms to my father wasn't help exactly. What is it this time?"

Ahmed Khan smiled, and paced the stone roof for a while before answering. "Ogilvie sahib," he said at last, coming to a halt in front of him, "movements have been noticed along the British line. I cannot say what these movements are – whether they are of infantry or cavalry or artillery, whether or not they are accompanied by ammunition and supply trains. If I knew all this it would be a great help to me in assessing the strength of the British on the peaks, in assessing how much opposition I must plan to meet when my supply column reaches the end of the valley. Do you understand?"

Ogilvie felt a prickle of fear. He said, "I thought you said you had spies planted in the British lines? Don't they –"

"Unfortunately, one spy only. Equally unfortunately, no reports have come from him for some while. I fear he may have been discovered. But on the fortunate side of the coin, Ogilvie sahib – I have you!"

"I don't see the point," Ogilvie said, playing for time. "Why do you bother? I thought you were confident you could get your column through to the fort, whatever the British did?"

"Oh yes," Ahmed Khan said at once, "I am confident still, of course. That has not changed an iota. Nevertheless, I wish to be in a position to estimate the strength of the British as closely as I can – because, you see, it is shortly going to be necessary for me to make my own dispositions. That is to say, I shall have to deplete the strength of the fort, and I wish to know by how much I should do so."

"You intend sending out a support column from here, to help the supply train through?"

"Yes, of course. Naturally, I expect, and am ready for, a strong attack, but I do not know how strong. I have to strike a balance between leaving the fort too unprotected, and keeping too many men here who could more profitably be used to bring the supply train through. Now I think perhaps you understand?"

"I don't understand what you think *I* can do to help."

"No? Then I shall tell you, Ogilvie sahib." Ahmed Khan stared into his eyes, standing very close to him now. "You will take the glasses, and you will study your formations, and you will interpret for me all that you see. With your more intimate knowledge of your own army, I believe you will be able to tell me things which I may have missed, or misinterpreted. And you will not tell me falsely, Ogilvie sahib. Because if you do, it will be so much the more unpleasant for you afterwards, when I shall have found out the truth." He pushed the glasses at Ogilvie. "Now, look, and look well."

"I'm not doing anything of the sort."

"I say that you are, Ogilvie sahib!"

Ogilvie shrugged, tried to conceal the trembling in his hands. "You can't make me."

"No? I wonder! Think, Ogilvie sahib — think deeply of whether or not I have means to make men talk!"

"I repeat," Ogilvie said, "I'm not helping you. You can do what you like!"

"Truly spoken indeed," Ahmed Khan said softly. He laughed. "And what I shall like, is to see you flogged." He lifted his hand, giving a signal to two of his followers who at once laid hold of Ogilvie. His helmet was taken away, his khaki tunic unbuttoned and removed, and the shirt. He was dragged across the roof to the battlements and held by his wrists across one of the embrasures, held tightly across the stonework. Looking over his shoulder he saw a tall man holding a leather whip, its many thongs weighted with lead pellets. He looked away, stared down the sheer side of the tower, straight down into the plain outside the walls, saw the rise of the courtyard towards the wall just where the side of the tower was built into it — quite close, that must be, to his own apartment if ever he saw it again now. He closed his eyes, and prayed.

Ahmed Khan moved behind him. "Now you will change your mind?"

"No."

"You are very, very foolish. This information that I want—it is not vital to me, though useful certainly. You would be guilty of little disloyalty to your comrades out there, who are going to be cut to pieces whether you help me or whether you do not! You will suffer quite needlessly, Ogilvie sahib."

"Then why go on with this? Is it just sadism, the sadism of Afghanistan, the sadism of a heathen?"

"Or of a dirty nigger?" Ahmed Khan said as softly as he had spoken before. "No, it is not this. Only I am not to be denied, Ogilvie sahib. My wishes are not to be set aside—my men know this and have often felt the proof of it upon their backs! They must see that the same is true of the British, that I, Ahmed Khan, am the master!" After this there was a pause. Ogilvie's eyes were still closed. He gave a convulsive pull against the gripping hands on his wrists as the first cut came down hard on his back; but he made no sound beyond an involuntary grunt. There was a pause of about ten seconds, then the next cut whistled down. After four more cuts, Ahmed Khan stopped the flogging and once again asked if he had changed his mind. He had not. The lashes continued. They mangled the flesh of his back and left him weak and in agony, and on the nineteenth he fainted. Salt, spirit and chillies were rubbed into his wounds, and he came to, and cried aloud.

"Now will you speak?"

He could scarcely have spoken if he had wanted to, but he managed to repeat the one word: "No."

"Then all your men will suffer," Ahmed Khan said, livid with anger. "Every one of them, and you yourself with them, will go at once to the courtyard trench and will remain there until I decide if I have any further use for you."

Ogilvie's wrists were let go; he slumped to the stone below the battlements but was dragged roughly to his feet. His shirt and tunic were pulled over his lacerated body. His feet dragging, he was half carried down the spiral staircase and out into the courtyard. He was dragged across towards the dungeon and thrown heavily against the wall. He lay in a daze of pain until he heard the men being brought up from the cellar and then somehow his pride brought him staggering to his feet. He leaned against the wall, his face white beneath its tan. Then he saw the Regimental Sergeant-Major being marched from his quarters to join the rest.

Somehow he managed to return Cunningham's salute. The R.S.M.'s face was stony and dangerous. He said, "This is a bad business, Mr. Ogilvie, sir. I'm that sorry for what's happened."

"It's all right, Sarn't-Major. I'm the one that's sorry. I've let you all in for it, now."

"That's no way to think of it, sir. We'll take what's coming, never fear."

Ahmed Khan had not come down into the courtyard for the men's incarceration in the trench. He was apparently still studying the British positions and movements and making his assessments for the action to come. Faiz Gheza was left to attend to the details, and he made no objection when Cunningham picked Ogilvie up bodily and laid him gently in the trench, then himself lay down beside him. Ogilvie's back was in torment as the shirt rubbed him and he felt the hard contact with the brick-like earth beneath. There was a moment of panic as the iron lid began to close and he felt he must suffocate. He cried out incoherently. Death could not be far off now. There was a dull clang as the lid closed altogether and they were in total, unrelieved darkness. He lost consciousness again, for how long he didn't know. Coming round to the horror of that close imprisonment he heard murmurs, curses, moans from along the line of men. He was thankfully aware of the proximity to him of Cunningham. By now, all footfalls from above had stopped. Some while later Cunningham spoke to him. The R.S.M. said, "Sir, it's an ill wind, as they say. The nigger may not have done himself so much good after all."

Ogilvie bit down on his pain and asked, "How's that?"

There was the briefest chuckle. "Because I've laid you down just where the inner wall is weak, Mr. Ogilvie. And I'm thinking you're the right build to squirm through . . . once that back of yours is better, that is."

"I don't see what good it's going to do us now. Oh, we'll be a good deal easier—but only till they open up and find out what we've done."

"Ah—but before they do that, sir, we'll be gone! If we choose the time right, that is. You see, the absence of sound from above means to me that the cellar door is not guarded—"

"You're right, Sarn't-Major, it isn't, but—"

"Well, sir, it's my belief it'll not be locked either. I have not heard them lock it after the men came up. Why should they bother, when it's empty?"

"Why indeed?" Ogilvie said dully. But soon he felt a faint hope and things began to slot into place in his mind. When the supply column neared the entry to the valley, Ahmed Khan, he knew, was going to deplete his garrison here in the fort—he'd said that. And there would be an excitement in the fort, an excitement that, especially if Ahmed Khan himself should be absent with his advanced line, assisting the passage of the supply train, could lead to a certain lack of vigilance. Once again Ogilvie thought of the piper, and the door through which the man had gone with his pipes.

Perhaps a second Havelock could yet bring something off!

They sweated it out through that day, waiting their time. They endured torture, gradually feeling the dehydration in their bodies, all those hours as the sun heated the iron and turned the trench into an oven humid with sweat. Ogilvie, with his lacerated back, was naturally in a worse state than any of the others; merely to lie still was painful enough, but after a while he was visited by an enervating restlessness that kept his body twitching but without the relief of being able to stretch any part of himself other than his legs, and those only in the one direction. And with them, moving his toes cautiously, he was able to feel through his boots the crumbling of the inner wall. Later, as the twitching died away at last into an exhausted stupor, he fell into a troubled sleep in which continually he heard the scream that had been torn from Colour-Sergeant MacNaught the night his shoulder had been shattered in the assault on the peaks. By evening all the men were in a semi-stupefied condition; no chink of daylight had penetrated but Ogilvie could tell by the cooling iron that the day's heat had passed off them an hour or so earlier; he could begin to reckon time in a rough fashion. By now it would be dusk, and soon it would be night—and still, after that, some forty-eight hours yet to go before the supply column was due to pass between the British positions.

They had much to endure yet.

As the trench gradually cooled, so their imprisonment, though not their raging thirst, became a little easier to bear and Ogilvie, with the pain from the lashes now receding into a background of discomfort, however acute, was better able to concentrate. In a whisper he spoke to Cunningham: "Sarn't-Major?"

"Sir!"

"How long d'you think the men can go on like this?"

"As long as they have to, sir. They'll be in no worse state than you or I, Mr. Ogilvie, will they?" He added, "I'd not like to see you scrabble around too much till you're fit, sir."

"I'll be fit as soon as the time comes to make a move—don't worry! I suggest we wait another four hours or so—it'll have to be by guesswork, of course—"

"By counting, sir. One—pause—two—pause—three. That's three seconds." He gave a throaty chuckle. "It'll be a wearisome business, sir, but it'll give us something to do at least!"

"All right," Ogilvie said. "Then I'll try to break through. If I can do it, the men can take turns to go down for spells in the cellar. If anybody's going to open up, we'll get enough warning, I imagine, to get two or three men up here again in time. How does that sound to you, Sarn't-Major?"

"Fair enough, sir. And after that, what?"

Ogilvie said, "We'll have to wait through two more days. Once the sun's gone down on the second day, we *all* climb into the cellar together. Then, soon after the column moves out from the fort, we come out of the cellar door."

"And do what?" The R.S.M.'s earlier optimism had gone.

"Cause a diversion. God knows how . . . but that's what I'm going to try for."

"A diversion where, Mr. Ogilvie?"

"Why, right behind Ahmed Khan's advanced line, up by the defile! If we can make enough racket we might sound like an attack from the rear, an infiltration from another sector of the British lines—a kind of outflanking movement, don't you see?"

Cunningham gave a low whistle. "By God, if only we could, sir! It just might give the brigade its chance if we timed it right." There was excitement in his voice at first, but it didn't last. "We'd never get there, though. There wouldn't be a hope in hell!"

"It's still worth aiming at, Sarn't-Major."

"I'd not hold out any hope at all, sir. There's too much ground to cover and we'd stand out like sore thumbs, especially if there's any moon at all. We'd not even get through the streets of the town, let alone cross the nigger's territory to his forward line, sir! They'd have us before we could move a dozen paces from the gatehouse—and even before that, there's the quarter-guard to be considered. No, Mr. Ogilvie, the odds are far too great against us."

"Well, I'm not so sure. This morning . . . when I was spread out against the battlements . . . I looked down through the embrasure. On the other side of the fort, the side *away* from the gatehouse, the ground rises towards the wall. If we could get to the top of the wall, there's not too long a drop to the open country—and it *is* open country, Sarn't-Major! Wide open. The fort seems to be built into the actual town wall itself—so on that side there isn't any town—d'you see? That battlemented tower is in a sense I suppose a sort of guard-point for the north-western corner of the town wall. We'd be right out in the open, and we wouldn't even have to worry about the quarter-guard or the gatehouse."

"Is that so? Well, then, Mr. Ogilvie, maybe that makes a difference, always provided we were not seen from the battlements, of course." Cunningham's reaction was cautious but there was a note of rising hope now. He was silent for some while then he said, "Aye, it seems the best we can aim for at the moment, as you said." And then he added, "You'll be assured of a good turn-out from the men, sir, I'll be seeing to that."

"Thank you, Sarn't-Major."

They spoke little after that, as they waited for full night to come down upon Jalalabad. When there was no sound from above beyond the distant clamour of the guns, and after he had counted his way through an approximation of the four hours— Ogilvie said, "I'm going to try to breach the wall now, Sarn't-Major."

"Very good, sir. Take care of your back now."

Ogilvie said, "Give me a hand, then. You, too," he added to the man on his left. He reached out, groping until he had taken each man's hand. Then pulling hard against them, he managed to slide his body forward a few painful inches until his feet had some leeway to press against the wall. Drawing his legs back until his knees met the iron lid above, he rammed them back against the hard-baked mud. He felt a slight give and there was a rattle as small pieces dropped into the dungeon below. He stopped moving; every man held his breath. But nothing seemed to have been heard outside. He pushed again. This time his feet

164

met solid resistance. He went on pushing, with all his effort behind his thrust, but nothing shifted beyond a few more small pieces. Sweat poured from him, mingling with the dirt of the shallow trench. "Keep it up, sir," Cunningham said encouragingly. "You'll get there if you keep it up."

Ogilvie was very near exhaustion in fact, after the day-long heat and dehydration and the claustrophobic effect of the close confinement; but he summoned all his will and he kept on thrusting out with his feet, trying as best he could to keep his back flat and unmoving on the earth, for still every move of his shirt against the flesh sent pain through his whole body and he felt the wetness of blood beneath him. At last he could move no more and he lay dazed and motionless. Cunningham spoke to the man next to him on the left, a man who had been trying unavailingly to smash away the section in front of his own boots. He said, "Try to get your legs across the officer's, Taggart, and see what you can do, all right?"

Heavy boots rasped over Ogilvie's legs and started banging away at the wall. After an age, as it seemed to the waiting men, Taggart, attacking from a fresh angle and with more strength, sent a whole chunk of the mud wall flying inwards. There was a heavy clonk from below and again every man held his breath. Still nothing moved out in the courtyard. By this time Ogilvie had recovered some of his own strength and was able to push again. When a second large chunk was heard to fall Cunningham said, "That may be enough, Mr. Ogilvie. If you feel able to move yourself ahead, I think it's time to try if you can get down."

Ogilvie squirmed painfully towards the hole they had made. He felt his feet go through. He moved his legs apart and felt the width; there was room and plenty for his body to pass through. Soon his legs were dangling down into the cellar; it was going to be a tricky drop. All at once he thought of Sandhurst, of that nightmare process that the newly-joined Gentlemen Cadets were forced to undergo, the ordeal of being herded down the impedimenta-strewn staircase. Possibly that hadn't been such a pointless exercise after all! At least he knew what it was like to trip over a chair and go headlong to the bottom. He pushed himself farther out, easing his torso into the gap. He heard Cunningham call out in a restrained voice, "Mr. Ogilvie, take a hold of my boot with one hand as you go through, then try to turn yourself to face the wall. You'll go down easier that way — and you'll not need to worry about pulling me through with you, for I'm stuck tight, I'll be bound, till the hole's widened out a good deal more!"

Ogilvie took Cunningham's advice. Just before his body went through, he reached out with his right hand, found Cunningham's ankle, and gripped it. He slid through, along with a shower of rubble. He fell back against the wall of the cellar. Then he slewed himself round, got a grip with his free hand on the lip of the hole, shifted his grip on Cunningham, steadied himself, and let go.

He slid down the face of the wall. It sloped a little so that in his slide he was able to check his descent, and he landed square on his feet without much difficulty. He moved around carefully, trying to locate the steps, tripping over loose stones, disturbing rats and strange slithering creatures that he felt upon his boots. Finding the steps at last, he climbed them. He pushed gently against the outer door. There was no movement. It was shut solid. They were locked in as firmly as if they had never bothered to make that hole at all.

It was a bitter disappointment.

Ogilvie went back down the steps almost weeping now with frustration. He was unable to find the hole in the wall until he heard Cunningham's voice directing him; he followed the sound and told the R.S.M. what he had found. Cunningham said, "Don't worry, Mr. Ogilvie, there'll maybe be a way yet for all we know. At least we can get down for spells as we planned and that'll keep us all fitter than being up here. With your permission, I'll send down three men right away."

"Right, Sarn't-Major."

"Then stand away below, sir."

"I can guide them down if they—"

"Better not, Mr. Ogilvie, unless you wish a boot in the face. They'll go down the same way as you." Ogilvie stood back against the opposite wall, thinking about the locked door, feeling a vicious bitterness against fate. He heard the sounds as the men came down.

"I'm over here," he said. "Keep as quiet as you can."

The men moved across. One of them said, "Sar-Major says, sir, if we have to go back up quickly, one of the lads'll be there to reach a hand down."

166

"Right." Ogilvie was wondering what the next move could possibly be. They were really no farther ahead, in spite of Cunningham's easy acceptance of that locked door. Ogilvie sat with his head in his hands while the men went back towards the hole and, assisted by those from above, who could now move much more easily, widened out the gap. Then at last he fell into a heavy, exhausted sleep, and remained asleep while at intervals the men changed over. Cunningham had given orders that the officer was not to be disturbed until he woke of his own accord; and when he did wake Ogilvie insisted upon going back into the trench after the Regimental Sergeant-Major had with some difficulty come through the hole and landed in the dungeon for his own respite.

During the next day there were many alarms when voices were heard from the courtyard. On one occasion the men below made it only just in time before the iron lid was wound back a little way and, under a strong guard, water was passed to them and a little food. They drank greedily; there was no stint of the water. Evidently Ahmed Khan still had a use for them — no doubt hostages could even now be useful in some way. There was hope of a sort in that; hope that death was not due to come just yet anyway. The door leading to the dungeon itself was not opened at all. The sudden alarms apart, they all got through that day a good deal easier, and even Private Burns recaptured enough energy and interest in life to start a low but bitter tirade against authority during his spell below. This time Ogilvie, who was below with him, found his nerves stretched to almost unbearable limits. He aimed a blow in the direction of the voice, which was close by him, and his fist landed fair and square on Burns's jaw. Burns gave a startled yelp but before he could give away their presence Corporal Brown had an arm round his mouth. "Shut your bloody racket!" the Corporal said. "If you open your mouth when I let go o' ye, Burns, I'll squeeze the life out o' ye — for the good of us all — and I mean that."

He let go. Burns said in a savage hiss, "Soon's we get back I'll have yon Ogilvie on a Court Martial, see if I don't!"

"That'll be a sight to see, all right," Brown said, "and we'll no' be seeing it, because nothing at all happened beyond the fact you stumbled and hit your face on a stone. Right, lads?"

A murmur of assent told Burns beyond all doubt that it was quite right. Muttering mutiny, he subsided. Ogilvie found it an encouragement that even Private Burns was instinctively thinking in terms of 'getting back'.

The hours passed, slowly; the day's heat faded once again. There was one more night and one more day to get through before there could be any thought of action, and in the meantime there was the first problem to be resolved: how were they to break through the locked door of the dungeon?

"All I can think of is trying to batter it down with some of the bigger stones," Ogilvie said to Cunningham, "but of course the noise stops that. Not that we'd be able to make much impression on it anyway, I suppose. If only we had some explosives!"

"Explosives make a lot of noise too," Cunningham said dryly.

"But with much more concentration! I mean . . . we could be out and away, and in hiding, before the rebels realized what was going on."

"Well—maybe, sir. But begging your pardon, sir, ifs and buts are not helping us now. We have to find a way with what's available."

"Which is just nothing, Sarn't-Major."

"We have our hands, sir."

"You mean dig our way out?"

"Aye, that I do, sir. With the buckles on the men's belts, and with boot heels, we should be well able to make some impression on the mud wall around the door. If we could break through near the bolts and the lock, we may be able to push the door open easily enough when the time comes."

"And be seen in the digging."

"Not necessarily, Mr. Ogilvie. If we start the digging by day, and not break through the outer skin of the wall till we're nearly ready to come out—that's to say, at night—we'll have a very good chance of not being spotted. It's a risk we have to take in any case, the way things have turned out."

"Possibly." Ogilvie sat with crossed legs, his head in his hands, turning the proposition over and over in his mind. His thoughts were hard to concentrate now; he was weary mentally as well as physically. His mind kept going back to the regiment, to the men under that sustained bombardment on the hill top. "How d'you think they're doing, Sarn't-Major?" he asked suddenly after a long silence.

Cunningham gave a slight start in the darkness. "Who, sir?"

"Why—the regiment."

"Oh—yes, sir. You'll forgive me . . . I was wandering. I think they'll be doing fine. The 114th never have given ground easily, sir. Never. There'll be casualties and heavy ones as like as not—but they'll be there when we join up with them." He sounded confident but Ogilvie believed it to be no more than a surface confidence; all at once he felt there wasn't quite the buoyancy in Cunningham's voice that he normally had, that he had had all through until now.

Tentatively Ogilvie said, "Sarn't-Major, you spoke of wandering. Is there anything you want to tell me?" He sounded diffident.

"It doesn't concern you, sir."

"I'm sorry—"

"No, Mr. Ogilvie." The Regimental Sergeant-Major reached out and put a hand on his arm. "I'm sorry too, for I didn't mean it that way. I meant only that you're not able to help. You'll appreciate the fact that a married man in this kind of situation faces worries that a single man does not. Mrs. Cunningham, sir, is a woman who worries a good deal."

"I'm sure she does. I imagine one could say the same of any soldier's wife at times. But she'll be in good hands, back in Peshawar, won't she, Sarn't-Major?"

Cunningham gave a sound of irritation. "Aye, that she will, sir, of course. That doesn't stop a woman worrying, nor the bairns either. For a long time it's been in my mind that a soldier has no business marrying at all. It's terrible for the women and the bairns. If a man leaves them behind in Scotland, he'll never see them for years and years. If he brings them, why—if he dies out here, it's ten times harder for them than if they were back home."

"They'd always be looked after, Sarn't-Major."

"True, sir, but with all respect, the Colonel and the Padre are nor the same as a woman's own kin at such a time. Look, sir. I have to get back to the lines. It's not just my regimental duty. It's Mary too." The R.S.M. seemed to be fighting his emotion. A few moments later he went on, "You'll pardon all I've said. It was nothing but a momentary weakness. And we're going to get back, make no mistake about it."

They sat in silence till it was time for Ogilvie to resume his place in the trench so that Corporal Brown could come down for his spell. Ogilvie thought about the R.S.M. He didn't in fact know as much about Cunningham as perhaps an officer should know of the Regimental Sergeant-Major. He knew Cunningham had three children, that he came from Invermore town, that his father had served in the 114th Highlanders and had finished his time as Colour-Sergeant, knew that he himself had three more years of service left before he went out on pension; and he had met Mrs. Cunningham at regimental dances and found her a pleasant, happy little woman still in awe of her husband after fifteen years of marriage. But he had not known her name was Mary. It was a small enough thing, and totally unimportant and irrelevant to their situation now, but he felt it gave Cunningham and himself a shared link if a few points were stretched. For one of the extraneous things still on his mind was the fact of Mary Archdale's existence; the girl haunted him and he wondered if she was aware of what had happened, whether the fate of a subaltern would make news enough for word to reach her. Probably it would, in the case of the Divisional Commander's son. He had felt quite strongly that she had reacted to him, had been drawn to him as he had been to her. But what of that? She was still married, even though she hated her husband. She was forced to accept the social conventions of the day and she would be unable to show any overt feeling for Second-Lieutenant James Ogilvie. Even a clandestine affair would leak sooner or later in the Indian hothouse, and invitations to parties and balls would very soon cease once the rumour ran that a Brigade Major's wife was seducing a raw, green subaltern of the line. There were the well-established conventions of sin as well as of rectitude; ranks and ages tended, on the whole, to stick together unless the man was the older of the liaison parties. And naturally, such a liaison would have the poorest possible effect on Ogilvie's career, while if his father should ever get to hear of it the results could well be catastrophic . . .

Ogilvie caught himself up sharply. 'It' hadn't happened; probably never would. He was running much too far ahead of himself, becoming too grandiose in his thoughts altogether. Nevertheless Mary Archdale — and it may have been no more than a train of emotion started by Cunningham's words about his wife — Mary Archdale became a goal to return to, something beyond the regiment and even his own life, to lead him out of captivity and sharpen his instinct for survival. And whether or not it had anything to do with thoughts of Mary Archdale Ogilvie, afterwards, couldn't possibly have said; but the fact remained for the record that, as he thought about her, and as he stared upward from his recumbent position in the direction of the iron trench cover that he couldn't see though it was no more than inches above the tip of his nose, the idea for the break-out came to him.

And, at the same time, he remembered the pipes.

On the hill-top held by Dornoch's brigade the casualties, as Cunningham had forecast, had been heavy. The artillery had been badly depleted and until reinforcements could reach them they had only four guns firing, while all the indications were that the northern peak was similarly depleted. Sir Iain Ogilvie, still with Brigade H.Q., was becoming increasingly alarmed as to the general situation and was not slow to say as much to the Colonel of the 114th over a whisky-and-soda as the field kitchens prepared the officers' luncheon.

"It's going to be touch and go, Dornoch. By all accounts, that damned supply column's very heavily protected." He had expressed this opinion many times already in the last few hours and by this time Dornoch was merely nodding his agreement. "Dammit, we can't afford to let it go through—we simply can't! Calcutta'll have my head on a charger, see if they don't!" He swallowed his whisky, then paced up and down for a few minutes before stopping, and, once again, lifting his glasses to sweep the enemy lines and the town and fort behind. "There's got to be a change of plan, Dornoch. I'm forced to the conclusion we can't go on holding the hills for long enough now. That damn nigger will hold his column somewhere up the valley till he's silenced all our guns—or what's left of them—hey? And reduced the men to a damn handful, too." He lowered the glasses and glared belligerently at the Colonel. "Hey?"

Dornoch said, "It's possible, sir, but what's the alternative?"

"Damned if I know! There has to be one, though, and I've never been stumped before, Dornoch, never! I remember once when I was fighting the damn Sikhs . . . but I dare say I've told you before, come to think of it—"

"Yes, sir."

"Oh. Well—thing is—what'll the rebel be *expecting* us to do? Work *that* out, and there you have it!"

"Yes, sir. He'll be expecting us to do what we're doing, I imagine—hold on for reinforcements."

"We'll soon be needing the whole damn siege line brought up at this rate. I can't afford to denude the perimeter too much, Dornoch. Some sectors are already beginning to look like a woman I saw once in Port Said . . . but never mind, never mind. That damn nigger'll break through as soon as he finds a weak spot—you know that." He paced again, gnawing anxiously at his moustache.

Dornoch said, "I think you may be wrong, sir, about Ahmed Khan holding up his supply column. He's not going to give us time to reinforce too well."

"No, I don't agree. He knows our strength, you can wager that! He'll realize what I've just said—that I wouldn't risk weakening the perimeter. I only hope to God the 88th come through the Khyber intact—and in time!" So far no word of the Connaught Rangers' progress had come through, beyond the fact that they were on their way; naturally, they would be forced-marching for all they were worth. The General realized now that he had acted foolishly in holding them in reserve at all—every man-jack was needed here before Jalalabad; he'd been guilty of underestimating the rebel and that was an unforgivable military sin that could be expiated only in victory. Victory was a most remarkable expiator of almost everything under God's heaven, except cowardice or treason. Sir Iain's face tightened at the thought of treason. He'd accused the boy of it, in a blind fit of unreasoning anger. He was sorry for that, though he would find it impossible ever to admit it; but all the same, there was a nagging anxiety in his mind that the boy could have done something damned silly and damned wrong. It was so *blasted* odd, he thought, that any British officer should urge his Divisional Commander to accept a rebel's terms—it was damned impertinence of a rebel even to suggest terms at all—and of course he had never forwarded those outrageous proposals, he hadn't had the time; he would do so, when he'd dealt with the supply column, after which Ahmed Khan wouldn't be in any position to dictate anyway. The boy could have been under threat and had given in. That was cowardice, if not treason. And if that should come out . . . Sir Iain's hands shook. Then his jaw thrust forward and his eyes hardened. Better—far better—if he should die! He would be a hero then, unless the facts were so blatant that the men talked about them afterwards. But then the Regimental Sergeant-Major would always support his officers, and put a stop to any such damned nonsense, such flagrant disloyalty. That was what men like Bosom Cunningham were for.

The boy's mother would miss him, of course. Curious, for a soldier's wife, and a soldier's daughter too . . . but she'd forgive him any military sin so long as he came back to her. Suddenly the General felt a strange pricking behind his eyelids and he went off into a fit of coughing, with his back to Dornoch and the Brigade Major, who had just come up, while he fished out his handkerchief. The moment passed and he swung round. He said irritably, "Oh, for God's sake, someone give me a suggestion. If it's too damn silly I'll say so. If it's any good, and it works, I'll give the credit where it's due. Come, gentlemen, speak your minds." He looked at Dornoch first. "Well?"

Dornoch said, "We must continue as planned. There are only two other courses. Withdraw, or—"

"I'm *damned* if I'll withdraw."

"Quite. Or form column and march west, then cut across the supply route higher up and hope to ambush the supply train. But we haven't the men to ensure success."

"Of course we haven't! Once we're in the open, the rebel will attack from the rear—we'd be sandwiched. Archdale?"

There was an uncomfortable silence from the Brigade Major, and not for the first time Sir Iain wondered how the devil the dead Brigadier-General had managed to put up with him. Archdale was a man of turgid mind, as well as body, and he had the most extraordinarily stupid face; nevertheless he was ambitious, and just astute enough to know that an ambitious man of small intellect should never, never commit himself when speaking to a Divisional Commander in what he privately believed to be a fairly hopeless situation. Sir Iain, realizing all this instinctively, glared at him and was seized with a sudden desire to torment. Sir Iain was the kind of commander who made a particular point of acquainting himself with all manner of small detail about the men under him, especially those closest, because experience had taught him that a commander is none the worse for having about himself an aura of divinity;

and that the revelation from time to time of minute personal data impressed both officers and men to an extraordinary degree with his sagacity, clairvoyance and insight; and, of course, he knew well about that confounded field lavatory and the spying activities of the duly executed bum-*havildar*. So he snapped suddenly, and turned away on his heel when he had done so, "Don't *strain* yourself, Brigade Major. If you prefer to keep your lips as tight shut as your damn backside, it's your own affair, I suppose. But possibly action will open them both."

During that evening and night, some reinforcements came in; but they were no more than bits and pieces, units and guns brought out of the line on a piecemeal basis from wherever they could be more or less painlessly spared. The Brigade was augmented by two batteries of mountain artillery, drawn now by mule-trains, a company of sappers for what they were worth, two companies of sepoys and — most welcome — one of the Black Watch. The Royal Strathspeys were glad to be joined by more Highlanders, and spirits began to revive despite the comparative paucity of the numbers. They revived still further when the news at last came through by the field telegraph that the 88th Foot, The Connaught Rangers, had cleared the Khyber Pass, albeit with some regrettable losses, and were marching post-haste to join the Brigade before Jalalabad.

But hard on the heels of this good news came a report from a runner sent by Brigade's extended scouting parties dispersed dangerously well down the valley towards the Hindu Kush. This report indicated that Ahmed Khan's reinforcements were already in the vicinity. A strong column estimated at many thousands of men with artillery, cavalry and wagons had been sighted that evening just as the light had faded and were believed to have halted in a position about thirty miles to the west of the peaks.

Working in silence, with men posted in the trench and just inside the door of the cellar to listen out for the first indications of any approaching footsteps, the imprisoned Scots had toiled under Ogilvie's direction at the plan he had thought up. Cunningham had agreed with him that it would have more chance of success than his own idea of chipping away at the wall beside the door-lock and bolts; for one thing, it would be less obvious, at any rate to a cursory inspection, if they should be interrupted. The new plan was this: Ogilvie had realized that the hole in the outside of the wall where the key was inserted to operate the cover mechanism above the trench, was in fact right above the hole he had made in the inner cellar wall; and that a little additional work should expose the mechanism, and that that mechanism would most likely be workable by hand from within. In the very nature of things in Afghanistan it was bound to be of the simplest and most basic construction. He had also told the R.S.M. of his idea in regard to Ahmed Khan's bagpipes. He had said, "If we can get hold of those pipes from the store, and get clear away from the fort with them, we can put them to work. Once we hit the rear of the rebel force across the valley — well, we spread out and start playing, all together at a signal from me! How's that?"

Cunningham had thought it sounded all right. "A good blast of wind, sir, to put the breeze up them well and truly. Yes, it'll help."

There was only one interruption during the day, again for water and food, and the sounds overhead when this arrived gave such of the men as were below ample time to crawl back into the trench before the lid went slowly back. Circumstances had forced them all to become excellent actors; the bleary, unshaven faces that stared up, shutting their eyes against the glare of the day, were beaten and docile enough for anyone's closest scrutiny. The water and food passed, over went the lid again and after allowing half an hour by counting, in case any-one should be lingering up above, Ogilvie and Cunningham got to work again. As dusk came down once more, the last dusk now before the arrival of the supply column, they had laid bare the mechanism of the trench cover.

Lying at full stretch in the trench, with his head inwards, Ogilvie felt carefully around the works, then, moving aside, he asked the R.S.M. to do likewise. When Cunningham had finished he asked, "Well, Sarn't-Major? What d'you think?"

"It's just clockwork, sir."

"That's what I thought."

"It should be simple enough, if heavy."

"It's going to be that, all right. Still — we're going to manage now." All at once Ogilvie was confident in spite of all the odds against them. "We'll leave it alone till we hear sounds of Ahmed

Khan moving his men out from the fort," he went on. "As soon as they're away we'll wind the thing back, then out we go. I think we can rely on all attention being directed towards the forward line."

"Aye, sir. There's just one more thing, if I may suggest it."

"Go right ahead."

"It's our uniforms, sir. With them we'll not stand a chance, wherever the attention's directed—"

"But we'll be over the wall and away from the fort and the town—just as soon as we've got hold of the pipes."

"That's true, sir, or anyway we hope it is. But we still have the courtyard to cross. Now, we can overcome this quite easily. I suggest we all strip to our underpants, smother our bodies with mud, and go out naked. The underpants'll look near enough like loincloths and if we're mistaken for Thugs, well, that'll be better for us than if they recognize us for what we are. Our shirts we can tie round our heads, turban-wise. D'ye follow, Mr. Ogilvie?"

"Oh, I follow all right . . . but isn't there a snag? How the devil do we get hold of any mud? There's dirt in plenty—dry stuff—but mud, no!"

"We're pretty dirty already, sir, from the sweat, but mud's easy made, if the men urinate."

"Oh—yes." Ogilvie hesitated. "All right, then, I'm with you, Sarn't-Major. It's a good idea."

"Then I'll give orders that that is to be done before we start to move the lid, sir."

"Very good, Sarn't-Major. When I give the word, I'll have everyone down in the dungeon and I'll brief them. Then you can have your muddying-up operation." After this, so that nothing should go wrong at the last moment, Ogilvie sent all the men back up to the trench and joined them himself with Cunningham. Then they waited. They could do no more for now. It seemed an interminable wait.

Ogilvie was feeling a sense of let-down, of anti-climax as the night wore along with nothing happening, a feeling that there had been a shift in Ahmed Khan's plans, that the supply column was not after all coming through this night. Keyed-up for the break-out as they all were, he felt they could never struggle through another day, another night, and maybe, for all he could tell now, more days and nights after that. And he was on the verge of giving way to a feeling of utter and total helplessness and abandonment when the brooding silence of the fort beyond the coffin-like lid was broken by a strident bugle call.

In his ear Cunningham said violently, "By God, this is it!"

All around, the men held their breaths once more. Within half a minute of the bugle call, the courtyard above came alive. They heard clearly the shouted, excited orders, the moving feet and the rumble of limber wheels. When this had been going on for some time Ogilvie heard the key slot into the hole in the wall and the lid start to move. It opened. They lay as if dead. There was a laugh above them and then Ahmed Khan's voice saying something in Pushtu and a few moments later the lid was moved back over them again. They lay listening, trying to interpret the various sounds. Soon there was another short bugle call, followed quickly by a trumpet, and then the sound of many men, horses and guns on the move. The column went by them quite closely, making for the gatehouse, and took a long while to pass.

At last the courtyard became quiet again.

It was a deep and absolute silence with an air of finality about it. Ogilvie gave it a while longer, forcing himself to count slowly to one thousand. Then he whispered to Cunningham to move the men down and himself slid towards the excavated hole. Within three minutes all the men were in the dungeon. "Now listen carefully," Ogilvie said, keeping his voice low. "Remember what I say, and follow out your orders to the letter. You already know what you're to do about your uniforms. Once that's done, we get the trench uncovered just far enough for us all to crawl out when we're ready to do so. Then we man the trench and we lie still. We all go out together when I give the word, and we all head at once to our right, and get under the lee of the fort wall. We follow this right the way around the courtyard to where it joins the main tower—that's the one with the battlements, you'll remember. Just before we reach the end of the wall, there's the doorway where the bagpipes are kept. I'm assuming it's not locked—it never has been to my knowledge. We go in there and grab those pipes. There should be at least twenty of them. If we can find any arms, so much the better, of course. We stay inside that door till I give the word to clear out, and when I do, we make as fast as we can for the

177

corner of the tower and we climb the wall. Once we're down the other side, we make for Ahmed Khan's advanced line with all the speed we've got. We make towards the left of their line, so we're heading in the general direction of the hill held by the 114th. And when I give the word on the march, I want you all to spread out left and right and play those pipes with every drop of breath you've got. It doesn't matter if you can play a tune or not—just blow. If we're successful in causing a diversion, we may be of some help to the regiment. Any questions?"

Brown asked, "What about the quarter-guard, sir? Aren't they going to see us?"

"We can only hope not, Corporal. They won't see us come out of the trench, not from the gatehouse anyway. They won't have us in view till we're more than half way round the walls, in fact, and I'm hoping they won't be worrying about what's going on inside the fort at all. They won't see any need to. If we're lucky, both the quarter-guard and anyone who happens to be manning the battlements will be watching out for His Highness's column coming back with the supply train—all ready to celebrate a victory! On the other hand, if they do happen to see us, since we'll be looking like natives I'm fairly certain they won't open fire right away. In the event of being seen we'll scatter, and it'll be a case of every man for himself. We'll have to skip the pipes then, and go for the wall and join up the other side. All right, all of you?"

Cunningham took over after that. "Strip off the lot of you," he said briskly. "Bundle up your uniforms to take with you, and when that's done, urinate on the ground and be quick about it. I want you all as mud-plastered as you can get, so don't waste a drop, all right, lads?" The operation proceeded fast and when each man had reported himself ready Ogilvie, stripped like the rest, sent a detail to stand face to the wall below the trench, braced to support him on their shoulders. Feeling his way across Ogilvie climbed up and, working entirely by touch, got a grip of the spokes of a large-diameter cogged wheel. The men below him staggered as he threw his weight on the wheel. He forced it over. He felt the inside edge of the iron cover move against his body as he went on turning. He bent down and called in a whisper to Cunningham, just visible now as an outline in the loom of light stealing down through the gap above the trench. He asked for more men to stand in line behind the others, and be ready to take his weight. They were sent forward at once; cautiously Ogilvie stepped backward, feeling for the next pair of shoulders with his feet. He turned the wheel again, went on turning and moving back himself until Cunningham reported there was gap enough. Then he jumped lightly down to the ground.

He looked up diagonally through the gap. He could see the tower across the courtyard—there was some moon, but it was fitful, and there was a good deal of cloud in the sky, he fancied, low lying and reaching out from the distant Kafiristan peaks.

"Right, Sarn't-Major," he said. "All up now, fast as you like."

"Aye, sir. Up you get, lads. Don't forget the bundles of uniforms." They went up fast, the first one giving himself a leg up from the shoulders of the men who had supported Ogilvie, then reaching down to give a hand to the next. They took up their positions in the line, lying prone and silent till the order came to move. In the moonlight Ogilvie saw that they looked as ruffianly a bunch of toughs as had ever been entitled to wear the Queen's uniform. The makeshift turbans and loincloths would look realistic enough at a distance, and they, like the men's bodies, were mud-covered and filthy. Ogilvie went up last of all, behind Cunningham and Brown. They lay silently for a few more minutes, listening, watching. Ogilvie saw that the courtyard was empty; nothing was stirring anywhere. As he listened he heard something start up that had been lacking the last couple or so hours—the guns along the rebel line—rebel guns, British guns, and possibly now the guns of the supply train as well. It was a loud and sustained bombardment. Well, at least it was going to occupy the attention of the quarter-guard and anybody else who had been left behind in the fort. A few moments later he heard another sound from his left, a more horrible sound than the guns: a baying hysteria rising from the townspeople of Jalalabad outside the gates as they heard the action from the hills. It was an exultant, savage racket that grew with every second.

"Swine," Cunningham said flatly in a whisper to Ogilvie. "Let's hope they'll shortly be celebrating on the other side of their faces, the black bastards!"

Ogilvie nodded; then he said, "All right, take it quietly, no sound at all. We move out . . . *now!*"

They went over the top as one, and in total silence, carrying their bundles of boots and tunics and kilts. Gently a light breeze stirred the trees growing by the wall. Ogilvie moved right, Cunningham and Brown waited to bring up the rear as the officer took the lead. Running fast and lightly Ogilvie reached the shadows by the wall, passing out of the moonlight that had unkindly lit the courtyard fully now, passing into the trees. They had not been seen; the whole contingent reached the wall safely and ran on fast. It was almost too easy, Ogilvie thought, soon something must go wrong and someone would find that open, empty trench. But that hadn't happened yet. Within a minute of coming clear of the trench they were all inside the storehouse in the wall where the bagpipes were kept. Cunningham shut the door behind him as he entered. There was no light in here, not unexpectedly, but, rummaging around, they found the pipes. The place appeared, from the smell of leather and the feel of saddles, to be a harness-room; they could find no arms, or at any rate no conventional arms. It was Ogilvie himself who had the sudden idea, after he had hit his head a crack on a pair of stirrups dangling from saddle-leathers thrown over a beam. He got hold of Cunningham. "Sarn't-Major," he said. "This might come in handy. Use it as a kind of sling!"

Cunningham felt the stirrups. "Why not, sir! I'll see if we can find some more." And he did; he found half a dozen pairs. This was armament of a sort, and when they had been through the store as best they could Ogilvie edged the door open. The moon was obscured and if they could reach the shallow wall by the tower quickly, they should make it with ease before the scud of cloud slid past.

"All out," he ordered.

They came out at the run, followed Ogilvie towards the corner where the tower met the outer fort wall. They all made the top in safety and were rolling down the sloping earth at the bottom of a fairly short drop when their luck ran out on them. A single shot echoed across the plain and was followed at once by a flickering line of rifle fire from the battlements. Bullets sang past Ogilvie as he rolled wildly away, and there was a short, sharp cry from one of the men.

"Get up and run!" Ogilvie called out. "Far away as you can before they reload!"

Cunningham came up, puffing. "You all right, Mr. Ogilvie?"

"I'm fine. Carry on going, Sarn't-Major. Who was hit?"

"Batson, sir, and he's dead. I have his pipes. I'll play them myself if I have the wind." Then he was gone, with Ogilvie running after him, running in between the piled sand-hills, away from the fort, away from Jalalabad with the Kabul River to the north, heading west for the rebel line. Soon there was more firing from behind, from the battlements, but no shots came anywhere near them and there was, so far, no pursuit from the gatehouse. In a little while they came past the spot where the three dead privates had been buried; and Ogilvie saw a man stop and seize the Union Flag from the ground and run on with it. He saw that the man was Burns and he shouted, "Put it back, Burns, put it back where it belongs!"

"Och, awa' wi' ye, ye great loon!" Burns shouted back at him, his muddied face lacking its outline but his eyes gleaming crazily in the moonlight that now came streaming out across the plain. "Those poor buggers've no more use for it, an' we may as well fight under some sort o' standard even if it's half a bloody Sassenach one!"

So, under the flag of England now, with Private Burns as the unlikely Escort of the Colours, the semi-naked band ran on for Ahmed Khan's rear.

Nine

A SQUADRON of cavalry came out from the fort, riding fast. The British heard the horses' hooves and the jingle of their equipment and went to ground just in time, before the cavalrymen swept past around a high sand dune. The horses pounded on. Ogilvie and the others emerged from the sand once they had vanished ahead. A few minutes later they heard them coming back towards the fort, and again they were able to conceal themselves, but this time the horsemen didn't come anywhere near them and in the moon they were able to see them sweeping towards the south. It seemed they were not heading out to inform Ahmed Khan that they had lost the prisoners; they had, perhaps, enough instinct for self-preservation to preclude such an unwise action until victory had been won. After this Ogilvie pressed ahead fast, making for the gun-flashes along the line across the valley mouth and on the hill-tops to the north and south of it.

The supply column was fighting its way along that valley and it was making good progress, though in fact its losses were reported to be heavy — heavier, indeed, than Sir Iain had by this time felt he could hope for. Heavy enough now to bring some encouragement to Brigade H.Q., where Lord Dornoch was watching the fighting through field glasses. The mountain artillery from both the British peaks was putting up a good account of itself, as he remarked to the Brigade Major. Archdale agreed, but said, "They've only two more miles to go, Colonel. The moment they reach the end of the valley, Ahmed Khan'll advance and join up with them."

Dornoch shook his head. "It remains to be seen, but I doubt it. He'll stay where he is and simply go on giving them covering fire from his heavy guns." There were some very heavy guns in the rebel line, brought up by elephants, as they had seen earlier. The elephants had now been unyoked and replaced by bullock teams, which were less excitable under fire. "If we could put those guns out of action, I'd recommend Sir Iain to send the infantry in to attack the supply column hand-to-hand. As it is—" He broke off; he had heard the whine and both men ducked instinctively as an artillery shell trundled overhead to burst some three hundred yards away against a rock overhang. There were screams from men and mules. Dornoch picked himself up and said savagely, "D'you know, Archdale, I've a damn good mind to send two companies of the 114th to try an outflanking attack on that devil's line. Trouble is—I'm short of officers. How would you care to lead an attack yourself?"

Archdale said, "Colonel, I'd like nothing better." His eyes were shining oddly, Dornoch thought. But he added, "I'm bound to say I don't believe we'd have a hope. We'd be mown down . . . like flies, Colonel."

"But we might draw their fire from our gunners, Archdale." Without committing himself Dornoch went back to his study of the advancing supply column. Already in the spasmodic glare of the exploding British shells he could glimpse the out-lines of covered ammunition-wagons and store-wagons pulled on by bullocks. They seemed to be without end, advancing out of the battle smoke and extending back as far as the eye could see in those all too infrequent explosions that burst upon them from the hills. In front of Dornoch, and farther down the mountain-side, the 114th Highlanders began to get the head of the column in their sights as they waited in cover of the crags behind their long-range rifles. But their fire would be no more than gnat bites. What was needed, Dornoch knew, was what they had not got: more and more artillery, to pound the column into fragments and explode the ammunition-wagons . . . he looked across once more at Archdale. He still had that idea of withdrawing the 114th from the peak and sending them down to carry out the outflanking manœuvre. But the Brigade Major, though certainly no coward, was such a confounded fool. He would dash to his death, which of itself wasn't especially important, but he would carry the battalion with him, and he was probably right in saying they wouldn't have a hope. They would be seen too soon, that was the trouble.

"When I give the word," Ogilvie said, "I want all of you to

spread right out across the enemy's rear — leave say a couple of hundred yards between each man." They were now within half a mile of Ahmed Khan's line and they still hadn't been sighted in that difficult, sandy terrain. "You, Burns, take the left of the line, nearest the southern hill. I'll take the flag and the Sarn't-Major will come with me. Corporal, you'll extend right, and the rest of you in between. All right so far?" He paused, then went on: "The moment I yell, every man will start piping — but will not advance. I want you all to stay in your positions unless and until I say different. I may pass the word to retire. If I do that, you'll all retire to the southward — to the left, then make westerly towards the hill where the battalion is, and try individually to reach our lines. You'll carry on piping, but do all you can to keep out of sight — it's important, obviously, that the rebels don't get to know how few we are. Now — into your uniforms."

The men dropped their bundled kilts and tunics and dressed quickly. When they were ready Ogilvie said, "Start spreading out now. For those of you who can really play the pipes, the tune will be a charge: On Wi' the Tartan. You all know that one. Play it the best you can. And good luck, all of you."

Silently, carrying the pipes tucked beneath their arms, they moved away, fanning out across the enemy's rear. Ogilvie, holding the flag erect, gave them a slow count of a thousand. At the end of that time he could see only the two nearest men, and those only as darker shadows against the general gloom of the night. He counted again, up to two hundred. Then he put a hand on the Regimental Sergeant-Major's shoulder. "Here we go," he said. "Now or never!" He held out a hand, which the older man took warmly. "Here's my wish you'll come through, Sarn't-Major. You've been a tower of strength all along."

"Allow me to say the same thing to you, Mr. Ogilvie. Are you ready now, sir?"

Ogilvie nodded.

"Right, then we'll give them a real good Highland yell together," Cunningham said. They did; a primeval cry from Scotland's heart ripped across to the rebel line and within seconds was repeated to left and right and then the dispersed pipes crashed out into the night, savagely, triumphantly sending out that stirring charge so often used in olden times by the great Marquis of Montrose as he led his Highlanders to victory.

184

Immediately, the firing from the enemy ahead wavered and there was a perceptible movement in the line, an instinctive surge away from the rear. The Highland regiments were renowned all along the Frontier for their remarkably unfeeling use of the bayonet.

"What the devil's that?" Sir Iain asked.

"It's the pipes, sir! The pipes!" The Brigade Major's mouth was hanging open.

"I know that, damn you. I have ears, you fool. Who's down there—who ordered an outflanking action? I'll—"

"Lord Dornoch—"

"No," Dornoch cut in. "I had an idea of doing so but I never gave the order." He stared into the night. "It's wheezy piping," he said. "I see nothing. Possibly Division has acted without letting us know, Sir Iain, but—"

"I am Division," the General snapped. "Division can't act without letting itself know—so there! Damned if I know what's going on, though! Does the G.O.C. not get told *anything*? How's the enemy behaving?" He clapped his field glasses to his eyes. A moment later, and just before a soldier dashed up with a report, he said in wonder, "They're milling around like flies. *They're in confusion*! But I'm damned if I can see any of our troops. I don't understand this! Any ideas, Dornoch?"

Dornoch said at once, "Somebody's causing a diversion and it's up to us to take full advantage of it. We must mount that outflanking attack immediately, to join up with whoever's coming up in the enemy's rear." He waited, impatiently. "Well, Sir Iain?"

After a moment the Divisional Commander gave a heavy nod. "Very well, Dornoch. I agree. Every man you've got—we'll leave the hill to the gunners. And by God—I'll accompany the attack myself—damned if I won't!"

Dornoch swung away, calling out for Captain Black. A moment later the bugles blew. Within five minutes the 114th Highlanders, supported by the men of the Black Watch and the remnants of the Mahrattas, were storming down the hillside for the plain. Sir Iain was in the lead with Lord Dornoch and Andrew Black and the Brigade Major. As they swept forward behind a rain of rifle fire from the charging soldiers on the flanks, Dornoch saw the General draw his sword and swing it round his head with all the agility of a youth, and in the light of a shell-burst below on Ahmed Khan's line he saw something else: from where the sound of the pipes was still coming a tattered Union Flag was streaming out along the night breeze and the tall figure who was carrying it, a man in the kilt of the Royal Strathspeys, looked remarkably like young Ogilvie. And he was about to be ridden down by a bearded native cavalryman.

Ogilvie had seen the advance from the British-held hill and was cheering like a maniac when he, too, realized that a horseman was riding for him. With the flag fluttering from its pole, he was — as indeed he should have been — the focal point. He read the fury in Faiz Gheza's face as the man rode nearer, coming along at the gallop with his sabre lifted high. It flashed through Ogilvie's mind that he might stand his ground, lower the flag, and use the pole as a lance to topple Faiz Gheza from his horse. But he realized equally swiftly that the pole, rotten with years, would snap like a twig. Then he remembered the stirrup on its saddle-leather that he had purloined from the fort's harness-room. He brought it out. He waited as Faiz Gheza came on. As he saw the sabre start its downward cut he threw himself forward, whirled the makeshift sling and sent his body crashing to the ground in the moment that the weighted leather strap wound itself round and round Faiz Gheza's cutting-wrist. There was a tremendous jolt and his body half lifted, then fell back to the ground with a thud. He heard a cry, heard the pounding feet of the horse as it galloped on towards the rear. There was a lump on the ground beside him. It didn't move. Neither, for the time being, did Ogilvie. He shammed dead as hordes of natives broke to the rear and fled past him. When he got to his feet he found that Faiz Gheza had his head smashed in, no doubt from a galloping hoof. Then he heard a tremendous cheering from somewhere ahead and saw the remains of his small force march in, still playing their pipes. Cunningham was one of them, Cunningham streaming blood from a great gash in his forehead, so blinded with blood that he could scarcely see where he was going, but every inch the Regimental Sergeant-Major just the same. Burns, completely untouched, was another — a jaunty, cocky Private Burns whose pipes were now playing cheekily, Oh, But Ye've Been Lang a-Coming, a Burns who, despite his views, seemed pleased enough to see

British officers that night. Four other men came in; and that was all. And as they came, and rejoined the battalion, they saw the rebel guns go into action once again, but this time in the hands of the gunners from Brigade. Now they were turned against Ahmed Khan's supply train, struggling to get away from what had so suddenly become a terrible situation. It was like the Charge of the Light Brigade all over again; within half an hour the rout was complete, the supply train broken, cut to pieces. Shortly after dawn Lieutenant-General Sir Iain Ogilvie led the Brigade into Jalalabad behind the pipes and drums of the Royal Strathspeys.

Later the General unbent to an unprecedented degree.

"Damn well done, boy," he said, his hand on his son's shoulder outside the H.Q. tent. "Damn well! Your mother will be most proud of you, to be sure. I'll send for her when we reach cantonments. You'll like to see her, naturally." He blew his nose, hard. "You'll do, boy, you'll do."

Ogilvie said, "I couldn't have managed without the R.S.M."

"He'd be the first to say you could — but I know his worth well enough. A fine man, James."

"Yes," Ogilvie hesitated, then came out with it. "Sir . . . may I ask . . . what about those terms?"

The General stiffened at once, and glared stonily. "Terms, boy? What damn terms? Never heard of any damn terms!"

"No, sir. I see. But if I may point out, sir . . . Ahmed Khan is still alive."

"That's none of your damn business," the General said promptly, and the matter had been left at that. But Ogilvie still didn't know how his father was going to get out of it gracefully. Ahmed Khan had been taken prisoner during the final fighting and was to be taken back into India so that he could not act again to undermine the authority of the Amir in Kabul; and he would be held until some decision had been reached as to his future. But James Ogilvie could not help feeling disturbed on another count: Afghanistan would now be left under an unpopular Amir through whom, presumably, Ahmed Khan's hated British would now virtually rule the country one hundred per cent; Ogilvie wondered if any real good had been achieved after all the fighting, all the dying. The single star on each of his shoulders told him he had no business to be thinking such thoughts at all; and that star meant something – though he couldn't at that moment have said just what it did mean. Reaction had come to him; his weariness had caught up with him as well. He had a nagging suspicion that he could never go through a similar experience again, that, knowing now what action was like, he would not be able to bring himself to the point of facing it again. For the rest of it, he would soon be back to routine regimental life – and the continuing enmity of Andrew Black, which was not a very pleasing prospect.

They came back through the Khyber Pass without incident, beneath those watchful strongholds on the crags whose personnel had heard the news of the great British victory; and beyond the Pass they rested by Fort Jamrud before marching in the last eight miles to Peshawar. What was left of the Division came back without the 88th, who had been left behind to garrison Jalalabad until the politicians had settled matters finally. They came back as seasoned men – not yet veterans, but men who had had a full taste of action and had so conducted themselves as to retain intact the perimeter of Empire, men who had earned the telegraphed but entirely personal thanks of Her Majesty in Windsor Castle. Ahmed Khan was riding in the column, under a Captain's Escort. In front of him, visible on an open commissariat cart, travelled the Brigade Major's newly-built field lavatory, having made its second trip through the Khyber within a short while. As they marched in to cantonments at Peshawar, the victorious column found that the whole garrison with its women and children, or such as were not down with the sickness, had turned out to wave and cheer them in. It was a Sunday, as it happened, and the British troops were in their scarlet tunics after church parade; it was a colourful sight, especially since the Commander-in-Chief India had hurried with his gilded Staff from Calcutta to greet the returning victors in person. He took the salute, his hand quivering with emotion, as the 114th marched past with the pipers, backed up now by a brass band from Peshawar District, crashing out Scots Wha Hae. The whole garrison was going mad. Andrew Black was still cantering officiously up and down the line; but he rode stiffly ahead with a scowl on his face as it became quite clear that most of the welcome was for James Ogilvie in particular even though he, Black, had done a not inconsiderable service to the Empire in catching the spy in his act of transmission. It had not taken long for word to reach Peshawar that Ogilvie and his fellow-prisoners had swung the rebel line and made possible the capture of the all-important guns; and his name, as their leader and thus the symbol for them all, was being cheered to the echo. There was one moment when Ogilvie caught a glimpse of Mary Archdale with a group of senior wives and he could have sworn she blew him a kiss; her eyes were shining and she was looking straight at him, dancing up and down in her excitement as she—even she—was caught up in the exhilaration of the triumphant march. There were low groans and some boos as Ahmed Khan went past; the rebel leader met them with a smile, disdainfully. The music went on; the pipes were now silent, leaving it to the brass to play the regiments to quarters on its own. The British Grenadiers, Lillibullero . . . Schubert's March Militaire. And finally, as the tail of the column moved into barracks, with some of the great crowd following and attempting to shake the soldiers' hands, the whole concourse burst with a roar of spontaneous emotion, that reminded Ogilvie of that day aboard the trooper in the Arabian Sea, into God Save The Queen.

It was a tremendous occasion. Nobody seemed to notice, nor would they have interpreted it correctly if they had done so, the curious flicker in the eyes of the rebel, Ahmed Khan, as he glanced at the Union Flag that the replacement bum-*havildar* had, with an excess of loyalty, placed in a prominent position on the Brigade Major's field lavatory just as it rumbled past the saluting base.